A Silent Cry

Sincere Ronoldi

Sincere Ronoldi

ISBN:
LCCN:
Interior Book Design by: www.TheLiarsCraft.com
Cover Design by: www.TheLiarsCraft.com

Printed in the USA

Acknowledgements:

To my family, friends & Daughter Maliyah,

Who I love here is my story and dedication to
you…Without you I am nothing. To my loving dear
brother, Rashaad Khalif Montgomery, may you rest in
peace.

1

A Heavenly Glimpse

"Now I lay me Down to sleep I pray the Lord My soul to keep for if I shall die Before I Wake I pray the lord my soul to take…Father, I plea to thee keep me If in need of your help for lord I feel as though I tried to get over so much that has been bestowed upon my life. For I have done sins that the word man shouldn't be what I am now. I know I was a coward lord; the pain that I have now God is overcoming me, GOD PLEASE! I need you I can't do it no more, I can't take this pain, I just don't know anymore. As you already know my thoughts, then you knew that this was coming and I'm sorry lord my life's sandglass, is on its last crystals. I just want the pain to stop, the thoughts, the mind battles and most of all the pain I caused others. As I know by now lord, committing this abomination there is no place for me in heaven. The Fiery pits of hell burns with the eternity of my soul. It's impossible for you to turn back right God? Time that is? I guess at least I won't suffer on earth….

As I was surrounded by cracking leaky walls of a cheap motel bathroom, while my insane thoughts started to ring the core of my eardrums. My hearing now became impaired. Picture perfects weren't the images that flashed in my head like caution lights, everything was playing so rapidly fast as my vision slightly decreasing by the seconds. What I felt was unaware of what exactly was happening but I knew I wanted it to end soon, while my back lies on the cold floor, wrist feeling tingling throbbing sensation... Something was up?

Insensible was what could describe me at that moment. My pupils started to dilate as a light burst inside it like a sun ray. This light was drawing me like the oceans current peaceful and angelic all at the same time. I was reaching out for it... Then suddenly my body began to be on fire.... AHHHHHHHH!!! Someone please help me it hurts, looking down at my body from above I realize that it isn't my body at all but my soul. I felt every piece of the flames, As I started to scream no one heard me, no one was there I was in darkness crying in silence away from everyone. I was left behind to be in pure solitary, and then a voice called to me that also made me weak every sentence it spoke... It was sucking the very essence of my life out of my body.

I began to quickly remember that my life use to be much different than this, it was peaceful, angelic. I dealt with many struggles that came with life that was a part of the norm system. This amongst all things was quite different you see, I didn't understand what was going on I was confused and stricken with so much fear. I had to know what was going on with my body, my soul and most importantly my life...If I still had one.

2

A NEW BEGINNING

"Ah yo Mom, Mommy, hey where are you?" "I'm here she replied." Hey could I spend the night over my friend Derek's house? "Please, Please, please" His parents already said "I could" Please! "No, Mar we just moved here and don't really know the people very well. "But, Mom I never really get to do anything or barley stay the night over my friend's houses like that. Why can't I never get to do anything? Why do I ways have to stay in the house? How come you guys always let Sam and Miguel do anything and everything they possibly want? "MAURICE ANTHONY, I SAID NO GOT DAMMIT!!!! Man, you guys always show favoritism I hate that; I hate being the middle child. I hate you just leave me alone... As I stormed upstairs to my shared room with Samuel my little brother and Miguel my oldest, I really hated being the middle child. Always feeling lonely, mistreated and attention seeking but deep down inside I knew that my feelings of neglect were especially when I hated were we currently lived at now. Really though, I hated Harrisburg, Pennsylvania. Everything seemed too small and in one big circle. To make matters worse we moved in some weird area Called Steelton, but I for one wasn't too fond of the environment. I was so use to Washington D.C.

Although mother thought it was a wonderful place to start off new, a great change for the best she would always say... better schools... better people and drastically "Hahahahaha" a better life, Whomp!

I hadn't really been to my new school yet Steelton Elementary School, because we just moved in the neighbor, but I knew I was ready, ready to learn and be social with peers. Really a chance for me explore the new town and its people and I was ready to go on my quest. "Mar, Mar!" "Yes" as I responded to her calling me my mom that is. I was thinking maybe she had changed her mind or something or decided to be nice for the rest of the night who knows due to her image I rarely knew at times. Mom's was built like a linebacker strong up top and lady at the bottom. She knew how to get her lady image on at times when she needed to, but raising three sons and two daughters, "hahaha I guess you can say she knew she had to be firm".

"Come down here boy so you can eat". "I'm not hungry I would yell because I was mad, but who was I kidding I love to grub on some food. She would say" You going to be starving then. Now come on now she knew I couldn't survive without eating, shit I was on the husky side, you know fat in the face and thick in the waist. It was a trait my father Senior would say, his name being the same as my brother Miguel's. Even as I remember it running down the hallway to pull one of my tricks out of the bag, to put on my sad face to see if that would get me in my mother's good graces. Boy! Was I wrong that women always stuck to her word? Well Mom, tomorrow being Monday could you and Dad at least discuss it and get back to me Friday about it please! "Yes, Mar me and your father will discuss this now sit down and eat your dinner. I was so overwhelmed half way out of my chair thinking to myself it's about time I can at least have some fun. Like always Samuel always had his two cents comments to adlib on everything "You know Dad's going to say no because he doesn't like you" Yes whatever I would always say because I know Samuel always sounded like a broken record "Like that's all you can say, that's all you can say as the words always rung inside my head. We bickered all the time like most siblings do when they're about 18 months about apart; we were always competitive with each other that even lasted us until our adult stage at times. Especially since Miguel was five years apart from myself and seven years apart from Samuel there really was always complaints and contests on looks, swags and styles… Hahahahaha it's what we did as brothers as we got older.

Like Miguel always the outgoing one out of the group the "Ladies man one my call him the sex gyro himself. Always sticking his fingers in the pudding if you get what I'm saying. To tell the truth if was in his nature he never really had to try hard really, he spoke with authority and always had ladies and clothes on the mind, literally always on the mind. Cared for his siblings though but always, wanted to be by his popularity friends, the "in crowd" is what I called it. Yet as he got older the responsibilities of fame, power and appearance took a rift on what he wanted out of a real woman which was love, comfort and most of all eternal happiness.

Sam, on the other hand was quite different. He was what we called "The quite boy" although he really wasn't quite he just gave off the appearance of being that way especially to girls. Tall, slim "thug like" in the walk but yet innocent as ever in the face so we say or he says… one of those. Yet, Sam was in the street life always either selling or smoking whichever of the one came first. I'll respect him in this book to say it honestly was none of the hardcore drugs like crack, heroin, and cocaine. Weed was the motivation for him or in his case motivated to get the weed. What could I really say there my brothers and I loved them both?

My sisters Tamika and Charlotte were nice sweet and always stayed to themselves no matter what. It was just how they were, although they did like hanging around their brothers laughing and joking it was just they're personality stuck in their own world of a different reality…. But sad to say this story isn't about them pre-say, the moral of the story is really focused on me so let's get back to that, shall we?

School days were rolling by fast to me so I could hurry and get my answer for Friday. Go home, finish homework, clean my room, do my chores and anything else that my parents couldn't use on me just to say no. I was doing my best at everything even not to argue with Sam just to stay the weekend at my friend's house.

To speak the truth, I was very skeptical not to keep nagging my mother. As I prepared for bed that night with the usual routine of eating, showering and brushing of the teeth, I honestly wanted the next day to come. For Thursday was sure creeping up on Wednesday by hours. I thought to myself "yes" keeping my toes and fingers crossed in froze position while I slept, thinking good luck was sure to come. I mean any child my age would be thrilled to have a little fun like this especially with the strict up tight parents I had. It was always school, study, homework or worst chores. As so many thoughts ran through my head that night as I was trying to fall asleep. Understanding part was the hardest as I was losing focus about my family's recent movement from one state to another. I always asked my mother "Why did we move?

She always replied to me to give you kids a better life". I was puzzled at times due to the simple fact that I felt our life was alright, although the smell of gunshot residues in the air always tickled my nose. As well as the crazy drunks and crack heads that lined up or circled our block like starving vultures seeking its next meal. Every corner I turned there were either old heads recruiting my peers to do their dirty work such as selling candy as they called it. Better yet, the hookers that ran from there pimps. I always had seen women getting smacked around for either not making that money or not fucking or sucking correctly, but hey this was part of my norm system growing up.

Although I really knew better to pay attention to all of this that was going on around me due to the ass whooping's senior would ditch out or the protection of Miguel never wanting none of his siblings to go through any of this street life. I often saw my peers or people in general on the news that was getting shot over the dumbest things. Some of the kids I knew because they were missing from my school at Samuel Chase Elementary School. Never really have I ever thought the worst but it was expected when you lived in the "GETTO" or "HOOD" life one might say. To be on the truthful side sometimes death could appear a couple times a day or sometimes within the same hour. I figured it was like a ratio or fraction I guess for every person that was shot or killed a woman was pregnant with twins or maybe triples to equal the quality and reproduction of life. For the most part that's how it was in D.C especially when it came to the hustle game, although I never really knew too much about it. I only understood it through the mind-setting and eyes of a ten-year-old.

For my mom's dukes or ma-va" was slang accent term to announce the recognition of your mother, didn't really let us outside that much. Every gunshot we heard was taken serous in our house as our bodies would quickly hit the floor we were tossing furniture against our brown shitty color carpets. However, she would let us go out for a few but her favorite words were "you better check in and bring yo asses back before the street lights came on or I'll have your father whoop that ass" I would just smile and say "yes or okay" because in my mind I knew my mother was over protective, it was like her outside image was tough. Plus, Bernice had a mean-like streak to her but inside was pure love and joy, she didn't express it at times but I knew she loved all her children. Yet something between us allowed us to love each other even more. I can honestly say without getting mad now writing this as an adult that I was a mommy's boy or her twin and loved and hated every moment of it at the same time. Since my father was really my father, which was something I heard two summers ago, up at my meme's house which was my grandmother on my mom's side...White people and their funny names for relatives as I chuckle at the thought every time I would say it. Sam and I would go up for the summer which I never really understood why since I never really like the women. Sadly, it just so happened I was eavesdropping on a conversation between Meme and my Aunt Christen "Now mom you know Bernice should have told Maurice that O is his real father" I thought to myself like wow there really discussing letters in the alphabet. Yet I just had to be nosey and sneak more information. "Well Christen that's none of our business that is Bernice's problem that she will have to discuss with him as he gets older as my grandmother stated."

"All I'm saying though mom is that sooner or later Maurice is going to want the truth and if he wants to know later in life that Senior isn't his real father then I will tell him. Plus, why would senior want to take care of a son or a child of that matter that isn't really kin to him, it doesn't make sense mother."

I walked in slowly pretending not to show any facial expressions over the gossip I just heard as the two of them stoop up from the table in Meme's apartment in Liverpool, PA. "Hey sweetie did you have fun at the playground." Yeah, I responded hesitated, as if they were able to pick the conversation that was going on in my head. Like WHAT ARE YOU FUCKING SERIOUS SENIOR ISN'T MY FATHER HOW THE HELL THAT HAPPEN? I hated Perry County nothing but white city and honkies everywhere that hated niggers although they say they don't trust I know better to believe that shit, especially when Meme hated my dad or step dad because he was black and just tolerated the half-breed kids on the strength of my mother for him being her husband and all. I often felt at times she looked at my mother's children as if mixed beings were infectiousness' germs or something don't really know nor care to explain her prejudice motives.

Moreover, the thoughts really disappeared because I never really returned to Liverpool for summer visits any more. I was alright being in my own territory in my hometown. Plus, I really couldn't wait to get back home to shoot some hoops with my best friend Keith at the time which was my childhood buddy. My homeboy one can say funny as hell but dumb as a brick wall...Meanwhile I got back home a week and a half pretty much away from school. Keith called "My crib which was my house you could say and told me to meet him at the playground so I replied to my boy "be there in a bit if I get past mom dukes" As I went inside my shared room like always put away my things and headed towards the door... And where do you think you're going mister" Bernice would say as she stopped me dead in my tracks, I often thought she had eyes in the back of her head because nothing got past her or beside her. "Outside ma" "Why, oh no school is in a week and you need to get ready for it. "Come on mom I have one more day to actually have fun before my first day of school." I looked at her as she gave me the evil eye and said "All right but I want you in this house by 6:30pm mister and not a second later do you hear me? Yes, as I replied jolting out of the door smiling.

So indeed, I met up with Keith on the courts to shoot some hoops. Yes, he was better than I was height and a "Slim Jim complexion" other than myself that was big and round. As Keith started to score more we hear large fireworks go off at least that's what it sounded like but this time it was getting closer and closer as we looked up the street two gangs known as the "Bloods and Cripps" started blasting off their heats or guns you can say like it was the fourth of July. Keith and I busted out running start for home. I ran so fast my heart seemed as though it was literally busting out of my chest. As I got to my apt door 302 in Arbor View I knew these grounds held my protection from what was going on the outside. I couldn't believe what just happened, I was somewhat scared but was use to this surrounding but not so much up closed... in front of my very eyes that is. I tried calling Keith's house an hour later after I was in my house but yet there was no answer. I figured he was maybe still in shock and needed to calm his adrenaline down like it was a road runner off a cartoon.

However, I managed to get my mind off things by going school shopping for the next three days with my dad and the thought of me being around him made me questioned a lot in my head like does he even know I'm not his son? Why is he still around then? Well if he's not my father then I really don't like or want him to beat my ass anymore save that shit for the real man that's kin to me. Senior would pick up outfits and ask "you like this one" I would just shake my head yes even though some of them I hated. I honestly had other things on my mind like the first day of school to see if Keith and I had homeroom together like we had the previous two years before. Senior, my brothers and I finished the school shopping off by buying some fresh sneakers as we discuss who was going to look the best and freshest on the first day of school until Senior stopped our competitive argument.

BING!! BING!! As the school bell rang for the kids to go inside I didn't see Keith anywhere, I reckoned that maybe he was up at the front of the line. So I walked through the school hallways seeing all the new pictures and phrases of learning I was excited about this year. Everyone got into Mrs. Jones's homeroom in which was the best class to be in there was never really a dull moment with this woman. She was sweet and nice, plus she was delighted to have me for another year. As we all got near our assigned seats as I seen That Keith's seat was right next to mines, All right as I thought to myself. In unison, we all stoop up to say "the Pledge of Allegiance" and sat back down in our seats. Mrs. Jones started to give her welcome speech as she eased into the tradition of roll calling... "Sammie White "HERE", as she started by rows Tamika Smith "PRESENT" Maurice Mayo "HERE" as I said so loud. Keith Woods... Keith Woods as she said it for the second time the principal walked in "Good Morning Children" "Good Morning Ms. Jackson, as well all sounded like a deep echo.

Mrs. Jones, may I speak to you outside privately for a moment, "yes you most certainly can as she spoke in her soft voice". The classroom started to buzz like bumbled bees flying around I could really remain in my seat. My gut was telling me it was about Keith and as the classroom was out of control. I managed to put on my 007 persona to be a spy and check on the scoop in which they were discussing in the hallway. I couldn't hear much nor make out what they were saying exactly. I inched a little closer to receive some kind of information. I heard Ms. Jackson say "He was shot in his back and neck four times... WHOA!! THIS

COULDN'T BE HAPPENING MY BEST FRIEND.MY ONLY FRIEND DEAD? This just couldn't be true, as my eyes started to water the door opened. I see Mrs. Jones face and it look as if she had been crying as she looked at me she knew that I knew exactly what was going on. I was ready to burst into a sob of tears. As she started to say something to me, I rudely interrupted her cutting her very sentence off and said "I need to use the bathroom." She responded with a dreary look and said "Sweetie I really need to talk to you about your friend Keith" I cocked my head to a sideways position and said "I already know my parents told me as I lied to her in which in a way she already knew." Now can I please go to the bathroom, hiding my face so she really couldn't see my soreness? Yet with a weak frown she gave me the look as if take as long as you need honey in a timely manner. I busted through that bathroom door as if a bomb had been dropped inside shaking the walls of the lavatory echoing its surroundings. I couldn't believe it; I was mad more than less I was hurt. Why didn't I at least look back? Why didn't a bullet hit me, we weren't far from each other? I should have done something. I hope the bastards that shot him rots in fucking hell. I wanted those dead just like he was whoever did it. As I let out a couple of screams and tears of rage I realize doing that wasn't going to bring him back nor help none. The best thing I could do was to remember him, his name and what value he had on my life. I wouldn't forget our pack we made to each other to always learn and make it out of the hood life. To be the best men we could in society, to leave our mark and tell our stories to our kids. It was the least I could do after all death is death nothing comes back after that.

BOOM!! That's not the god damn point Miguel" As I was startled and disturbed from my slumber from my parents arguing and slamming doors. I heard my mother

12

yelling at my father and I really couldn't make out what they were saying. As I got out of bed sweaty realizing I must have had another nightmare about Keith's passing that hunted me at times when I slept. I never really told them I felt as though that they wouldn't have cared so when they asked about him I would lie and say "he moved to Philly with his aunt." I started to creep down the stairs from my room not to make a sound. As I got closure I could hear my mom screaming at my dad. "Miguel he is getting older and he makes good grades why can't he spend the night at least the weekend at his friend's house damn let the boy have some kind of fun. "BB, which was a nickname he called my mother when he was serious.

The point is we just moved here and don't know anyone like that, we don't know the kind of people around here and his little ass needs to be focus on sports instead of trying to hang out all the damn time, bad enough he's already soft and feminine. "You know what Miguel it's a damn shame you can't even love your son like the other two, you don't even see that you're pushing him away. Honestly you both are pushing each other away". Bernice don't play that bullshit on me, I love Maurice just as much as I love the other two. "Well, Miguel you sure don't act like it". As I heard her even louder this time, "We tried that remember when he stayed at Nikki's and Tyron's house with their kids and what happened? Honestly, I really didn't even know what they were talking about at that point. It must have been something I forgot growing up as a kid or was too ashamed due to my father that I blocked it out of my head somehow. I mean I remembered just scattered pieces about it? But not like they both had so it seemed. "You do! You know! As he screamed? "Yes, Miguel I do, but the fucking point is the past is the past for a reason, he's much older now and understand more and he was younger then what he is now and is aware of what's wrong and what's right. That's the point to teach our children good ethics and hope we don't stir them in the wrong direction. "Bernice I will not let my son turn gay I will disown his ass like he isn't mines. "Well you know what you already do it now so whatever." As I heard the both of them getting closer to their bedroom door I quickly ran to the bathroom. It was a good thing I did because my mom came out and knocked on the door. I flushed the toilet pretending as if I just got done as I opened the door she looked at me surprisingly. "Shouldn't you be in bed and sleep for school tomorrow? School isn't for another three hours so yeah I might as well go back to sleep as I stared in her eyes. As I past my mom I quietly said to her "never mind mom I don't want to stay the night at Derek's house I rather just kick it at home." The look she gave me knew that I heard everything as I walked away silently going up the stairs back to my room.

Hours later I woke up to the sweet smell of eggs, bacon, sausage, grits and pancakes which was weird because it wasn't Sunday and mom didn't really cook like that unless she was in a good mood. I rushed down the stairs to get my grub on. She pulled me to the side and said "You can stay the weekend under two conditions. I started to cheese with a big Kool-Aid smile and said" sure mom anything. "Well check in with me after school today and call me before you go bed and last but not least Maurice Anthony "Mom that's three things!" "Shut up before I change my mind and be here Sunday before five do you hear me? "Yes, mwah as I kissed her cheek, thank you thank you mom. "Don't thank me, thank your father. I didn't want to but I did because my mother asked me too. "THANKS DAD." "Yeah, yeah," I ran up those stairs to grab my pre-packed overnight bag kissed my mother again on the cheek and ran to school which was up the block

14

from my house 159 South Front Street in Melton. I couldn't wait to tell Derek video games all night and junk food until I farted and passed out I was really happy and excited for once.

3

SSHHH!!! NOT A WORD

It was the last half an hour of school and I couldn't wait for that last bell to ring then free weekend here I come. Derek and I had our last class together which was Mr. Neuhard's class indeed it was English. To tell the truth I never really was attentive in school. School just really came to me naturally; I mean I never studied or really took effort on homework. I knew I was smart but I acted dumb to just fit in at times or to get attention from my peers. That's exactly how Derek and I met which was in a gifted class for highly intelligent kids our age. BING!!

"Don't forget to hand in your projects when leaving out of the door; the basket is near my computer desk". Mr. Neuhard would say with his child-like features and pale blue eyes complexion. He seemed too young to be a teacher as if he was fresh out of college. I hurried up and grab my back pack and books to meet Derek outside of the classroom as he waited for me. "You ready dude." "Hell Yeah, as I responded to him with his bifocals making his eyes look three times bigger as I told him. Oh, there's just one thing man I just have to do which is call and check in with my mother." "Dude don't you hate that about parents?" "Of course, man who doesn't exactly why I'm so happy and relieved to be out of the house especially when mines could drive me crazy and get on my nerves, as I was speaking to him directly by his side. We both chuckled over the similarity of parents driving us nuts. "So what are the plans this weekend, and plus my mom wants me home by five on Sunday. Just please don't let me forget to call and check in or I won't be able to ever even do this again."

"Well I just got the new Harry Potter game which was the Sorcerer's Stone on the computer so we can play that and oh yeah Saturday we can go dirt bike riding. I do have one pair extra safety pads in the house for you". "WHAT YOUR JOKING? Man you can't be serious I got the same game at home and shit I would love to go riding although I really never been so yeah let's do it."

"Well here is my house Maurice and yeah just the heads up please don't pay no attention to my father he's... well he's just him but I really don't think he is home. "Okay, as I gave him a funny but awkward look." Yet the look he returned wasn't one that I was used to seeing, a look of fear and despair which was very odd for him when he was the kindest person that was always laughing and smiling at the dumbest things. As he put the key inside the door handle and we pass through the door frame, he started to yell "MOM!!"

"Be down in a minute sweetie." "Hey Mar, did you want a snack or something to drink?' Naw man I'm fine as I started to look around the house noticing a dragon framed chess board and pictures hanging on the wall. We quickly went upstairs to drop our book bags in his room then back down the stairs we went. It seems as if his parents had nice taste... strange but nice at the same time. Really what I wanted to know where the hell they went wrong at their son's room because that crap was just bizarre... Out of the ordinary and from the stairs coming down someone said "Hello how was school boys" Her voice was soft and very raspy and low pitched. I turned around and seen a small petite woman. I couldn't really make out her face too much as if the shadow of the light from the kitchen was trying to hide it.

"You guys hungry, I'm pretty sure you guys have built up and an appetite how does pizza bagels sound?" I grinned because once again I wasn't going to turn down food especially when it was pizza bagels. "Sure Mrs. Patton as I smiled towards her." "Honey Derek sweet heart did you wants some?" "Well maybe just a little mom as he turned and looked at me funny, "Oh yeah man where's your house phone at remember I have to call my mother." Derek threw me the phone as that shit almost clocked me in the head because I had slippery butter fingers. I dialed the number as the phone started to ring waiting for her to pick up.

"Hello" As my mother sounded like she was coughing with a heavy smoker's hackle toned voice. "Mom I'm here, "Alright you having fun- yeah trying to cut her off really quick because I knew my mother. She was very disrespectful in a polite voice but yet she spoke with intimidation in her tone. "Maurice Anthony, don't play with me what are you guys doing and where is his mother you know I want to speak to her? You want to come home? "No, saying in my mind like yeah whatever white lady but I'll respect you though. Mrs. Patton my mom would like to speak with you. As I went in the kitchen to give her the phone Derek tried to stop me to give the phone to her but I managed to bob and weave around him and as I handed it over I was able to take a glimpse at the side of her face. She was so trying to hide it she looks at me with a sad but cheerful glee and said "oh honey this is nothing I have slipped on the kitchen floor and hit my head on the kitchen dining room table. "Here my mom wants to talk to you."

"Hi, Mrs. Mayo" I turned around to go outside to play football with Derek and some of the neighborhood kids. I was troubled a little to tell the truth because I couldn't help but to still ponder about his mom's face. That shit didn't seem normal at all. She said she fell but, I so knew better than to believe that shit, because that was some fall. That dining room table must have beaten the hell out of her. I mean if you were beaten like that what is the whole purpose of trying to hide a bruised that big. I have seen mark's like that on women before not from my own mother but girls around town back home in D.C when they were trying to escape or get away from their pimps. Who really knew to be honest? Mark's like that mean she really must have did something to someone of that matter to really want to hurt her in such a way. I really didn't care though as long it was not my mother I could give to craps, and really Bernice didn't play that shit especially with Senior. She would go toe to toe with him if she really had too, even if she wasn't a match to him.

Wait just one minute as I thought to myself maybe it was Derek's dad. Wow no wonder he said "his dad is just his dad" without any explanation. Was his dad beating on his mother? Oh no! As I was sounding so sarcastic in my mental state of mind as if I had an animated voice speaking for me. Derek's dad is a women beater, but that's still better than being a killer like most of the thugs I've seen back home.

"Throw me the ball", damn I was wide open a boy shouted to me named Reese as I was quarter backing on the team. Derek was always on my team I wasn't going to allow anyone too punk my white boy, not along tackle him differently like they always tried to do. Man, we were pretty much down by a couple of points we just really needed one touchdown. I grabbed the ball "Blue 42... Blue 42 HUT! HUT!" I Backed up three steps and launched it towards Derek who was wide open in the touchdown zone.

To my surprise, he caught it and yes ladies and gentlemen it was indeed a touchdown teasing and screaming at our arrivals. So, Derek and I walked back from the park to his house. "My dad should be home now it's like close to seven o'clock." "Okay as I said" With a confused look on my face. "I'm just saying as he laughed, plus I really hoped my mom cooked. "Yeah man I really second that motion as we both were laughing and walking up the steps of his house.

We walked through the front door, "Hey you guys hungry I order pizza, Maurice you like cheese and pepperoni's? "Yes, ma'am I do just not cheese." Good you boys have hands so dig in just wash your hands first." As she went upstairs with a plate of food, we really didn't wash our hands. We just dug in heavy piling pizzas on our plated until a voice stop the both of us in the middle of our feast. "Don't be such a fucking pig Derek he called out." I'm not even going to lie his voice gave me goose bumps on the middle of my spine. As he came into the kitchen light from the living room, I now saw what the problem was. He was really messed up in his appearance. His cheeks on his face looked like craters or zits were constantly popping all over the place on his skin. He always seemed to have a scar like mark underneath his eye that was obvious a small child hood mark that remained noticeable throughout his life. "You boys ready to go dirt bike riding tomorrow" I looked at Derek then looked back at his dad and with a smile I said "Hell yea, I mean sorry sir I'm just really excited because I never been before but yes. "You don't need to say sorry my boy the only words you can't say in my house is bitch, fuck and red neck as he was laughing along with Derek and I. Derek had this fake smile and laugh on his face that seemed as if he was hiding something. I really couldn't get a grasp on it. We took the remaining of the pieces of pizzas upstairs to play video games. The night went on and on with game after game after game. It was really close to midnight and Derek's eyes were beginning to get blood shot red. He began to give some sad story saying he was tired and yea tired of me beating that ass in madden.

"Hey if or when I go to sleep do you think you can try and fix the harry potter game on the laptop because I'm always stuck on one part. "Yea sure no problem man where is it exactly because I really don't see it around as I responded to him still playing and trying to score my final touchdown on the game. "Well it's down stairs I believe it's on the dining room table in the kitchen somewhere near the back door just be very quiet because my parents are sleep." Aye captain looking and joking with him like I took him serious as he was dosing off. As I got done with the game and was walking down the stairs towards the kitchen in pitch black and smelled a foul and terrible odor. I flicked on the kitchen stove night light you might as well say to find the trash can to see if the smell was coming from that but it wasn't. So, I went near the back door and there it was the apple laptop. I turned back towards the kitchen door frame to head back upstairs but something strange caught my attention.

A Cloud of smoke was hovering off of the kitchen ceiling. It was coming from the living room. I place the laptop on the dining room table and creep towards the living room; I tried to flick on the lights but the switch wouldn't work. The Smokey air smelled like cigarettes which was a smell I was use to because of my mother being a smoker. I squinted my eyes looking around to see if I see anyone or anything, but I didn't. At this moment, I was scared a little and grab the laptop, turned off the kitchen light and went back to Derek's room where the bogie man wouldn't get me. As I told myself that little joke to calm my nerves down, as I got into his room he was knocked out in a deep slumber. Derek! Derek! As I called out his name

21

thinking that would shock him out of his sleep but it didn't and shockingly he still remained sleep. I began to start logging into the computer realizing all I had to do was click ok because it didn't require a password since it already been recently logged into. I uploaded the "Harry potter and Sorcerer's stone" game to see what the problem was but, there wasn't one just the computer being really slow at games. As I started to get on the internet many files popped up as "special" at least that was what the documents name was. I was certainly half tempted to open it up too see what 's inside, but I felt like someone was watching me, hovering behind my back like a spy although I quickly spun around and saw that there was no one but dim lights in the room. I felt like I was being victimized like a villain did to its prey in a horror movie. I could hear the drastic suspenseful music now ringing in my head like "Jaws" ... but really I just had to know what exactly was so secretive? So I clicked file open and I couldn't believe what the hell I just saw....

"OH MY GOD... LIKE... HUH, as my mind was astonished to what I was seeing. WHAT THE FUCK IS THIS SHIT? Thinking in my mind not to yell or scream. This man was really sick, a lunatic, crazy, psycho path. I really couldn't believe neither what I just saw nor what to do as my eyes were glue to the images and my feet were paralyzed as I stood. The man being Derek's father had nearly a whole entire collection of child porn. I mean photos, videos and even email accounts of children my age and a little higher. Some of the kids looked younger if not actually younger then myself. Kids were in adult clothes, swimsuits, underwear's and even nude. Some kids even had what seem to look like lotion or cream on their bodies that was coming from out of his penis. I just was disgusted with what I was seeing and thought to myself I had to get out of here to tell someone at least my parents because this man was a bad person a child molester of some sort. Something isn't right about this man seriously.

"What are you still doing up Maurice? As Mr. Patton's disgusting voice echoed the walls of Derek's room." "Oh nothing just got done playing a game."

"Oh yeah so what are you hiding behind your back then?"

"Nothing, I was just about to shut down and get some sleep." I quickly press the "ESC" button with my middle finger, back face towards the laptop and face looking dead into his dark like eyes so he wouldn't see what I was snooping into.

"Oh, ok well, Derek shouldn't have given you my laptop so I'll just shut it down so hand it over." As he headed towards me staggering, I turned right back around and hit "Ctrl, Alt and delete to quickly close out the document to shut it down. He yelled at me and said "Boy I told you I would do it." Sorry Mr. Patton I thought I give you a hand and what in god's name is that awful smell? "Boy that's the sweet smell of whiskey would you like some? Sorry no my parents wouldn't approve, but thank you for letting me use your laptop anyway I'm going to the bathroom now before I go to bed. "Yeah, yeah you will sure enough pay for meddling into things that don't belong to you as I heard him utter over my shoulder as I was exiting the room and you better hurry up and get back to bed as his tone started to get a little louder as he spoke to me.

I entered the bathroom to urinate gathering my thoughts because I really didn't know what to do or how to handle this kind of situation of news. I was pacing back and forth as I was too consumed with fear to be around this man. I was stuck trapped inside of a four-sided box as it appeared there was nothing that I could simply do. **"Okay this is me the author of this book writing this, unfortunately what you are about to read next is very**

detailed and holds too much intensifying emotions that if possible may make you want to put down this book in which this story only gets deeper from this point. Sad to say there isn't no happier nor calm vibe from this selection of the book more like rage, so if you are a person who can stomach the weakest things and cruel and usual then keep reading it gets better so I thought... As I got done and flushed the toilet and ran the water to cleanse my hands, I heard footsteps entering the bathroom. My heart dropped to my stomach as I was unaware to what was in reality, about to happen. I can feel and hear the pulse from my hearting beating harder and ringing in my ears.

"I see the way you been looking at me boy, switching that cute little round ass you have." "What are you talking about Mr. Patton I really need to go to bed? "SShhh! Not a word, you don't have to call me that just call me Shawn after all we are friends, right? As I was trying my best to inch towards the door with hesitation, His voice manages to strike my movement. "Ummmhmmm I never really had a nigger before I bet your sure going to taste good." You really don't know how much fear started to consume my thoughts and control the motion on my body. "Just come over here and talk to me I won't bite unless you ask me to... hahaha. "Mr. Patton, please don't do this I beg you...PLEASE! As water began to feel within my eyes it really didn't make a difference to the atmosphere that filled the bathroom. I was beginning to shake and shiver more than ever, afraid and petrified... It was as if I was living a real-life horror moment from the movies you watch. "Do what boy? All boys go through pain that's how it is you want to become a man don't you? "Come on Mr. Patton your drunk plus I'll scream and wake everyone up or better yet I will tell my parents." "Oh, is that right? Then me and my good oh friend will have to just take care of your parents and if you scream I will kill your black ass. You fucking niggers are always doing shit taking our women and making fucking half breeds you make me sick. It's okay Maurice I'm going to take excellent care of you trust me you won't feel a thing just remember to take a deep breath. He tapped his two fingers on his side reassuring me that he had a gun of some sort and that any sudden move for me was vital. As he flicked off the lights I saw a glimpse of his sliver gun reflecting off the moonlight that was coming through the bathroom window. I tried to run towards the door but I was captured by a firm grip around my neck. He swung me around as a heavy blow was stuck across my face. My body hit the floor as his hands began to wonder over my temple. I did however manage to kick him but his strength was much stronger than mines as hitting him only made him angrier. He ripped off my clothes and placed me on my stomach gagging me with a wash cloth. As he pinned me down unlacing the shoe laces from his shoes, using them as bondage to tie my hands behind my back and my feet together. Controlling me, Place me in a submissive position of a mere peasant. As he formed salvia in his mouth and spit on the aperture of my backside, there was a quick second of silence... "SSHH NOT A WORD OR I'LL KILL YOU I SWEAR I WILL. IT WILL BE OUR SECRET...

A sharp pain inserted my body causing me to wiggle and swarm as well as mumble painful cries. Rapid motions were hitting the inside of me as if I was shoved and pushed in a big crowd back and forth and back and forth. As he pulled out of me and spat once more on himself again, this time shoving himself back inside of me even harder than before. I could feel his sweat dripping on my back. It was either deal with him rapping me or gag to death due to the fact from lack of air from the cloth being still in my mouth. He was making my body move as if an earthquake was knocking down my walls. He preyed on the innocence of my body like a lion did with its prey devour then deposed of the remains. Although he was penetrating my manhood, my ego, integrity yet I felt my soul was untouched. I felt like he was riding and breaking me in like a new stallion. I was thinking to myself I can't breathe it hurts too much I want my mom and dad which was statement I would say all the time in trouble or in need but in this case, no one could hear me. A silent thought, a silent voice, silent hope, silent tears and the continuous of my silent cries. This man who I thought was a real father; a real man was still proceeding with his statutory scène as if I was his true "American beauty" still fondling his new toy.

"Yea you like that, don't you? I love this boy pussy you have, hold on baby ugh I'm about to come soon, I know you like it you little fucking nigger. Tell me you like it. TELL ME! AND I'LL STOP. Hahaha that's right you can't say shit you better not either or fuck your brains up how about I stick my gun in you see how you like that? Huh yea you like it." So, he did exactly what he said, he stuck his gun up inside of me. His gun was cutting through my flesh. I can hear him playing with the trigger, Afraid that one may come out of the chamber. "I decided to hold my breath until I couldn't breathe any more. Counting in my mind from 10 to 1 trying to speed up the process since I was under so much tension as I began 10...9... "Don't you be getting wiggly on me boy, 8...7...6...? Ugh! As he made sounds of enjoyment expressing himself on his sexual gratification roller coaster, trying to reach that serial killer climax high. Not really trying to focus on his voice and escape in my head to imagine myself in a different place not paying attention on the affliction he was bestowing on me, 5...4...3... "I'm almost done, I told you that you were going to like it you want, some more don't you? 2...1... I felt a warm liquid sensation as if I was being stuffed with a lethal injection, as this point my body was left with his venom. He took his penis out into his hands I reckoned and began to piss all over my body laughing. He bent down and gave me his last words I heard him say to me before I passed out was "Ah boy I need to keep your ass around you have the best boy pussy then half of these women walking around and you can have whatever you want." He turned me on me on my side as my body looked like a deadly corpse, "Just remember SShhh not a word about this to anyone because silence is golden." He kissed my forehead while my eyes were still open what seem like a pass out state wasn't really a pass out just me lifeless you can say. I was numb to the very core. The darkness in his eyes will always be the image I will remember. His shudder some voice was the last ringing sound that vibrated my body with chills...

The morning sun is what woke me up that Saturday. I really thought I died or was in another world. I was granted to experience such a tragic moment although I pass out a little. My hands were untied but I still had marks and bruises on my body. I felt so weak and worn as I attempted to fully stand up yet I fell on my knees. I managed to pick up the fragments of my pride but found it difficult due to my clothes cover in blood. I wanted to forget what just happened, but I was forced to remember it all. I tried to convince myself that it was all just a nightmare yet my thoughts repealed that image. I finally stood up gathered my belongings and forced myself through agony to slip out of the bathroom window.

Soon as I got outside of that window I ran like hell or at least I tried as my insides were on fire...Literally feeling like someone just struck a match and was dancing inside of me. I was catching jagged throbs on my lower area near my penis. I took street alley ways to get to my house so he wouldn't catch me if he saw me leave or anyone asking any weird questions. My heart was beating so fast from running slash jogging as I reached the grounds of my elementary school. I hide in the jungle gym confused of my next move because I soon had to go home to tell someone but I couldn't or he would kill us all. If he can do that to me imagine what he can do to my family. I see a garbage dumpster and through my bloody clothes in there and just kept my shoes, shorts and the top half of my shirt that wasn't cover with blood. I began to be in a Trans wondering and asking myself what did I possible do god to deserve such a pain? Why me? Did I do something wrong to you? I should have listened to my parents and I shouldn't have trusted that man period. There was no way I can tell Senior and have him banish or disown me for something that wasn't my fought. If senior ever knew I would be the faggot son, he continued to be disappointed in. I was mad as hell this man broke, torn and mentally destroyed me. I felt bizarre and different about my body yet ashamed to be a boy. Thinking to me this probably wouldn't have happen if I was a girl. What am I? Who am I at this point I don't know what to do. Do I now have to get use to this from every man? Did this man really change me from the boy that I was to the man he made me?

Needless to say I returned home on Sunday before five and spoke of this to no one only to myself within my head. Consumed to be miserable with my thoughts and feelings as I prayed to god constantly for answers or did I really want to forget about god for really abandoning me in my time of need. My father always told us as children, whenever we needed God the most to simply, just call out the name Jesus and he shall answer...

Dear God,

I have suffered and torn into many pieces as thy flesh remained a broken vessel. Yet I prayed and plead to thee, no response on thy cry. Thy has been brutally beaten and ripped from inside to out, while thee looks from above and does nothing, but watch as in amusement. Oh, how my sweet sorrows of despair don't reach even the core of your mercy... as grace her twin doesn't see nor meets thy eyes. Thy fury is more intrigued then my heart for it beats no more sounding like a throbbing drum but now of pure silence... I thank thee... for false hopes... Don't pretend to hear thy cry I been hearing echoes instead of thy heavenly voice. Who are you? Speak up! I choose to renounce the importance to me that you have... FAIRWELL FOR YOU HAVE LET YOUR SON SUFFER AND FALL FROM YOUR CLOTH OF PROTECTION... Amen

4

THE BEST OF BOTH WORLDS....

"Alright now that it's over, our story is going to get much deeper as you continue through the memories and truths of my life it gets much deeper... go ahead read more... I probably shouldn't tell you that Maurice battles more than just this but a whole life style that is felt with many colors, emotion blah you know the whole deal. Better yet or how he ends up on top so I say with love, respect, confidence, beauty... I really can't say because you have to read more, who knows really death could mainly be the end for him?" Matter of fact put down this book right now, there is no need to read, He dies, everyone is happy, clouds are blue and the grass is green and everyone is felt with rainbows...

What could I say much time has passed from me being a weakling ten year to now being fourteenth identity of my own and an attitude that could manage whatever came my way? I now had a body that was thick built, solid, wide hips, long brown hair that was like a white woman with the right conditions if you feel me. To be real though I didn't have the look like my other two brothers so I pretty much remain in my shell sheltered and unconfident in everything that I did. Moreover, I felt whatever I am me. I didn't really give to flying fucks something I would say when I'm pretty much pissed off about something that I can't control such as the way I looked and was built like a linebacker. I felt like everything was changed about me when that man did what he did as I often call him that because saying his name puts him into an existence and I really didn't want to do that although I felt like he hunted me at times in my sleep and also in my thoughts everyday all day. Especially how god never helped me out about that no matter how much I prayed he stayed in my head through those years and in some cases I felt as if he influences my anger and attitude at times.

With that being said, he really worked my nerves the most in my new school Swatara middle school which I was now attending in the eighth grade. My family lived on 795 Highland Street within the Dauphin County District inside of a big green and white house. The year was pretty much 2006 and what can I say time was still ticking for humanity. Moreover, school was school I had about seven teachers and nine classes including lunch and free period where I could do pretty much whatever such as computer lab or free gym time. I was now an athlete with gymnastics, soccer and wrestling and honestly really loved it somewhat semi popular in school. People respected me for not sports or smarts sad to say but because of my mouth and my insane out bursts and non-caring attitude. I was always getting into trouble with the school and my parents. Ass whooping after ass whooping and the more I got my ass beat the more fury I had built up inside towards everyone especially senior. I often felt at times Senior and I never saw eye to eye on anything. I felt as though he secretly hated me. Senior wasn't the type of father to say to his children I love you,

I'm always here, Great job, I'm proud of you wasn't the words you heard from his mouth. He was more of the type of father to show up sometimes at games or yell and scream and beat the skin off you. I just became numb to yet that I stop paying attention to him. Really I didn't care because the more I got scolded for anything and everything there it all went in my number one journal I'm writing right now as the ink is on these pages, I just really feels though if anything came about me or the worst come at least someone would know my true story. Also writing this has made this my project for my English class which was Mrs. Roof who inspired me to write more and embrace this even if anyone didn't listen or understood me longs as I did. She told me it's a way of us as writers creating and escaping the real world when whatever goes wrong. So I did just that writing my truths and memories and pain in the best way I possibly could on this paper and the memory I had to relinquish was me currently in middle school now.

As I remembered it there I was in my second to the last class of the day which was Mrs. Roof's class before our end of the school year prep rally following our gymnastics routine my team had to do on May 25th a week before school ended on June 8th. My classmates and I were all fidgeting in our seats waiting for that bell to ring so after the rally straight home we could go. Our class was just felt with the last ten minutes of talking and not really paying attention to the teacher because if you ask me she really wanted that Friday to end soon as we wanted too. I was busy talking to a couple of girls in my class about their plans for the summer as well as my plans getting first job and making some money. I spoke to Jennifer Gross, Jenna Knobbles and Felicia Bright not he prettiest girls but I thought were in my category as middle school went by the jocks, geeks etc. like pretty much in any school really. So the girls were telling me that this summer was going to be really good because Jennifer had a birthday surprise for me that I was really going to enjoy. Something that was out of this world as I thought to myself because this girl was just a white girl not my taste and just weird the way she talked. I just dealt with her because she sucked my dick a couple of times and yes I did say she suck my dick heavy. I really didn't know about sex too much but hey to me I thought she was literally trying to make me bust a piss not a nut but a piss because that's how crucial her dick sucking game was. Shit, Senior nor did Bernice every give classes on sex and honestly that topic was really weird in my house. It's like you were scolded or yelled at for asking certain questions that went against the strict guideline of being a son or perfect kid in some sort. So thanks to the "The Man" good owe Shawn I already was ahead of my peers in the sex world, but really never really went all the way such as penetrating. I really had to soon though because I was getting sick and tired of the rumors in school about me being gay liking men and being a complete faggot. I mean sorry if a man raped me and fucked up my head a little and having a soft voice and built like a girl really didn't help none either so really I didn't give a fuck because I was going to hit some pussy anyway by means necessary in the summer time. I had to my image depended on it and most importantly my straight image listening to what society wanted a man and just a woman together not faggots.

Somehow Felicia and Jenna were going to come with her too they said which I already knew because those bitches sucked my dick too numerous of times especially when my parents weren't home. Just the sight of all three of them taking turns stroking my dick fondling and handling it in and out of their mouths back and forth the shit for the moment. Shit girls I don't care about your dam looks I just want my dick to see the back of your throats girls. I mean these bitches did some nasty freaky shit to me literally eaten my ass, sucking my dick sideways, backwards, upside down I mean any possible way you could think of even my balls were attended too front to back like their tongues were Huggies wipes for babies. So, a little sex was on my schedule for the summer time if it's meant to happen because the thought of the ideal of me really meeting that special someone that I could love and be with me for me wasn't really going to happen anytime soon. Moreover, I didn't care because I was going to get some sex anyhow. Happy to no longer be a virgin I suppose.

Next thing I know the bell rung and my peers and I jolted towards the exit door of the room ready for our school's rally. So, we all entered the gymnasium as the noise was so loud that is sounded like a football stadium. The cheerleaders went on doing their normal routine followed by football team screaming at the stop of their lungs like "Yeah baby, we our number one". Next to come was my team which was tumbling. I aced my all my landings like the movie "Stick it". What happen after the rally was more important though? I cleaned the sweat off my body and put all of my clothes and materials in my gym bag ready to leave the locker rooms as my principal,

Mr. Gordon entered and stated great job out there. So, imagine at this time I was getting dress. He held a small conversation with me about going to nationals to represent my school which indeed made me delightful and thrilled I was actually great at. So, as he started to walk past me to leave he smacks my butt and said "keep up the great work". Next thing aside that came after that was wow your butt really feels soft. I thought he was leaving but he actually wasn't he turned back around unzipped his pants and the length of his man parts fell out. He looked at me and said to me "do you know what to do with something like this?" In my head, I just thought of Mr. Shawn and what he did to me if I rejected or said "no". So, I told him, in return he came closer to me and told me don't worry I will be your coach. Mr. Gordon said "there is nothing to it just remember you still want your teeth, and keep your eyes on the tattoo bird which was exactly seven inches down from his belly button. In my head, I was crying but, yet I showed no weakness. I did exactly what he said; I knew he was happy about it as I was more fearful then ever frightened that he would hurt me like my last hunter. As I closed my eyes to take the image out of my head of what I was doing at the moment, my head was felt with a question to God "why me lord?" … Mr. Gordon started to get much louder with his juvenile pleasure of me as his last scream of orgasm let me knew he was finished, but I knew that already as I had the remains and the effects of it on my face and in my mouth. I gagged and threw up coughing and spitting left and right. He said exactly what Shawn said "SShhh… not a word to this to anyone or I swear you will pay for it.

Indeed, I did heed his warning like I did the last man's. More importantly I was mad more at God then anything because I felt as though he was laughing from above and knew exactly what was about to happen. Once again he didn't step in to help me nor punished the man for what he was doing to a child like me. I felt as though God wasn't really God but something that the world has created as a higher power for nothing. I mean what kind of God would do such things like this; I was only just a child, a mere boy at that. Nothing could replace the fear, the rage, the unwanted emotions that I had inside of me. If God himself or herself couldn't fix this problem, then I was stuck to deal with this shit on my own. No one would understand me. I have no one to listen or to vent my tears in. Once again I was alone with silence and the deal with the demoniacs of thoughts. Tears always flooded my head but never really shown anymore through my eyes. The more I thought about God, the more I became felt with rage and anger. I didn't want to listen to anyone nor really cared. I was stuck to deal with it all and with that being said, my personality switched for the worst. I became the most devilish thing in the world which was the best of both world's straight like imaged but sweeter than a sugar cane. I was going to make every man pay for the shit that they bestowed upon me and curse that God influence. I was going to be the icon that every man wanted and wasn't going to allow them to take charge of my life no more. Instead I was going to be the aggression and the predator preying on the weak and innocent. I was going to change my appearance inside and out but still remain my angelic image to family and friends as if no one could ever tell the difference. I wanted to raise hell and revenge was screaming for me to devour... So, I did as I prayed to God in rage and ignorance...

Dear Lord,

Why must thy cursed thee with a curse. I forsake thee in every way. Yet thy will has been broken, harmony has been taken and yet peace isn't still any more. You have allowed your fallen angel of music chimed thy soul with evil and hatred. He swept thee off my soles and cluttered my thoughts with a kiss of death and ye wonders with the question "why my poor child? No longer will I be yours, I rebuke thee, I rebuke thee or father that is no longer mines... I rebuke thee and every existing factor you no longer exist to thee anymore... Yet the taste of both worlds is the sweetest fruit I have bitten and yet better than your daughter eve biting her fruit, O I have loved this Adeline of sin.

5

SIN EQUALITY

I really didn't care what God wanted from me anymore because in my eyes and thoughts I felt as though he really didn't exist anymore but a mere thought.

"Sad to tell my reader's but the story line for my character Maurice tends to get much deeper and graphic, so if you don't like the homosexual thoughts and displays of sexuality then, I advised you to put this shit down because it only gets worse. I mean this shit gets downright nasty and disgusting trust me, I didn't even want to write it but the show must go on" .... or shall I say silence.

Believe it or not life seemed a lot different in high school as I was a freshman at Cedar Dauphin East High. As it was my first year beginning with the year 2007, I was now sixteen with broad shoulders, long hair that went to the middle of my back and an ass for days bigger than half of the females in my school. I had a nasty attitude like fuck the world because deep inside me really didn't care. Most importantly my relationship with my parents began to get worst the more I got older. The more they tried to control me the more I rebelled and became more defiant with the things I wanted to do. Moreover, in high school, I really only had two good friends which was Monique and James. Monique was tall chocolate toned, long hair for a black girl, big ass, nice tit-ties and a smart-ass mouth hence why I loved her. On the other hand, James was my homeboy who was in Christ but also had a bad boy image to him if he was pissed off enough. He was also dark complexion and very short like a hobbit. These two kept me on my ass literally in school with jokes and gossip.

So, there I was in choir rehearsal with James practicing on the upcoming music fest as our whole class gave it are all. James taped me on my leg and asked me was I going to Amber's party a girl in our school that was very cool. I really didn't care since popularity wasn't hard for me; I tend to fit in due to the legacy my older brother left behind for me, which was fuck every bitch and keep it moving. His model was having that bitch swallow your kids and never get a girl pregnant. Sometimes I followed this but, however I was shy when it came to girls. I mainly faked the funk in school to pretend I was fucking all these girls when actually I was still a virgin. I didn't even know what pussy smelled or taste like to tell you the truth. My dick has never seen the inside of female lips. Instead it's seen the hands of a man. I mean my body was use to men but never women, and to be honest on that note, I was scared to even let a woman view my body because I really didn't know what it was worth sure I was sexy and finger licking good but I couldn't tell my thoughts that as they always interfered as I would approach a girl and get nervous then leave her presence. Shit, I really wanted a girl though all of my friends were already out their fucking bitches and me I was too scared according to my friends to even touch some pussy.

I finished with choir with James and told him I would call him later so he could pick me up since he was a grade higher than me and already had his license. Monique and I had to get ready for our buses and talk about some things mainly people. Maurice! "Yea as I responded to her while my face was pointed towards a direction of a girl I like, but she never took notice to me." Well I have to talk to you about something important that can't wait whenever you have the time. "Well, girl what is it? "I'll call you on the phone because I don't want to say it in person in front of your face, just please make sure you call me when you get home. What are you doing this weekend? "Well I really don't know maybe just working at my job which was "Fuddruckers" at the time.

"Okay well whatever you do, just please don't forget to call me Mar"

"Alright, I won't I promise. She got off the bus and my stop was soon to come. I had many thoughts in my head that just kept me from being the age that I was but more matured and adult like. Although I just wanted to be a normal teenager I was far from it very far. I got dropped off by my bus went inside of my house dropped my things in my room and packed my overnight bag and told my parents I was going to stay the night at my older brother's house in "Penn woods" which was an apartment complex. There at my brother's crib I could practically do anything and everything I wanted to do without being cursed out by my parents, so that's exactly where I spent most of my time at. Plus, my parents didn't care they felt as though my big bro was going to take care of me and wouldn't allow me to get into any trouble.

I got over my brother's house and what you know the door was lock as usual, but I didn't care either the spare key was underneath the rug or one of his windows was unlocked. I knew my brother that's how he was at times he was probably on his pussy mission to devour and conquer being a legend like always. I looked underneath the rug that was at the door of 5125 apt D of Manayunk Rd. went inside through my belongings on the couch and started to plan my weekend. I called up James and asked him if he was still going to that party of Amber's. He was and so was I. I told him he might as well come over because my brother wasn't coming back anytime soon. Juju agreed which was a nicknamed I called him and said he would be here within the next hour so I told him just come through the front door since I was going to blast the music for the party mood and hop into the shower. I began to run the water and sing gospel music since that was the only thing that kept satan out of my mind because he always seems to alter my thoughts not matter what I did and tried to do. Singing was one of the greatest gifts God did give me since he wasn't good at nothing else. I began to get deeper and deeper and started to feel it more because he made me smile to know the range I had. I had a big voice inside this tiny body I had. *"Know that I am always with you; don't give up my son the battle isn't yet over. I haven't left you nor forsaken you, for what shall happen next will cause you great pain and suffering just call on me and I shall be there, believe in me and I will come. For no temptation, my son has taken you except what is common to man, for I am faithful, who will allow you to be tempted above what you are able, but will with the temptation also make the way of escape that you may be able to endure it. For I didn't give you a spirit of fear but the power, love, and self-control, Believe. Believe and I shall be here"*

I felt as though at the moment God was talking to me. As if he was trying to reach to me and make a connection. "No don't listen to that remember he allowed you to get raped and allowed you to suffer. If he was really who he said, he was where is he now. Where was he in the beginning when you called for him nowhere but looking at you as if you were an insect? He doesn't care. The only person that cares about you is yourself. Trust me he will allow you to go through it again as he has done already before. Get that out of your head Maurice. Curse his name. Curse who he is and every heavenly thought that he tries to bring because I'm here with you and always have been since you have gone through it all. Remember I told you revenge would sound better. I reminded you that pain can be brought to others if you just listen to me instead of the so-called thing you name as God. I am your savior. I believe in you. I have always heard your cry. Have I not been there always? "Es esmu satīna. Savu nekustamo Dievs un mūsu Pestītājs. Elle ir svarīgāks, un sniedz jums visvairāk flameful dāvanu, tad debesu kādreiz var. Par manu vārdu ir Leģions, let manu armijas lietus galvu un plūdu jūsu sirds, un jūs ir valdnieks visu, ja tu stāvi ar myside." (I am Satan your real god and savior. Hell, is more important and gives you the most flame-full gift then heaven ever can. For my name is Legion, let my army rain in your head and flood your heart and you shall be the ruler of all if you stand by my side).

My singing began to cease as these two voices began to battle in my head I was confused and struck with terror. I didn't even understand the language that was ringing in my ears. It sounded like Hebrew then I thought it was Latin. The crazy thing about the whole ordeal was that I understood it because I was talking back to the voice in Latin. I never knew I could speak that language nor understood it. I was chanting "par manu vārdu ir Leģions" over and over again in my head and was laughing and smiling the whole time... My chanting began to stop with a bang at the bathroom door. "Hey man are you almost done I been out here waiting in your brother's living room for about a half an hour now." It was James. "My bad man here I come. My eyes were wide open as I took one foot out of the shower followed by the next one. I wrapped my towel around me and open the door he was sitting on the couch texting on his cell phone. I walk past the door framed to walk towards my brother's room to change my clothes and I managed to catch a glimpse of his face and eyes. He was staring at me and the look of his eye had a dark glow in them. "Why are you staring at me nigga? "WHAT! I'm not I'm waiting for you to hurry up and get dress so we can zoom to this party now stop playing and let's move it along please" I totally forgot about the whole party and snapped back into reality well my mission to have some fun.

I manage to finish up my outfit and threw it all on and adding my final touch with curve cologne and baby lotion. We hopped in his car and drove towards the party as we both was hyped. "Here drink some of this it will relax us and have us twisted for the party." I took the bottle and looked at the label in front of it which read "Vodka Absolute". Man I don't drink you know that... "Just drink it trust me man it's powerful" That voice in my head told me it was okay go ahead the only thing it would make me do was think clearer and be myself. So I did and boy did it burn my chest and before I knew it I have consumed the entire half of the bottle to myself. James and I got into the party seeing mainly everyone from our school. Everything was spinning around like crazy but I felt good and warm inside. Like this feeling made me giggle and constantly tingled and warm all over. "Hey since I been drinking like you, you mind if I stay the night at your brother's with you since I don't want my mom to know I was out this late and plus I already told her I was staying anyway because I felt like you wouldn't mind." I told him yea because I already knew my brother wasn't going to be home so it didn't bother me, that's how it was anyway on the weekends I stayed I pretty much have the house to myself every weekend. Man, I was in that party acting a pure ass dancing with so many bitches and feeling on asses like crazy. James looked at me and gave me a head nod like "yea man we in here marking which girls was going to get it" Hey! Don't forget Maurice I need to tell you something later and talk to you about something important for real." "Okay as I told him while I was finishing dancing with this one girl throwing her ass up in the air and dry humping her like I was really fucking her on the dance floor."

The party was the best it pretty much lasted for four hours from 10:00pm to 2:00am. We were already late by an hour because of me taking my good ole slow time getting ready but we didn't care because James and I had a blast a night to remember. I started to feel dizzy and drunk as I told him. "All man that's normal it will wear off trust me." Well I seemed to be more drunk then he was since he was okay to drive us back to my brother's house which was only ten minutes away from the party. We got to my brother's house and were laughing about the whole night. I was falling and stumbling all over the place even constantly throwing up in the bathroom toilet. I got out some blankets and pillows for him to sleep on the couch while I would go to my slumber chamber which was my brother's bed.

He came in the room to get his phone charger; I asked him "Can I see your phone? He started to hand it over to me as I smacked it out of his hand trying to be playful and making jokes since I was twisted out of my mind. The phone landed on the bed near the right side of me. He crawled on the bed staggering too cursing at me like "why the fuck would you do that?" What James is cursing? You never curse, so I grab the phone from him teasing him because he was short and couldn't reach it while I had it held up in the air. "Give me my damn phone Maurice" UGH NO! HA as I cackled with laughs. He jumped and jumped but just couldn't reach it and next thing I know I started to bring it down from the air and he grab my arm leaned in and kiss me. WTF I was shocked... I didn't know what to do at this moment. We both looked at each other and stared in one another's eyes for a minute than he kissed me.

My eyes were closed because I didn't want to imagine this and then reopened them because I couldn't believe this shit was real. I wanted to push him off but yet I never had someone kiss me on the lips not along a guy. I was so use to men just taking advantage and rapping or abusing the shit out of me, I couldn't handle this situation. I was curious to why? In my mind, it seems right and something kept ringing in my ear telling me no and that I need to stop this. Next thing I know his shirt came off and so did mines. His pants dropped from his waist line. He reached for mines and I told him no. He looked at me and said "This is what I wanted to tell you that I like you and I'm not going to do anything but kiss your body."

I listened and I was intrigued to what was about to happen as we both stood there nude now in the dark. He couldn't see my body nor could I see his as our finger tips were the eyes. He caressed my chest and pressed his lips against mines. His tongue slowly entered my mouth swerving around like he was licking the taste buds off my tongue. As soft kisses started to go down from my chest to my nipples, and even slower down my stomach; making this memorable. He cuffed my balls with his small hands. As he blew on the eye of my snake I felt a warm sensation overcame my body as small hairs stood up on my arms and back. I looked down and couldn't believe what was happening. His head was turning so hard in circular motions as if he sucking on a Popsicle and he was sucking and licking every flavor of it to core that it wouldn't exist anymore. His nails went back and forth across my chest and as if he was tickling me while he remains on his knees, submitting to a sexual endeavor. I never felt this before from any person especially a man. He was juggling my balls in his hand as if they were Chinese stress balls and still choking the hell out of my chicken. I felt no teeth but yet a pleasure hole. Like his mouth held all the treasures in the world and I was his golden rod. Next thing I know he takes it out looks at it spits on it and says "you like that don't you" … I remained silent because I wasn't use to talking. He went right back to making it all disappear in his mouth he was Houdini. My eyes rolled back in my head, as my body felt so good and relaxed. I felt like I was in another world. He was taking it out again smacking it against his tongue playing with it in and out of his mouth as he felt me with more pleasure.

I was overwhelmed with fear, sin, and joy and shamed all at the same time. It felt too good for me to stop. Finally, I thought to myself someone isn't hurting me but showing me satisfaction. I was nervous what was about to happen next as bullets was blasting out of my gun as I took deep breaths and moaned silently. He ran to the bathroom and spit up as my kids were dropping from his mouth hitting the carpet floor. All I could hear from the bedroom to the bathroom him throwing up and coughing as my mind began to play tricks on me. "See I told you Maurice you would get revenge… Doesn't that feel good! There will be more to come in the future if you just follow my directions and listen to me." As that small little voice echoed in my head, I was content to really listen since what it was saying was actually true. This time I didn't get hurt I wasn't forced to do anything but enjoy something that was for me. I wasn't bossed nor threaten. I didn't have a gun pointed towards me. I didn't have him telling me SShhh don't tell anyone or nothing. I laid on the bed looking up at the ceiling like what I just did felt good but something was strange about this. It seemed wrong. I was disgusted with myself that I allowed this to happen. I felt god was pushing me again. Correcting me in my head like he was very disappointed but he just told me that I just got revenge. He was confusing me. I didn't know what I did was either good for the goose or bad for the hatchlings. James came back in the room and climbed into bed and laid his head on my chest and wrapped his arms around me. I didn't know what to do as I laid there like a dead body motionless. He took my arms and wrapped them around his body as a our stench smell of sin. Before he dosed off he whispered something in my ear and said "Don't worry I been through the same things you have and trust me I won't hurt you. I will always be here for you as your best friend and whatever else you need. I didn't know what he meant at that moment because I had so much running through my mind. I tried to sleep but yet I still was looking up at the ceiling eyes wide open as I was at a slow pace dosing off...

UNFORGETTABLE

"For we all have sinned and fall short of the glory of me. If you confess your sins, I am faithful and righteous to forgive you the sins and to cleanse you from all unrighteousness. Due to the mind of the flesh is so hostile towards me; for it is not subject to my law, neither indeed can it be. Those who are in the flesh can't be pleasing to me. I tell you, no but unless you repent, you will perish in the same way. Blessed are the merciful, for they shall obtain mercy...

These words came to me in a dream as if someone was speaking to me directly. As if they were ashamed at what just happened the previous Friday night. The words touched me but yet I didn't know exactly what they meant or where they came from. So, I avoided them at all cost and erased them out of my head for it was untainted gibberish. Something ranged more loudly in my head which was "par manu vārdu ir Leģions" It woke me up from my slumber that Saturday morning on my brother's bed. I turned my head to the side looking out the window. The house was quiet; I already knew James left early so he wouldn't be faced with questions of my confusion. Although I had a smashing head pain didn't erase the scenes that happen last night. I didn't know what to say or do. My mind was blank until something told me now the fun begins from here on out. I quickly searched for my cell phone grabbed it and called Monique as she picked up she cursed me out on the phone for not calling her exactly when I got in and talking to her about what she wanted to tell me. "What was it you can tell me now I'm really sorry?" "Well, Maurice, it doesn't matter now I either forgot it or can't really say right now." Alright I figured she really didn't have anything to say in the first place because I knew her.

If it was really important she would have remembered it. Honestly, I lied to her saying that I couldn't talk on the phone anymore because I had to do something. I really didn't have to do shit but focus on my thoughts sense the night before still played rapidly in my mind. I mean was I gay because these misfortunate events that have happened in my life. Lord, knows this isn't nothing that I wanted and far from it. For James to be my friend, best one at that; I felt as though he really took advantage of me especially when we were drinking and he pretty much knew about my whole life. He was the only person I told about my Shawn. Part of me felt like he used me like the other two men, yet why did I feel that what he said about never hurting me? Was this possibility true? Was this my destiny? Was this something we were going to share together or just act as though the night never happened? I really wanted to know seriously because I didn't want to set myself up for embarrassment nor disappointment. Don't get me wrong James was my homeboy but if something could be much more, I would feel awkward about it but also curious to know. Since really the only person I have ever trusted more than family has been him. To believe it or not, I always felt a weird vibe from him but never acted on it like he did with me or better yet said anything to him about such things since they remain as erotic dreams. I really didn't want that though to be honest with my best friend encase things won't work out I would be struck with confusion and more importantly loss of a good friend. I really wanted a woman. I wanted her to be everything if possibly able to heal and mend pieces in me that I couldn't myself try to fix. I wanted her to love me for me and make things work no matter what the cost, problem or disbelief is because I have a lot of love to give. I know it sounds crazy like how can you give love if you have never known what it was nor received it. I wasn't pressed about her body or looks but more concern with the contents of her mind and the music that her heart could bring me so that our souls would dance eternally in harmony and peace. Specially to deal with someone like me with a lot of baggage, demons that weighed tons. I wanted her to be strong and never give up because it's what I always wanted LOVE... something that family nor friends couldn't give me, which were the comforting, gentle warmth and true affection of a woman.

For her to work with me and mold me into everything she is possibly looking for and to complete her. I felt as though the value of my heart was priceless and the measures of my love that I could give would be 3-D dimensional. I just needed one to be there no matter what. The chances of something happening like that were very slim since I was nothing like my older brother in that department nor felt like just fucking bitches just to fuck them. I wanted much more. I wanted... compassion and love. Not just any love. I wanted indestructible, long lasting, undeniable, courage, true love. I wanted the girl of my dreams that is to look me in my eyes and see past all the ugly that was inside of me that was there not by choice but by many experiences and pain. Let me catch my thoughts because waiting on this fantasy was never going to come so

I had to face reality and come back to terms with myself that no one wanted to be with someone that had such skeletons like I did.

Moreover, that Saturday was more confusing for me than ever in my life as my friendship and thirst for affection was driving me insane. I even went to work thinking that it would get my mind off things but yet it didn't. The lover's quarrel scene was still playing tricks on my emotions and sentences that formed in my head. As much as I wanted to cry over this I couldn't because of work and due to the simple fact that I really didn't have emotions inside of me just pain and neglect. Everyone seems to treat me like that or that's how I made them to be, to simply protect myself from actually being vulnerable. I was scared at work to either get a text from him thinking he is going to blame me for the whole thing. To hear him say "Oh, sorry Maurice I can't be your friend anymore. It's not anything that you did but more so on my part." I didn't want to lose James as a friend but deep down inside part of me didn't want that to EVER happen again and the other half was curious… eager to learn where this could have led me. As I often thought to myself that I looked unattractive and disgusting as most girls in my high school didn't really want to date me. Especially after my other two girlfriends' one is being Crystal who was small, petite, Rican with long hair and a models body but very conceded and stuck up. She was cool but only likes to use me for material things and I wasn't really down for that especially when she was James's friend. We almost got close to having sex but I didn't feel like being her score points in high school for virginity being taken, neither did I want all of my friends and folks knowing my business. Next on the list was Jasmine and God O mighty she was built and thicker than a government's paycheck. I mean long beautiful hair, caramel skin tone, soft lips, and a VERY big ass. I mean she had a grown woman's ass only to be fifth teen. I would have really wanted things to work for us but her father didn't like the ideal of her dating boys so are relationship pretty much ended very quickly no matter how much we tried to hold on to or savor nothing never worked... So the ideal of me keeping James around as my friend was normal until things started to fall from friendship or lovers as he text me at work that day telling me that nothing was going to change for us that we could still have fun and still be nigga's. Do not get me wrong I mean reading this I know it seems strange but at the present time I felt as though love didn't exist in genders and I was very open minded until the correct ethnics came to mind and changed me for the best instead of the worst.

I got off work that night at my usual work place and James picked me up. I already told my parents that I had a ride so I was okay and they really didn't seem to care much as long as I checked in. We rode around the city of Harrisburg talking and laughing as if we were two school girls. I loved the attention he gave me all the time I was around him. He made me feel special and unique. He had a way with words and making me laugh about the dumbest things even if they weren't funny as long as I was around him I was already felt with joy. He dropped me off back at "Penn woods" and told me he would call or text me later, as I still stood there staring into his eyes to see where I was supposed to depart from him with a kiss or the usual homeboy hand five or shake... It was a shake, I wasn't mad I just figured we both would never be the same from that night and that some things are normal for us to feel skeptical around each other especially with are moods around one another.

School was that Monday; I was excited to meet him again but nervous at the same time. School relaxed me from the unwanted affection and arguments that home always had waiting for me. Senior never showed affection and Bernice was still trying to do the best she could be filling in the holes her husband couldn't due himself. I really didn't care because I had James's attention and affection and Senior was just a pebble compared to a boulder like James in terms of endearment. I was gathered around my locker as I always did before my last period of class and I heard the most beautiful noise. It sunk in my head and the melody made me feel accomplished and overwhelmed with peace. I slammed my locker door and started to follow the harmony to its origin. I turned the corner from the end of the hallway, made a right and seen that it was coming from the last door on the left. As I came closer to the door, I peeped in the window and seen the school's gospel choir. "Go in and share your gift son" was in my head and I started to want to walk away but my feet like glue was keeping me bonded to the very spot I stood.

If it wasn't that then I don't know what really made me open that door. I walked in and the choir was singing a song called "Now behold the lamb" I felt like all the negative energy I had in my body was release. I didn't feel out of place here but more like acceptance and I felt wanted. I especially knew this song and was humming the lyrics inside of my head. "Hello, is there anything I can help you with" as a slim, slender built white man started to walk towards me. His nose and eyes seemed too spaced apart. He looked very strange. I hesitated and said "no, I was just amazed at the music I was hearing. "Well, do you sing and if so would you like to join us? "Go ahead, sing to me so that I may hear your cry, sing to my praises and feel thy anointing" as the voice echo the walls of my head. Well I'm not perfect as I told the man and by the way my name is Maurice but my friends tend to call me Mar as I spoke to him. "Well that's fine Mar and also I am Mr. O'Neil and I am the gospel choir director here. Would you like to sing a song for us so that we may see where you are at with your vocals? REALLY! I'm shy singing in front of people and don't really know what to sing. "It doesn't matter sing whatever comes to mind long as it is gospel and there is no need to feel nervous everyone has been nervous here before, trust me you are amongst friends and a whole new family here. "GO ahead and sing son, I'll feel your heart with a song." There was that voice again. Well since you insist Mr. O'Neil here it goes, "Bless in assurance that Jesus is mine, O what for taste of glory divine, He's the heir of salvation...." "Stop, stop you have an amazing and powerful voice, but it needs work and true power from which you have potential but you need the strength of Jesus Christ to build upon that and to make it so much more than just a voice but your testimony." Thank you, Mr. O'Neil." Your welcome Mar, here is a bible for you and if you want you can join whenever you want there is no rush and you come when you are comfortable and all that we ask is just if you make a commitment with us your making one with God also and bettering a relationship with him by sharing a gift that he has given you. Your gift is perfect and nice and just needs to be replenished in the spirit of God. It's there but you will never know what you are capable of if you don't train it and feel it with the power of God."

I wasn't even going to lie, singing in that room made me feel special and I really wanted to join and see where exactly it would take me... "You don't need that shit remember Maurice you are already special. Remember how James treats you as if you really are special to him. What you are looking for is there and holds greatness for you than a mere God could ever give you. Someone who wanted you to sing so much never really gave a care on how you would hurt and suffer the way you have done. Just remember Maurice who has been here for you no matter what through all of the pain you have received and who has taught you how to deal with these things in the most incredible way. Just remember who we both are together..."

At that moment, I really didn't want to listen to that shit that was filling inside of my head. I really enjoy singing and wanted to do this just to see where it would take me. If a relationship came along with God, then so be it. I was more excited to how many fellowships I would have if I joined the gospel choir at school. I thought long and hard on it for the moment and really didn't know what to do. How could I join something religious when I had James still hanging on me? If he was my friend he would understand. Somehow, I felt like I needed his permission for some strange reason. Scared and lonely I decided to join this organization just to give it a try. I would never know what it holds for me if I never put an effort towards it so I thought to myself why not?

Dear Lord,

I heard thee whisper in thy ear like the wind blows on the earth. Is this a symbol of your affection? Does it taste like honey and delightful to my tooth? Or will it shock me with its sour after taste and rot the essence of thy mouth. What do you want in return of time submitting? Does thou want to trick thee in to damnation? I want to know thee more and sip thy gift and warmth as if it has never been done before. O father I'm so confused on what it is that is being asked of me. Yet I don't know so I will remain being the cold-hearted muscle that still beats with hatred that pumps through his body, help me! Help me please O lord.

I decided to get more intrigued with this religion thing. I figured I really didn't know how to do this pray thing nor speak correctly. Guidance and correctives was all I really needed to build me up to the right person to sing and do the good lord's will. I didn't want god ashamed of me nor did I want him punishing me any longer. Yet the emotionless personality I had just really didn't give a fuck. I was bad to the bone and really enjoyed it to be honest. I mean the only person that cared about me was James. The chances of me telling my folks that I wanted to do the lords bidding was nothing but jokes as if I could hear it now all from their mouths. I decided to call James that night to ask him some questions on this religion thing just to get a second opinion. I called the first two times all I got was a couple of rings then the voicemail. I hated when he did that, like that shit really pissed me off. Then just before my mind started to run away with my emotions my cell rung and it was him I picked up the phone to Hey baby, yea anyways, James I have some questions to ask you about religion as I stated with an agitated tone. Just to run some ideas off you I want to join the gospel choir at school and feel like it's weird when I know what I'm doing with you isn't right either. Is it possible for me to still join?

Like is god going to be mad at me singing to his graces and still fondling around with you? Like am I going to die from this or go to hell? Like dude help me out here like I just really don't know? I don't want to tell my parents because I may get laughed at, so that's why I'm asking you, so what do you think? I started too rambled like crazy on the other end of the line, before I could keep it up he stop me with a "whoa". I replied what? He told me that joining the choir would be great for me that god forgives everyone and that he loves all his children unconditionally. He told me that I didn't have to worry about what we experience that we didn't have to do that anymore and just be friends the way things used to be before that night of a fairytale. What about my parents I asked? I didn't have to worry about that either and just to tell them I was staying after school for some kind of math help. He told me he was in the gospel choir at school and he wasn't there the day I sung because he was in detention for tardiness to classes. I started to form questions in my head again but stop when he said, "Look I do care about your past being my friend and would never stop you for trying to neither better yourself nor change who you want to become. Far as our intimacy that can stop with no problem it will be as if we still bust it up with laughs and talking about girls or the usual conversation. Don't worry you won't lose me as a friend; I told you I'm going to always be here no matter what. "BUTTONS" which was a word we both said as a code like I love you or care about you when family or other people were around something we both understood and enjoyed.

I got off the phone with him that night and just laid in my bed thinking and dreaming hard on what I wanted my life to be like within the next five to ten years. Something that most people tend to do you know, set goals and accomplish them. I knew I wanted to go to college to become a writer or a great doctor of some sort. Yet the ideal of me writing and others enjoying it created negativity in my head to push that far back into the mist fog of my not caring attitude. I wanted to see myself succeed you know, fall in love, have kids while living in a big house with a white fence and a poodle name biscuit. I chuckle at the thought because that dream was only for the rich and famous. I often juggled that I didn't want to be famous just known for me and the talents that I possessed. I wanted to create my own writer's name like I don't know Sincere Ronoldi or doctor thoughts laughing out loud to myself at these crazy author names. I wanted to become somebody and not just anybody. As I got done with the daydreaming and staring at the light on the ceiling in my room I began to get my things ready for school and off to bed I would go. Then suddenly the strangest thing came to me telling me to pray, I shook my head as if it was just a whisper on my shoulder. Then surprisingly it came back again. I laughed because I didn't know one thing about praying yet know how it was done. So I just talked out loud to myself as if I had an audience: Oh dear lord, baby Jesus, god well whoever you are which one I don't know I ask you. I don't know teach me more of who you are. Let me know you are hear. Are you real? Can you even hear me? If so show yourself, I want to see what you look like. Are you a man, woman, child or even a creature? Why can't you appear to me? I started to giggle and get into bed as I knew I was crazy you know like maybe this whole thing of god wasn't true. That maybe I just had a way with my conscious running schemes in my head. I drifted off to sleep that night with James in my head high hopes and the addition his drug that I was thirsting to have more of LOVE.

"You called me to ask me who I am; I have always been here Maurice deep within you I am the lord God Almighty. It seems as though you need me, call on me when you really need me the most. Thou shouldn't take thy name in vain. What you are doing my son isn't right for you fight against it, be strong the battle has yet to begin. I need you to seek me more for without me you will experience more pain in your life then you ever have yet to do. Obstacles and trials will come your way, it is up to you to decide was is right or wrong for you, seek my name, seek my word, taste my grace and mercy. You know what you have to do, let me in so that I may show you the path of true righteousness. Remember Maurice the law of the wise is the fountain of life to depart from the snares of death.

Mar, remember me I will always be here to hold and love you. I love you too James as the voice started to fade away. Surrounded by the dark bliss yet another voice came close to me Maurice... Maurice yes! Who's there? It's me. Me who? Come find me Maurice. How I don't know where you are? A red light cracked in the deserted dimension, I could see my hands but not my face. I walked towards the light looking back and seeing nothing but darkness. I stretched my hands out to touch the red light and I was pulled into it. Why do you continue to keep hurting me Maurice promise after promise you say you are going to change and I believe you ever single time? Looking around to see where I was at it looked like a kitchen but whose kitchen was the question? I walked out of the kitchen towards what looked the like the front door and opened it to see what was outside. I see a blue two door sports car in the drive way of the house I came out of and right across the street was an apartment complex called "Whisper woods". So are you just going to leave out of the door and not listen to a word I'm saying? I turned around to look at the voice I was hearing to match it up with a face and jumped.

That shit freaked the hell out of me her face was blurry. Like for some reason I couldn't figure out who she was or yet so she thought I was. So are you going to just stand there and act dumb founded it or Do you even love me Maurice because I can't keep going through this tell me what's going on. Why are you hiding something? Is there something you want to tell me? I looked around in the living room where her voice drawn me to there was a computer in the dining room, a big screen TV to my right and a couch and loveseat to my left as she was staring and standing right in front of me. I glanced to the far right behind her and seen a picture of us well me holding her body in my arms as she kissed me. I was wearing a red shirt with a hat and it seem as though I was her boyfriend that we looked happy yet in love. Are you going to answer the damn question as she screams? Whatever I did baby or whatever you want me to do I'll do and I'm sorry for whatever. I love you always and forever. I got close to her to quint my eyes to unmask this mysterious woman and she responded to me I love you too bay always and forever. She kissed me and places her hand on my heart and I felt this connection we had this bond, this electric magnetic pull that she was my soul mate. The red light came again. I was lying in bed with her on top of me this time I could see her eyes as they were brown, big, bulgy and seen past everything in me. As if her eyes burned into the core of my heart. She kissed me again and said as she looked into my eyes I love you, please don't ever hurt me. I looked deep into her brown eyes and said I love you more always and forever. I felt like my body was drunk either off the moment or something else. We both began to indulge into a continuance of passion of affection. I entered her and somehow, we became one. The red light came once more yet this time was different it flashed quickly while we were love making. I see everything about this woman, everything we shared together from tears to arguments to laughs from kisses to hugs. It felt good, I seen from when we got married to having kids' two sons. To us getting old and still loving each other constantly. As the sexual scene still played into effect with more rapid motions and a climax soon approaching of pleasure the light got even stronger. I then seen her face a quick glanced as the connection started to enhance. Then the horror came, I seen fight's us screaming and yelling at each other quick scenes of her saying you're still messing with men. I was verbally abusing her as I broke her down emotionally into little pieces as if she didn't matter to me.

I saw games that I played on her. A broken promise false hugs and kisses and even lies that I told. I had seen myself cheating on her heart, while she cried in the background. I had seen me doing sexual acts while she remained faithful. I saw our child being born and me ruining her life and shatter all her dreams and ambitions. I had seen her telling me you never cared you choose to have you fun and then try to always come back when you wanted. I can't wait for you to get yourself together me and my son is fine without you. Goodbye Maurice. The sexual connection broke as the red light took me to another place. Was I-time traveling? Was I dreaming if so I wanted to wake up fast, this didn't seem like a dream it feels real? I felt every emotion and pain. There I was again surrounded by four walls and unaware of my surrounding. I heard a juggling of keys at the door and decided to hide behind curtain in the bathroom scared that someone or whoever was coming in would be sure to find me. The voice barged through the door yelling "Fuck everyone no one cares, not my mom nor my dad. Not even my girl and I lost her too. God, you did this to me you said you would always be here, you are a belligerent bastard. Now thanks to you I can meet you early and come up there myself to tell you how I truly feel."

This man's voice sounded like me just older, not of a sixteen-year-old boy's. I stepped out of the shower tub to get and glance to see the man. I inched closer to the opening of the door way as he screamed you can come out I know you're here. So, I came out scared and petrified to look this man in the eye face to face. He screamed again some awful sound laughing at as he was drunk and falling over. He lifted his head and I see his eyes match up with mines. HE WAS ME! I was bugging out like what the fuck man was this type of shit. This man was me just with a deeper voice, facial hair and with a haircut. I need my drugs wears my coke. He was drinking a bottle of vodka and popping pills at the same time. I tried to go over there to stop him, well to stop me from doing this to myself but when I would touch him, my hands would go straight through him like what the hell this shit doesn't make sense to me like is this some type of Christmas carol shit my past my present and future type deal. I listened to him weeping and crying about him losing Lauren, fucking other men when you knew it was wrong. He was crying about him losing his son well our son. He was going insane while I was just standing there watching myself blow up right in front of me without being able to say nor do anything. I couldn't really believe this moment right now. Screaming at the top of my lungs WAKE UP MAR! YOU NEED TO WAKE UP NOW… GOT DAMN IT. "Why are you trying to wake up so fast the best is yet to come?

As he snuffed the powder off his wrist gulping the last of the bottle while sitting on the bed looking at me strange, I knew this shit was ballistic. Wait! You can see me? What do you think Glaze! Or shall I say Glaze in the making. I'm you and your me dickhead. Why are you trying to leave? You did this to us. You made us what we our ok? So don't give me any sad look and confused retarded gesture. You choose to sleep with men, you choose to shutter yourself from the world, you choose to lie, steal, cheat, connive your way through people. You choose to listen to him when you knew you were called for better, for greatest. You held the power life and death on your tongue as well in your mind. So, despite all that you choose I am what you become; I am what you are because I AM YOU! I became you when you shelter everything inside. Your fears, your silent cries of a world of emptiness. You didn't want to listen to the wise one, did you? You decided this path for us and now you want to leave because the going is tough. Look how pathetic we have become. We can fuck a man, lie to the love of our life and love ones around us, cheat life, rob and hurt others yet we can't take responsibility for our own actions, I can't even look myself in the mirror anymore because of you. Wait I don't understand. WE OUR NOT MENT TO UNDERSTAND WHY DON'T YOU GET THAT, WE OUR GIVEN CHOICES AND IT'S UP TO US TO CHOOSE WHAT IS RIGHT OF ACCORDING TO HIM. Who is him? As I was talking to me, just forget it because you're never going to nor learn, nor care about anyone but your damn self. Trust me I know. So, guess what I have for you nothing but death. The dream like me reaches in closer and I kissed myself on the lips. Then pushed dreamlike me away saying what are we doing. What are you doing? You're so afraid and deranged that you didn't even realize you can't even love yourself. So with that being said I guess that kiss meant nothing to us, yet that kiss will lead you to your death well our deaths. Are we ready? Wait I don't want to die; I don't want us to die. Too bad too much damage has been made, you see you ruined every opportunity you had to do different in life, you asked him to give you love, a child, peace in mind and yet a life worth living and what did you do you gave him your ass to kiss literally by ruining every blessing you had so you don't deserve to live, that is why we are going to kill ourselves and be done with that... maybe will meet god or maybe not who knows let's just find out. As I stood right in front of me laughing and caring on like an animal he pulls out a razor from his left pocket. I run towards him to stop him yet I was going right through my body. What's right me? Are we a little afraid? Here we go love. He rolled up his sleeves to both arms as mines began to roll up as well. He slashed his right wrist as blood squirted out fiercely so did my right wrist. I began to feel like this wasn't a dream at all because it hurt. Tears were coming down from my eyes because whatever he was doing to his body mines showed the same since we were one. Are we having fun yet? No, please stop, we don't have to do this to our self. We can change. We our worth living for. PLEASE! Oh, no mister you're not getting out of this that easy it's time to go all the way and meet our maker. Ha as he laughed and silted our other wrist bleeding out so fast both our bodies were drench in blood. I fell to the ground so fast even the impact took life out of me. The reflection of me walked slowly over to me while I was on the ground and whisper to me "It's time we pay for everything we did, we are not god. You know that Latin you say in your head all the time. It means we our legion, we our many, we our hell itself. Its ok SShhh not a word. Don't cry, we let him in it will all be over soon. I looked myself in the eyes and seen that is was no longer me, but an evil demonic appearance of me. Then, I was glaring at myself then dreamlike me vanished into flames at I stared at the brown carpet slowly dying. A last tear hit the floor as a voice echoed my head roaring like a beast untamed...NOOOO!

Immediately I awoke out of my dream soaked in tears still crying. I got out of bed crying even harder asking myself is this true? Will that really become of me? I was terrified and didn't know what to do as I was pacing the floor of my attic bedroom, crying and soaring inside. I couldn't believe this I just thought it was an awful dream until I cut on my bedroom light and seen my shadow on the wall move from my body I screamed and rubbed my eyes and looked once more my shadow was there. I was now spooked. I grabbed my cell phone to call the only person I know that would listen to this story of mines. Ring! Ring! Sorry you reached the voicemail of James I can't pick up my phone right now so please leave a message after the beep... Beep! I hung up and tried again still crying, please James pick up I need you right now. No answer. I began to get more terrified as my head kept feeling up with questions as to who was I going to turn into? Who was Lauren? What did this whole dream mean? Was it real? Was it a warning? What did god want me to do? What did I mean by I let him in? How did I lose my child? How is it possible I was able to have kids? Was I really loved? Did I really have it all? Stop, stop, and stop it as I pounced on my head with my fist. My thoughts were tearing up inside. I dropped to my knees and began to weep crying out God WHY? Why me? What's wrong with me? What did I do god? HELP ME, PLEASE FATHER HELP ME:

OH, Dear God,

Please I'm losing you. I don't want to die. Show me what to do god. Show me who you want me to be. Strengthen me. Give me courage. God please. I feel god I been spiritual touch by another that is not of you. I don't want to go to hell. I'm sorry god for everything please. I feel as though there is not left to give and sorrows of my tears that I can bear no longer as I am on my last. Let your mercy touch the crown of my head. Let your grace guide my soles. Let me be open to hear you're calling and receive your love. Please god, I need you. Hear me. Hear me! Answer so that thou may listen to your tone. Reach out to thee. Touch thy spiritual core and crack open thy gifts that you long bestowed before birth.

"I will always remain here son, push to do better, and push to do my work, keep calling on me so that you may know me more. Change your ways of being wicked and lift up my name, repent so that forgiveness can swim in its deepest ocean. Turn and be righteous for anything asked shall be given if you uphold me in your heart. Your mind remains focused on me, and you confess with your mouth and heart your sins."

What do you mean god? I need more I do not understand? As I got up off my knees confused to what was a sin and what exactly was I supposed to do? How to look and search for him? The voice of thunder left my head again as it periodically came and gone when it felt like it. I apparently had a gift to replenish. Yet this dream would remain in my head or the layout of my life. What is my next objective? I needed to know yet find out more. I have to find answers to these questions.

WAKE UP AND SEE

As the dark voice spoke again to me what seems as though the spirit realm saying "you've started good but lets us take a look at how you fell off" As another memory slip inside my brain I saw myself as the young man I was Seventeen and running wild....

The next day seemed more unreal for me as I manage to respond to Lauren's text message I found it really difficult on how to explain myself. I knew if I sent the text she would call immediately. I tried to avoid it that morning, yet I didn't succeed. She called again and I finally pick up with a hesitating tone. "Hello" Hey what are you doing as she responded. I told her nothing just thinking. She again replied is there anything you want to tell me? Umm... Ummmhmmm I guess sure... Well go for it Mar I am all Ears right now. Where Do I begin?

So, I went in and told her the whole ordeal what I been through my curiosity with James that is only just a thing without emotion, yet it wasn't a part of me anymore. I'm learning to be more of myself and get over my past anger neglectful pain. I explained to her that I truly did love her and please don't give up on me. I swore to her that I was worth the fight. As she sweetly scolded me and explain to me sure no problem but whatever is in your past keep it there and learn to grow and move on to better things. I'm going to pray more for your recovery as long as you make an effort to give up your thoughts and strongholds. The more you hold on to those the more you set yourself back. I asked her was she ok? She told me yea but her mind was wondering and she was confused and nervous. As we both sat there our ears to each end of the receiver quiet awaiting on who was going to break the awkward silence. Finally, she did telling me she had to go to basketball practice and that she would call me back later.

As I manage to get myself together in my room I was startled by my mom and senior screaming my name COME HERE MAR! BRING YA ASS DOWN STAIRS. I rushed down thirteen stairs from my attic room and said yes walking fast down the hall way... YES yelling also until I got to their room. As I bent the corner to the hallway and walked through the door frame Senior seem so furious... Come here as he told me. Is there something you want to tell me and your mother? No I told him while looking at both of them with confusion. He looked at me like he wanted to cave my chest in. He stared me right in my eyes and told me "Well tell us why your friend Monique called the house saying that you let some guy fuck you and how you were bleeding all over the place or better yet that you caught some STD from him... As I started to speak up for myself and explain the situation fully senior hit me smack in the middle of my chest cage and knocked me clear on my feet. As my mother shouted "Hold on give him a chance to answer" Senior really didn't care at that moment as he shouted to me "No son of mines going to be a faggot, and if your ass becomes gay, I will disown you. If you don't want to abide by the rules of this house, then you can pack your shit and leave. I had so some many tears coming down at that moment as I jumped up and ran to my room in rage. In my head I was screaming and shouting, YOU NEVER GAVE ME A CHANCE TO EXPLAIN, YOU DON'T EVEN KNOW ME, YOUR NOT EVEN MY REAL FATHER, I FUCKEN HATE YOU DUMB ASS BASTARD, YOU CAN'T EVEN PLEASE YOUR WIFE USING VIAGRA YOU OLD DIRTY BITCH...

I shifted around the room gathering some small nick-necks I could. I wasn't longer going to live here. I fucken hated my life and hate being in this dumb ass house, you guys always treat me like shit as the middle child. This time I ran down stairs even quickly past their bedroom and Bernice shouted to me "Come here Mar!" I totally disregarded her, grab my car keys, jump inside my car, and speeded allowing my anger to be my fuel. I tried to call Laruen so that she could calm me down but I realize she was busy after I got her voicemail several times. I was tapping my head on my phone trying to call someone...yet I had no one really to talk to. Talking to God at the moment seemed pointless because it wasn't really going to help out my current situation. I couldn't call Monique because she is the reason why I am into all this shit in the first place. I manage to scroll through my phone in search for someone so I finally came to Chocolate; she was Monique's older cousin who recently got out of jail for eight years for fighting a police officer. Chocolate was a Dark skinned 5'11 women with brown eyes, slightly wide hips from having too many kids and she barley just had a butt. Her hair was long and jet black that was very curly and thick. She had the funniest and outrageous personality and you can tell that she was filled with good intentions.

Therefore, I manage to call Chocolate and was talking to her about my whole situation including what her cousin did and how it affected my family life with my parents. I was venting to her because I had no one else. I told Chocolate That I left my parents' house due to my dad hitting me and that I had nowhere else to stay. She went ahead and told me to come over that I could stay with her until things settle down and for me to get a good night's sleep before school the next day. I went ahead and did exactly that. I arrived at her apartment at Presidential Halls located near our city's Harrisburg East common mall. I knocked on the door a couple of times and she welcomed me with open arms. She told me I could sleep on the pull out couch and she had it all set up for me. Chocolates house smelled like cigarettes and skunk. I lay down that night looking up at the ceiling and try to process everything that was happening. My mind was trying to break it down in simplest terms but I couldn't. Tears formed as I swallowed the knot that was in my throat as I thought to myself if only my parents knew what I was really going through yet if they could snap so easy over something like that then they didn't want to hear the real story. I turned my right side to the direction of the TV and nick-at-night was the only thing I was interested in, it's because my mind was still coming up with negative thoughts that wouldn't allow me to sleep. This kept going on till like three in the morning.

Wake up Sugar foot... As Chocolate yelled at me from the kitchen how do you want your eggs runny or sunny side up or scramble. I responded to her doesn't matter. It was eleven a.m. I manage to oversleep and didn't remember to set my alarm for school. Chocolate came in the room, handed me my plate, and said "Don't worry about school take the day off you had a really bad emotional night last night." I told her thank you in return. She told me no problem. As she was walking away she told me to shower up and get dressed that we were going to the grocery store. She also explains to me that if I was going to live with her that nothing was free that I had my part to part take in within her household. She had two of her nephews she was raising since her other sister Nita was in Jail. She told me that I had to be responsible to pay one bill which was electric and nothing else. I agreed to those terms because I Was still making good money at the nursing home. She also told me that she wanted me to meet someone later on that day. I looked at her and asked her who? Yet she smiled at me and told me that I would see later that I might actually like this person. I overlooked what she was telling me and turned back on my phone. I had ten missed calls two from Lauren and the rest where from my parents.

The voice messages from them were just completely horrible things like if you come home, you won't get an ass whooping. Please come home your father isn't mad. Honey we are worried and the more you keep running the worst it is going to be for you. Your father didn't mean to say any of those things just please call me so I know where you are at. Your father said if you don't want to return are calls then fine you are no longer welcome back in are household. We will remove you off our health insurance policy, all of your belongings will be sitting on the front porch in bags for you, and either Samuel can bring them to school for you when he sees you or you can come get them. Lauren's voice messages were more of her showing her concern that she just wanted to know was I ok and where I was and that she was here for me if I wanted to talk about it and to give her a call or text so that she would know that I was ok.

I had so many emotions and things that were clouding my better judgment inside of my head. I just wanted to think clearer without anyone hassling me. Although I gave Lauren a text message and told her that I was fine that I was staying with a friend and that I loved her and I would talk to her later once she was available from her college busy schedule.

Chocolate and I shared many laughs as we were leaving the grocery store. She didn't drive so that required my assistant. She told me to take her to Regina ST. in the inner city you could say hood area of Harrisburg. Therefore, I did exactly just that. We pulled up to a house that had tons of people outside of it on the porch doing nothing but smoking cigarettes and drinking either old English or colt 45. She told me to stay in the car that she would be right back that she had to pick up something. I waited in the car what seem like forever, when you're waiting for someone time goes by slow. She got back in the car and told me you ready to have a fun night. I looked at her puzzle with a grin and said ... "Sure". We got back to the house and she began to cook and banged her music loud as hell... I didn't seem to mind because it drowned out the thoughts I had inside my head. She cracked open a beer and asked me if I wanted one. I looked at her and then to the beer and was debating if I actually really wanted to try one. She said "I'm not your parents, longs you take your ass to school, pass and follow the rules then I have no complaints on what you do. I looked at her and laugh and said no problem because going to school wasn't an issue of any sort for me. I was just more afraid of people disliking me for what was going around in school. I mean it made the walking in hallways difficult yet strange and not to mention that Monique still cut her eyes at me all the time. Suddenly there was a loud ass knock on her door.

I heard from the living room, the man step through the door way and said to chocolate what's up Bitch as she chuckled with laughter and responded nothing you a nasty bitch. I paid no mind to it until she called me into the kitchen. She introduced us and said "Mar this is Hershey, Hershey that is my nephew Mar" He looked at me with a strange smile and said nice to meet you. I stared at him for seconds and said "Likewise". Chocolate took me into her room and told me that he was her best friend growing up and also the god father of her two kids. She told me that she wanted us to hangout a little because he wanted to get to know me because he been through something's just like me and he fully understood where I was coming from. In my mind I felt something was strange with this setting. I could put my finger on it nor wrap my mind on the plotting that was about to happen.

He yelled at chocolate stating bitch come finish this dinner a bitch is getting hungry. I never thought a man would refer to himself as such. Yet who was I to really judge after all we were all sinners in my eyes. Chocolate finished up dinner and we all migrated to the living room sitting down. Hershey pulled out a leaf stick, told Chocolate go head, and fires it up. You can spark it. I looked at chocolate and him with amazement and curious to what exactly they were about to smoke. Chocolate told me you don't have to be in the room when we smoke weed if you don't want to. If you feel uncomfortable you can leave. I told her no I was fine. Hershey then looked at us both and said "All shit choc he wants to hit it too" I said "Naw is not like that, I'm a singer and I don't believe in smoking it kills people." He turned to me and said whoever told you that lied to you because that's not true at all. There blunt went in rotation between them two three times then Hershey finally looked at me and said "Do you want to hit it? I paused... As my hand reached out and my mind panicking like man what are you doing. I grabbed the blunt with my finger and said "I don't know how to smoke as I laughed" Hershey explained to me that it was like inhaling air slowly and exhaling it. Therefore, I did exactly that. After four puffs or pulls of the blunt you can say I was high. Everything was spinning around in the room. I felt good, relaxed and calmed. I didn't have any care in the world to what was going on. It felt as though everything that I had on my mind just melted away. I was laughing for no fucken reason and smiling too. Chocolate and Hershey both were catching there giggles off me. I tried to stand up but my body just wouldn't move. For a moment I really did think I got up and got me something to drink because I had cotton mouth apparently from smoking. My mouth was totally dry. Yet I didn't even notice that Chocolate brought us all something to drink. Hours went by with us smoking and carrying on. I forgot how many I smoked with them I lost count after six and apparently I passed out.

I woke up on the couch to Maury being on TV and Hershey literally sitting so close next to me. I knew I had to have been sleep for hours because when we started it was light outside now it was like 9 o'clock at night. I had two text messages from Lauren saying that she missed me and love me. She also told me that she wanted me to come down to her school with her mom in the next couple of weeks just to get away. I really didn't like her mother Mary J too much. I mean at first I did but that women looks like a linebacker with broad shoulders and sometimes she just creeps me out. Moreover, I responded to her texts with the same reply miss and love you too. We rarely talked much due to my current situation and her busy school load. Yet she couldn't see at times that I just needed her in person to comfort me yet that was so difficult with her own goals she had going on in life.

I got up from the couch and stretched, took off my du-rag and began to take my braids out so I could wash my hair before school tomorrow. Hershey looked at me and said if you need help taking your braids out I can if you want. I told him no thank you but I really don't like people in my hair. Not even men as I was thinking in my head like what the hell do I look like having a nigga play in my head, yeah right. He then asked me have I ever had my hair blow out before. I told him no, I don't believe in putting chemicals in my hair. He laughed at me and said no crazy I'm talking about blown out as in blow dried straighten... you know like a wrap. I can't say that I have because I don't even know what you're talking about. Hershey laughed and said cool don't worry about it come with me. I asked him where he was taking me he told me don't worry about it that we were going to one of his friend's house out 33 G Hall Manor aka out the south. Therefore, we did exactly that.

We got to this girl's house out the south which was another project ghetto homes you could say. He banged on the door until a girl shouted "BITCH STOP BANGING ON MY MOTHER FUCK-N DOOR GOT DAMN I SAID IM COMING." She swung open the door looked at Hershey and I laughed while saying girl don't be actin crazy like that at my door thought you was the cops for a minute... honey child. Hershey introduced us hey Booters this is glaze aka mar and mar this is my home girl Booters aka Besha. She was a very short girl with a big apple ass and hips that could wrap around you for days. She had a Carmel skin tone complexion with the reddest rosy lips I have ever seen. Yet the only thing that made her unattractive was her teeth. They were fucked. She could really open a can of tuna fish with them bitches. Her mouth literally looked like a Family Dollar can opener. Cute to look at until you seen them teeth. Anyway, Hershey asked her for a favor if she could wrap my hair for me. She rolled her neck in a circle motion at Hershey and said bitch you better have some fire to spark me up because a bitch don't do shit without her meds. Shit I need to get high. Hershey laughed at her and said but of course I got you cousin. She sat me in her chair and took off my fitted. As she took my hair out of its pony tail bun and said "Got Damn you have some pretty hair, oh yea I'm going to have fun doing this shit. So, she did exactly that she said she was going to do which was washed, condition, blow dried and put oil shine into my hair before she straighten it. As she was getting high while she wrapped my hair around my whole head and put a hair net on it to keep it there. She twisted the next two times around my head to make it tight as she told me don't let it come off and also when you unwrap it in the morning before school just take a comb to it and you should be fine papa.

I looked at Hershey and said "are we good to go because I am ready to go home and go back to sleep. In reply he told me yea let's go, I need to get you home anyway before Chocolate yells at me... See ya Booters as he yelled to his home girl as we were leaving her house. As we pulled up in my complex, Hershey told me that I was a cool dude that he didn't mind hanging out with a young-n like me. He slid me a piece a paper with his number on it and told me to text him tomorrow so he can see how my hair turned out. I got out of his car and thanked him for everything because with my girl not being home it was difficult for me to find someone to braid and do my hair. I went inside the house and seen that is was almost going on midnight so I went straight to sleep.

The alarm went off on that morning so I quickly got up brushed and washed and drove myself to school in my car. I got there just two minutes before the late bell rung. I went to the bathroom to take off my hair-net/do-rag and my hair began to unravel before my eyes. I couldn't believe the way I look. My hair had volume and bounce and it went all the way down my back. I didn't even know my hair was that long. You could have called me Rapunzel. I was nervous a little to walk around in high school looking alike a male Barbie. After all long hair doesn't care and a braid was the shit in school. In addition, if your outfit and shoe game was on point then it really didn't matter. Here I go as I was my palms were sweating, OH MY GOD MAR! Your hair is so cute, damn boy I didn't know it was that long. Throughout my course of the day I really didn't have anyone with negative comments. Perhaps it was because I only stayed for four classes then left at lunch time. I texted Hershey with a smiling face and told him thank you, because I never thought I could look like that. On my way driving home from school I would get on the phone with Lauren and boo love. I would tell her that I really did miss her and that I couldn't wait for her spring break to come around. I just wanted to hold her and kiss her so badly. I need to feel her affection.

I enjoyed our conversations because it was nothing but pure laughs all the time. Sometimes we would even stay up on the phone all night long until we both had school. I would listen to her snore which she states she doesn't do at times but she does. We talked about numerous things like are life's goals, are future, are careers and even children. She made me content and happy. She overwhelmed me with joy. This was our second year being in a relationship and the things that I have gone through and told her she has kept to herself as she was my personal diary. The person I could bury my fears in yet the one who I could cry endless with and wouldn't be judged. We had a mutual understanding of one another like are hearts would beat as one. Are problems and hardships only made us stronger and unstoppable? We were truly indestructible.

After my talk with Lauren, I went to work like I normal did part-time. I left work, went home, and was thanking my lucky stars that it was the weekend. Chocolate was inside the house getting her partying on to her loud old school music. I went into the living room and drop off my work clothes and school bag because you could say that was my room. Chocolate came to me and said "I love your hair boo looks really nice" I responded thank you. Hershey walked through the door and said I got weed and who got blunts" I wasn't really in the smoking mood yet it was the weekend. Chocolate pulled out her large bottle of EJ and we all began to listen to music and chill. So many blunts were going around. I was even taking shots. I had about eight you could say and I was really feeling good. So, good

I had my first puff of a cigarette and it felt like it boosted everything I was on literally. I was so high I could literally make myself think I had powers. I know sounds funny but that's how I felt. The music was so loud chocolate had some other friends there and so did Hershey. I was surrounded by plenty of people that I didn't even know like that. I was feeling disoriented in this house party so I passed out on the couch.

I was having the most exciting wet dream. My body felt all warm. I dreamt she was everything I was looking for in a woman as she grabbed and cuff me in her hands and began to swallow me whole slowly. It fit so real. I was biting the pillow trying my best not to talk but she felt so damn good. Her mouth was like my Niagara Falls with a splash of an organism. I was telling her hold on I'm about to cum. Please don't do this it...it feels way too good. Just as I was about to release I awoke from my dream and seen that it wasn't a dream at all. Instead Hershey had seemed to unzip me, pull my soldier out, and toss it around like he was playing with it on a battle field. WHAT THE FUCK ARE YOU DOING? As I jumped up feeling dizzy and blurry to my surrounding, His response was "Do not act like you didn't like it Glaze because you know you did. That ass was about to nut huh? I YELLED AT HIM WITH ANGER, NIGGA NO ONE TOLD YOU TO DO SOME SHIT LIKE THAT, LIKE WHO DOES THAT TO PEOPLE WHEN THEY ARE FUCKING SLEEP. I brushed passed him and went to the bathroom to take a shower and seen a big as hickey on my chest and neck... damn how drunk and fucked up was I as I thought to myself. I imagine him doing that while I was sleep and made me throw the hell up in the toilet. I hoped in the shower to wipe away his scent and even poured Listerine on my dick that shit was fowl he lost my respect. I got out of the shower and he was gone. It was Saturday morning and chocolate just got up because I could hear her making coffee in the kitchen being loud with her hang over.

I said "Chocolate I really need to speak with you about your friend something isn't right at all. She looked at me and said "what's wrong nephew"? I said your friend Hershey validated me while I was sleep and I don't like shit like that because I am not gay and even if I was he is way too old for me. That shit is just not cool at all. Chocolate looked at me in my eyes and told me Mar I'm sorry that happen but he really does like you and part of you living here is to make me happy and what makes me happy is seeing that he is happy... Just give it a try you never know Hershey can look after you and protect you. BITCH I CAN PROTECT MY OWN DAMN SELF AND I DON'T NEED TO BE WITH NO FUCK-N OLD AS NIGGA THAT IS EIGHT YEARS OLDER THAN ME THAT SHIT ISN'T RIGHT CHOCOLATE AND YOU KNOW ITS NOT. I DON'T GIVE A FUCK IMA TELL HIS ASS WHEN I SEE HIM. She went off on me yelling and screaming saying "well if you didn't like it you could go live with someone else. Yet I had nowhere else to go live at. Only thing you have to do is keep him happy so he can keep coming around and bring me my drugs. I'm sorry Mar but I need to smoke I have too.

I stormed off pissed and upset. Most importantly I had to tell my Lauren. I know what she will say she would probably break up with me. I didn't want to hurt her nor make her unhappy. Should I just text her and tell her it's over or tell her what happen maybe she might understand. Before I could even finish my text Lauren calls. I picked up the phone to her soft voice telling me morning baby I miss you and what are you doing. I replied to her nothing just waking up and chilling. What's wrong she asked, I said nothing? Well something is wrong just tell me please. Are you still coming down with my mom next weekend? I don't think I can baby I'm sorry. Thinking to myself; just give her an excuse that you're busy or something but I couldn't lie to her like that she seen past all that and to be honest she was too good for lies. One thing I admired most about us is communication and friendship we had together. Mar! Tell me what's wrong. This guy Hershey made a hickey on my neck, I'm sorry baby like I really am I really don't know how it happen one-minute I was drinking then the next minute I was passed out. I'm so sorry please forgive baby please. She was silent once again on the phone and then when she did speak her voice was trembling as if she was crying and then I began to sob with tears because I felt like it was over.

Mar! Its ok I am upset but please still come so you can get out of that kind of environment. Fine, baby what is your mom going to say about this hickey? Just cover it up until you get down here and I will tell her that I made it. In my head I was shocked as to why? Why would you do that for me? Better yet for us? What kind of love is this? In returned I told her no I was too a shamed to face her and that I couldn't make it still. I know she was sad and depress because I did that to us. I politely told her on the phone. I don't think we she be together and its really nothing you did wrong I just have too much baggage that you shouldn't have to deal with because you deserve so much better I'm sorry baby but I can't do this anymore. I banged on her and turned my phone off as I let my face drown in my own pool of tears. Hershey came behind me, heard my whole phone call, and whispered in my ear "See Glaze that wasn't so bad, she will get over it and learn that she has to share. I have great plans for you. As he kisses the back of my neck. My skin prickled up because his breath was hot and smelled like ass. As he smacked me on my ass and told me to get dress we had a trip to go to a ballroom and that we had to go shopping for it. Tears continued to fall as my mind would call out to God. Help me please I need you.

Dear Lord,

For my vessel is no longer pure as demonic people attack me like a sheep in your flock. Is there not shepherd to tend to your flock? Are you glaring at me and show no mercy? Father why won't you answer my call? Is neither my melody off key nor the pitch in the right tune?

Must I fall on thy knees and beg... yet thee loves to see me suffer and cry out. Why? Oh, why my lord? Good thing that I no longer hear you nor see you nor feel your presence. You are worthless to thy customs of protection. Harm has overcome my body. Evil has pierced my heart. Yet Lucifer has corrupted my soul. My mind is no longer mines... we shall see Father who will suffer through the length of time. You no longer rent the space in my head, yet an eviction is what you get in return. Get out and stay away I am not longer a child of yours. A father is supposed to protect me, heal me, and teach me. Yet you punish me with these ungodly acts of abominations of filth... MARK MY WORDS ONE DAY YOU SHALL PAY FOR YOUR FALSIFYING STORIES OF FAITH LOVE AND TRUTH.

Your broken son,
Maurice!

THE AWAKENING OF GLAZE

We went to several outlets that day, shop for so many things. I tried on so many clothes from tight jeans to G-strings and male thongs. Hershey explained to me that if I wanted to walk sex siren at the ball then I had to look the part. I asked him depressed like to what a sex siren really was. He told that it required me too practically wear no clothes just a thong or shorts of some sort and dance or prance down the aisle. To think and walk like a God of Sex. Demand and crave lust over every man that catches your eyes. We arrived in Philly at the KITTY KAT FIGHT VOGUE SHOW. Hershey took me into the back room and preps me before the scene. As he was talking to me my phone was going off with Lauren calling me but I couldn't pick up. I had to do my duty as a roommate to do as my master wish you could say. He pulled out make-up and supplies. As he brushed glitter on my entire body from face to legs, he told me that it was okay for me to be nervous. I would be fine as long I focused and remain on beat. The object was for me to go out there and sell sex with my looks and the way I walk. To make them the crowd crave and lust for me without actually touching me. Hershey pulled out a bottle of tequila, pours me eight shots, gives me grey-blue contacts, and tells me to drink it will calm my nerves and when I am done to put in the contacts it will give me an exotic look. For the sadness in my eyes will catch the hearts of the crowd. As he was leaving out the dressing room his back facing me saying make me proud bitch and you better work, and don't forget to get all your tens when you are done. (This was the score at the end). When your music comes on come out on stage and remember don't look at the people but straight ahead.

As my Vogue music came on: IN THE NAME KARAN, WE WELCOME GLAZE, IN THE NAME IN THE NAME, IN THE NAME YASSS, KA-KA-KA-KA-KARAN, I DON'T LIKE THAT BITCH, I DON'T SEE HER, and DO YOU LIKE TO VOGUE AND THAT'S A FACT WELL LET ME SEE YOU DIP WITHOUT BREAKING YOUR BACK. The music came on and all I could remember was me lifting up my head in the spot light. Everyone was staring and glaring at me. In my mind, I was so nervous and scared. Yet the attention I was seeking was breathe taking. The people were out of their seats saying you better work boy. As my hair was down my back, my size 38 snug tight shorts, every muscle bulging excessively as you seen my sapphire blue geisha eyes piercing through each man drowning them in a deep ocean as that gazed upon my beauty. My hair swung as I walked down the runway. My thick solid muscle thighs where glistening with sex appeal. As I strutted more down the runway, I could hear some say "Damn that's a Tarzan man, His eyes are so beautiful, and I never knew a man could have a round fat ass like that. As I returned back to my normal spot where I first began before I fully walked down. I gave the crowd one last look at me before my music ended and I exited the stage. I was trying to walk oh so fast back to my dressing room but I found it difficult as a man grab me by my arm and swung me around. My heart beat so fast like it was about to beat out of my chest. Hi, as he said to me. "I didn't mean to startle you but your performance was amazing and your body is a masterpiece. You have some beautiful eyes boy." He could tell that I had fear inside me. My name is Rocky some just call me Rock. I would like the chance to work with you so that you could make some real money. What you made out there was child's play money; if you have the chance to come work for me you can actually make some good money, as I looked up at him while he handed me his business card. He was 6'3 tall very body built with tons of tattoos. His eyes were hazel and drawn you in with every second you stared in it. He smelled like curve cologne and his hands were three times big as mines. His chest was so solid and built as if he laid down a couple of years within the prison. As he walked away from me smiling saying "oh by the way you should keep that name Glaze it fits you, should I be waiting for your call? I told him that I would think about it. He smiled at me with the prettiest white teeth saying I'll be waiting then.

GLAZE! GLAZE! DAMN IT WHERE ARE YOU… As I heard Hershey's voice call out my name like something was wrong you killed it and you made $800 dollars within one-hour bitch I told you, you better work. Hey who was that man that was talking to you? I told him that his name was Rocky. OH HELL NO… Glaze you don't want to get involve with him. He is the worst kind of person that you want to do business with. He is a pimp, a drug dealer and a thug. You don't want to be caught up in his mess. He is like a spider with prey once you're in his web it is very hard to get out. Yet, in my mind I didn't give a fuck because in some sort of way you are too. Using me to make money and do whatever you like with me just for me to have a place to lay my head. Here as Hershey said handing me $200 dollars. I took the money and placed it with my belongings. I really didn't care about the money. I was now starting to feel my shots more and all I wanted to do was go home and sleep. Yet, with Hershey the night was still young. We ended up partying with some friends of his as I sat back and watched the fuckery that was happening all that night just complete bullshit.

I manage to text Lauren surprisingly she was up that late. She asked me what I was doing and in reply I just told her up laying down in bed think about my life. I didn't want her to know what I just recently did. Our relationship was already suffering due to Hershey. Due to my sickening addiction of drugs and cigarettes, yet I told her that I smoke she was disappointed and she rather me smoke a black-n-mild which was a cigar based tobacco rather than cancer sticks. As much as I wanted to yell out to her what was going on and how it was affecting my life I couldn't. I was just trying to protect her fragile heart. She was too much of a good girl. In addition, I knew the more I would tell her the more she thought different of me. The more she would become disgusted with me. We talked through via text message for a couple of hours cracking jokes with each other. We were trying to compete with each other who loved whom more and who cared about whom more. My early morning conversation with her ceased as she was finally lying down before practice as, she reminded me not to forget that she was coming down for spring break. I was so thrilled and excited. I couldn't wait to hold her and kiss her again. Maybe we could possibly go to the movies, out to eat, skating etc. It didn't matter really long as I had her with me I was fine.

Hershey and I got back to Harrisburg that early morning and it was too late for me to go to school. It really didn't matter to me anymore because I was missing too many days of school although my grades were fine, however my attendance was unnecessary. I went to school when I felt like it. It seemed more for chocolate to benefit from me not going to school and making her money doing the ballroom scene. That money train made her happy and Hershey happy all the damn time, although Mar was never happy just given orders and told what to do and how to do it. I really didn't care about anything anymore. My heart was cold as ice and my mind remain crowded as always. Senior and Bernice were signing me out of school as they reported to my school that I no longer live inside their household. You thought I cared about that shit hell no. I was getting fed up with chocolate and Hershey schemes and plans for what they had in stored for me. Therefore, I decided to take Rocky's business card out of my back pocket and give him a call. When I did I got his voicemail. I told him that it was Glaze and for him to give me a call when he had the chance. Immediately after I was done with the call he texts me and said "What's up baby boy? I replied to him nothing and that I wanted to take him up on his offer and do business with him. In reply he told me to text him my address and that he would be there within an hour to pick me up. I showered and got dress and waited for him to patiently call or text me. As I remained in the living room waiting while watching chocolate and Hershey get so high off crack which was a drug, I didn't get into. The two of them were nodding when he pulled up. His music was so loud. I grabbed my charger and my jacket and ran out the door. As I took a look outside he was driving a new 2007 Cadillac escalade truck that was cream color and sat on 22 inch rims with chrome. He had class and style. As he got out of the driver seat to come to the passenger side to open the door for me, as I hoped in he smiled at me and asked me how I was doing? I told him still living unfortunately. He asked me was I hungry I told him just a little. Good he replied. I have a restaurant I would like to take you to. We got down to the Baltimore inner harbor to a seafood restaurant, as he told me please order whatever you like. Therefore, indeed I did. Rocky seemed so comfortable to get along with, his personality was so warming and gentle.

So, Mar, what I have in mind for you is being a "sugar baby". I looked at him and lashed out and said I knew it your just like everybody else what do you want from me. WHOA! SLOW DOWN LIL DADDY, it's not even like that. What I have in mind for you is good. I won't treat you like the rest of my boys, whatever you want you can have. I have clients that would like to wine and dine a young man like you. There is no sex involving maybe a little skin to show but nothing else I promise. I'll even come with you on your first gig. I just want you to be comfortable and relax. My business plan for you is to be use strictly for your beauty only not your body. I have clients through all out of Harrisburg, Philly, Jersey, NYC and even here in Baltimore. They pay you only for your time which I get 50% of and on the other hand anything they give you is yours to keep whether its pocket money or gifts it doesn't matter it's all yours to keep. I have four main rules for you as follow:

1.) NEVER SHOW EMOTION, MAKES YOU A BITCH
2.) NEVER FALL IN LOVE WITH CLIENTS
3.) NEVER GIVE YOUR HEART OR TAKE THERE'S
4.) AND DON'T FUCK WITH MY MONEY

On the other hand, you are more than free to do whatever you want. If you are ever in trouble or in need of my assistance never worry you will always have one of my men close by you. Here is a cell phone that is used only for business. If you have an emergency call, let it ring than hang up. So, what do you say? I don't know Rocky; it seems nice but… Listen Glaze I really need you to be a part of my team. As long as you are with me no harm will ever come to you I promise. No one will ever take advantage of you nor place a finger on you. In my mind, I was debating on what I should really do. He made the money sound so easy and assured me that everything would be okay. I was thinking I should talk to Lauren first about it. Yet, I would have more money to please her with and to be my age young and grinding, which would be nice. So, Mr. Glaze what do you say? You will never have to use your real name and you can always protect your identity. I will give you 5-10 clients weekly depending on the festivities that go on. I will contact you through phone. You stay with your client as long as they are satisfied and please with you.

Rocky I don't have no clothes no shoes nothing to make me look presentable. He looked at me and said "your so cute with your innocent face don't worry I took care of that" As we got done with lunch he told me that I already had a client set up later on that night back home in Harrisburg and that it was ok for me to be nervous, just be myself and talk to the man. He showed be a picture what he looked like and told me his name. Rocky, embrace me with a hug as he drops me off at the Hilton hotel. He finally told me, I choose you papa for a reason please make me proud. Your hotel room is underneath Jamal Glaze. I walked into the fancy hotel and asked the guest service agent at the desk what number room was I? She asked me my name and I told her. She told me room 202 so I walked to the elevators and got in to go to the second floor. The elevator music was soothing as they played "Don't stop believing by journey, I got off the elevator and made a right because I saw a sign that pointed my room out. I walked down the hall to three doors to the right and there was my door. I slid my card through the key holder and the door open. I flicked on the light and seen so many shopping bags. I had a bottle of crystal and roses in my room with a card from Rocky. Stating: remember have fun tonight, no sex, and no worries and call me if anything. In addition, there is an envelope with instructions on where and what to do with your client. You have to be there by nine p.m. so take some time for yourself and have fun with your gifts with concern Rocky. It seemed so strange yet that man had a way of making me smile for no reason. It might have been his charm or smile. I couldn't believe all of the bags of shoes and clothes he had got me. I looked inside the bags and pulled out clothes there were name brands I never even heard of such as Armani, Calvin Klein, Ralph Lauren, Gucci, Diesel, Hugo Boss Burberry Porum and many more. This all seemed too fancy for me.

I looked at the envelope that was on the bed and opened it. As I pulled out the picture on the back was the client's dislikes and likes, fantasies what kind of man he was looking to cling with. It was six o'clock and I only had three hours to get ready for what I had to do. As I ran the bath water in the hotel room and poured myself a drink I was so nervous I started to have second thoughts. I took my hair, braided it into a ponytail, and wrapped it into a bun so it wouldn't get wet. I eased my foot in the steamy warm water to soak it before I went too engaged in this act. I got out of the bath after I felt like my body was turning into a wrinkly raisin. I dried myself off and lotion up and spray Versace cologne on my entire body. I manage to open to fresh pack of Leo underwear that was super tight. I place on a pair of skinny silk black jeans and dress socks rolled up. I slipped inside these blue and black Stacey Adams and loved the way they felt. I ripped off the price tag to the Armani V-neck shirt that was royal blue. That shirt hugged my chest and arms so tight it felt more like under amour than a shirt. I made myself another drink and a couple of shots because I really didn't know what was exactly in stored for me tonight. I took another look at the man's photo. I couldn't' believe it this man was the mayor of Harrisburg. Mayor Reedner. I was more shock and surprise I didn't recognize that the first time. As I left from the hotel room walking down the hall towards the elevator hips swaying from left to right, I felt like a runway model. I managed to stop and glance at myself in the mirror and my reflection spoke for me. Do whatever it takes to collect the payment. I unraveled my hair from a bun and let it drop down my back.

I knocked on the door to room 216 and raspy voice speaks back its open. I walked inside nervous for what tonight holds for me as I seen this salt and pepper middle age man approach me with a long pointy nose, green eyes, red around the neck, medium build with average tone arms that can only lift a 5lb crow bar. "What would you like to drink? As he spoke softly too me, the vibe in the room was very calm. Tequila I responded. "Is ice fine? No I stated straight up is perfectly fine for me. The goal was for me not to get too drunk that I couldn't get the job done or not be aware of what is going on tonight. He came up behind me wrapped his hands around my waist turning to my right side to hand me my drink. I took it straight back and said "now let's get to the point I am on a time frame. I really wasn't according too Rocky it he was a 5-star client. He looked at me in amazement and smiled saying you know what I enjoy a man that knows what he wants. In my mind, I'm like sure if only you knew I was barely eighteen. He took my hand and walked me over to the bed as he sat on the edge of the king size California mattress, sheets gold brown and beige. His hands rubbed up and down my body mesmerized of my stature while looking into my eyes. He asks me is this your first time. I smirked and told him no now shut up and be my dirty little pig. As he ripped off my shirt and tore the buttons off my jeans as I stood in front of him butt ass naked. He began to twist and pull on my nipples whispering you like that boy. Instantly I pushed him off thinking about my encounter with Shawn. What the fuck is wrong with you kid? Either you want your fucking payment or not! I'm calling Rocky I told him not to set me up with any fucking amateur. I yelled at him NO! Don't do that. Well, shit give me one reason not to. I leaned forward and kiss his lips and took his small dick in my hands and stoked it and told him just give me a second I haven't felt my tequila yet why don't you go and strip down my and get another shot. He looked at me and giggled and said you're lucky for being so fucking gorgeous. As he walked to the bathroom, I turned around walked over to the mini bar and grabbed the bottle of tequila.

Fuck a shot I began to drink that shit like it was my last night living no cares no worries. I pulled the bottle away from my mouth as I began to fill an instant rush. He came out of the bathroom saying you ready to fuck my dirty little hole. Inside I wanted crawl in a ball but there was no backing down now. I turned around and barked orders: shut the fuck up you don't talk unless I say so. When I speak, you say yes daddy? Do I make myself clear? Yes, daddy and as he got excited jumping into the bed back first. What are you going to do to me? I snapped back in a deeper tone, did I ask you to talk? "No daddy as he was submissive to my dominance" I grabbed his wrist and tied them to the bed post with the king pillow case sheets. I walked around the bedroom looking at myself in the mirror that was right above the bed, I tilted my head to concentrate on who I was looking at really and realize it was now time for Glaze to show up my self-conscious innocence's was in the back of my mind. "PUNISH ME PLEASE DADDY PUNISH ME" So you think this is a game, I took my underwear from the floor and gagged his mouth, climbed on top of him and began to grin on his tiny little pink balls with a dick that looked like a pixie stick. I saw his eyes rolling in the back of his head thrilled over his sickening fetish. I stood up took the drawers out of his mouth and planted my ass on it as my back face the head board. I told him to eat me like a fat-ass at I-Hop. His tongue began to move so rapidly on my prized possession, I just couldn't let him finish I stood up again jump off the bed grabbed my belt from the loop of my jeans and cracked it in my hands. OH PLEASE! YES! GIVE ME MORE OF THAT SHIT. STICK THAT COCK IN ME.

Now see your being very naughty as I told him, you're not obeying my rules. What did daddy say? No talking, right? He didn't say anything. RIGHT!! As I yelled at him, looking at his pathetic ugly face, He responded sorry daddy I won't listen until you fuck me hard. I jumped back on the bed stood up as I looked down at him, feet at the side of his hips. I took my pipe and started to hose down his body. MMMM please more as he moaned. More you want I say. I step close to his face and began to piss in his face like a water fountain dispensing water, I grabbed the tip to drain it took the belt into my right hand and began to lash out on his chest with blows from left to right. Tell me you want this dick. "He screamed at me daddy please I'm begging give me your cock. Now ...now we have been through this little piggy as I strike him with another blow. What did I say about following and obeying what I say? PLEASE DADDY! GIVE ME YOUR DICK!!! I looked at myself in the mirror again as I stand over his body, smiled tilted my head winked at Maurice from dying inside. I looked backed down at the little piggy untied his hands from the bed post as I took my belt and hog tied my piggy by his wrist and ankles ass lifted up in the air on the edge of the bed, I walked away from him back to the mini bar to grab my tequila. As I hear him in the back-ground chanting on yes please give me that fat cock, yes daddy please. His voice was killing my vibe as I had the bottle in my left hand I picked up my drawers and placed them back in his mouth, I sat on the counter lit me a fucking cigarette, - I flicked the cigarette bud in the kitchen sink scratch at the voices in my head, screaming please don't do this. Sorry Maurice can't come out and play. I flicked the bud in the kitchen where the mini bar was at walked over to him stood on his right side while my left hand griped the belt, I freed his mouth and shoved my piped down his throat he gagged, I chuckled don't choke, wait to you put me on your will first. I took his head and bobbed it up and down on my dick as I pre-cummed all down his tonsils and voice box. I pulled away and smacked my dick on his face. Shoving his flesh light mouth back on my dick like a toy, I pulled out again smacked his face, spit in his mouth and shoved him back on it. I pulled away again took my left hand lifted him up in the air with the belt. Wait daddy wait there's condoms right behind you on the bathroom sink. I looked behind me walked over and grabbed a golden ticket from the sink, ripped it open… "There's lube in there also. I looked at him said "Aww isn't that cute. Who needs that when you're a pig getting breeded, I placed the condom on my dick pinched the tip, spited on the outside of it and spitted right on his dirty hole. As he moans waiting in silence, I tapped his flesh twice with my pipe in hand and rimmed myself inside him. I kept fucking him harder each time I pulled back lifting my head towards the ceiling not in pleasure but in shame. He kept streaming moans saying yes and harder. As flashes in my head of Shawn, James, Lauren, Hershey, Rocky, and SShhh not a word, I just kept fucking harder and harder to get the images out shaking my head, feeling his warm flesh on the extension of my objective of destruction. I can feel him tighten up on me like he was trying to close; I pulled out and thrust back in harder than before. He belted out daddy I'm Cumming, ohhhhhhh, ahhhhh yesss!!! Cum in my dirty hole and make me your filthy slut. As I brought my head down from looking at the ceiling while I was working, I saw that he did cum all on himself. I pulled out and took the condom off my dick, stroked the tip of my man's and bust cream on his face. Tapped his fore head twice and drained it, unleashed him from my hold that I had him in with the belt. I took my underwear began to place one foot inside of the other and pulled them up on me. He looked at me and said got damn "Rocky was right Mr. Glaze you are a rare jewel. Whoa that was intensifying, I looked back at him with my nose flared up with a smirked gathering my scattered clothes among the hotel room floor. I gathered everything, He pulled the covers over him and said payment is by the door in the enveloped $6000 as promised, I don't have to tell you that this stays right here in this room, Rocky advised me that you make good on your word to remain DL. I responded back to him? DL? "Yes, as in down low? Oh, yea absolutely I grabbed the money in the envelope close the door behind me, with my clothes in hand and walked the hall with nothing on but socks and drawers to take the stairs at the end of the hall. I placed my hair in a bun as I got back to my room. As tears started to fumble out my eyes, I place my body in the tub sat down and let the hot work peel the sin from my body cleanse me of activities. Crying out baby, where are you? I need you. SOMEONE! Anyone help me please. I don't want to do this anymore. Lauren, please forgive me I'm sorry baby, I'm so sorry as I began to sob... GOD!!!! Can you hear me? GOD!!! ANSWER ME!!!!

I cleaned my body with soap, all-purpose cleaner. I even put Listerine on my own dick. I got out of the shower placed on some comfortable shorts and tee-shirt, grabbed my cell phone looked and Lauren and I's picture we took at her basketball game before I crawled into bed. I was still drunk and began to develop an headache. I looked up at the ceiling thinking and praying to myself before I fell asleep.

Dear God, higher power

Love is stated as an unconditional gift yet it's something that you don't give me, you state everything is a choice but this life was already written for me before my time. Some ole powerful being you are if I had just enough power to smite you down off those clouds you hide behind up there, I would show you a thing or two. Yet, like air I can't see you, like a gentle rose I can't feel you, like a heatwave, I feel no warmth just a blizzard, a hurricane storm of empty silent cries... soaked land of tears. Although, I walk through the shadow of death, I shall welcome fear and evil luring... Waiting for you is like waiting on faith to show up with hope. Point of it all god both sisters died reaching out to those you didn't let them seek passage too.

Sincerely,
My Cry...

9

TEARS FROM THE BLUE JAY

They say God only gives his toughest battles to some of his strongest warriors, somehow, I believe my fate for fighting to live or die was nearly hanging on by a thread. You never really realize how precious life is even though, throughout time you try your hardest to be different to change the things to come and grow from the things that have past. Currently at the moment I became a father. I lost the women I buried my soul into, my parents only seen me as a son who is a faggot that I am, I somehow became an underground escort male whore you could say and turned and spread his legs to the highest bidder.

Somehow deep down I came to an understanding that my thot-less life meant nothing but to cause misery to others and spread my legs wherever I could find a coin. Yet a one-way ticket to hell seems far more appropriate for me. I was tired of running from pain, running from life, guilt, tired of running from one bed to the next, especially when you're running around in the streets of death. It's either put me out of my misery or somehow, I believe Rocky was going to do it one way or another.

My grandmother use to tell me that every Blue jay sheds a tear when it's alone in the world without love, without its flock, without its heart and even more so without it's family. She told me those birds tend to have emotions like people. She would say "When a blue jay is happy, its wings stretched in flight it can be the most remarkable and most beautiful thing to see. However, seeing a blue jay soaring in the wind was rare and if you see one wish upon it and that wish came true. Although if a blue jay flew to close to you trouble was nearby, Grandma would also say that if a blue jay is near you and it sheds a tear while looking at your death would be soon claiming someone around you or you yourself. She smiled at me and pinches my cheeks and tells me "Baby God has a plan for you, just keep the faith and he will do the rest. He always has a plan for all of us. I would always smile back at her. Grandma always understood me no matter how awkward I would be to other people she just knew who I was deep down. We've always had a strong connection. Even when she passed away I would always see her in my room at night as a child. She often would reach into my dreams humming and singing to me her favorite song. I miss her still till this day and although god has called her home, I just know she has to be a lovely angel somewhere in that make-believe place called heaven.

As I still stood awake in the darkness out in limbo suffering from the past transgressions, that I remember so many things and some I can't seem to fabricate some of the blurry memories. You have no choice but to think about the malicious things you said to individuals, the hearts that you have shattered, the lies you have told just to get by. The roaring of the thundering voice spoke out to me again in the black dwelling.

"At times, we all fall short to the true understanding and mercy of god. You have cut off all connections to the vessel that binds the core of what and who you truly are

95

profound to be. Having spiritual gifts among the world is rare and you have done nothing with them but disobey his calling. You have been marked and chosen before your time, before the body of you was even created. You have failed and desecrated the temple of God. You shall pay and understand that life is a privilege and death is a blessing.

I lashed out to the voice screaming back at it show yourself you fucking coward I can't see you. Emptiness is what I could describe myself right now at this moment, the voice left me again and yet another appeared far away with a fate tune and a blue light. The voice came through in my ears of a song a chorus I use to hear as a child:

"Oh blue jay, my sweet little blue jay,
With tears of sorrows and troubles follow
Cry blue jay, Cry the song of Tears.

I somehow knew and could remember this song my grandma use to sing it to me when I was a little boy. She told me it was one of her favorite songs and that her mother once sung it to her when she was a little girl. I called out to the voice Grandma? Is that you? Oh grandma I'm scared please I want to go home. Grandma! Please help something is keeping me here alone in the dark and I can't seem to find my way out there is no doors. The voice got louder this time approaching me as the tiny blue light shined a little brighter, I opened my hands and the light still sing sat in my palms:
"Oh blue jay, my sweet little blue jay
With tears of sorrows and trouble follows
Cry blue jay, cry the song of tears."

Only thing I could do was cry and weep, grandma I know that's you please help me. I want to go home. I don't know what is happening here or what I did wrong.

The light began to get even bigger and brighter and stop singing, it pulled away from my hands and transformed into a being with wings. She was beautiful with long blue crystal like feathery wings that stretched very far. Her hair was white like a fleece of snow and her eyes were deeply blue. I was astonished by her beauty. She spoke unto me?

"Maurice, my sweet boy you are here by trial to understand the choices you have made in life and no one can get you out of this abyss but yourself. Everything has a purpose and every being has a core that must be judge by him and him only.

Who is him? What can I change?

My sweet blue jay you're running out of time. Grandma! PLEASE HELP ME! What does he want from me? The question my blue jay is not what he wants from you but what do you seek of him? Do you truly understand the value of you? Do you comprehend the love that is within you? Do you understand the love he has for you that he has given his only son to man? What are you willing to give that separates you from many among the world? Your soul has been tainted my evil, your spirit as scorch by the fires of hell. Sacrifices are made for the greater good my sweet blue jay. The question is who truly pays the price? An Empty hole can't be filled unless you have the proper tools to fill them. Understand who you are baby and never forget who he is, I love you always and I'm always watching. I can't help you fight this battle and if he knew I was here guiding you there would be consequences. Remember every blue jay has a cry when it can't fly.

Her wings began to flap faster blowing me backwards and further away from her light. I was lifted off my feet and saw another light as I turned around. I felt as though I was being transported and shifted into another plane.

I heard a man yelling we're losing him Sharon; get us to the hospital quickly. The man in the ambulance as I hover over his head stood over my body, I was looking down at him and me from the top of the truck's ceiling. He looked like a paramedic to me but I couldn't quite see his face all the way, it was a bit incomplete. She yelled back at him "how is he holding up Derek? His pulse is very weak, the machine next to him that was plugged up with cords attached to my chest and one on my right side under my chest area made a flat solid sound. Beepppppppp! He's coding Sharon. I'm going to have to use the defibrillator, charging to 100 vaults 1, 2, 3 clear.

As I was still up above his head, I could feel the shock the magnet pull towards my body as my spirit was trying to move towards my body I could hear the man speaking to me saying please kid come on don't die on us. Give us something to work with. He attempted again repeating charging to 110 vaults 1, 2, 3 clear as my chest pumped up. Once again, this time it felt painful, it felt as though I hand a million hands grabbing me downward and tearing me apart inside piece by piece. He looked at the machine and still no pulse showed up he waited what seemed like a couple of secs. "He was stating out loud as if he was back in one of his clinical classes in school, Charging again to 120 vaults 1, 2, 3 clear, BEEP!!!! As the sound prolonged out, the man waited a couple of seconds. He called out to the women driving. I think we might have lost him.

I screamed out at my lifeless body BREATHE GOT DAMN IT BREAVE!!!!! PLEASE I DON'T WANT TO DIE!!! WAKE UP YOU SON OF A BITCH. WAKE UP NOW!!!!! While I was up above James's head, I heard my own voice inside my head ringing like a beacon's call those very words. Then suddenly a small steady beep appeared on the monitor. Beep! Beep! Beep! He's back with us Sharon just get us there we don't have a lot of time. She yelled back at him "I'm trying Derek".

"Derek leaned over my body and whispered to me, I don't know what happen to you buddy, or who could have done this amount of damage to your body. I don't know who you are but someone is watching over you, you just die for two minutes and came back. God has a purpose for you, I don't know if you did this to yourself buddy but suicide is never the answer. You are loved. You have to believe you are meant to be here. Every purpose isn't fully understood until the man upstairs reveals to you why you are meant to be here. Just hold on long enough until we can get you to the hospital buddy.

I could hear the continuing beeping however, I couldn't open my eyes at all on the stretcher, and my spirit was crying tears as well as a single tear fell from the corner of my right eye. I leaned over my body and tried to reach out and touch myself but my hand just went right through it. I began to shout WHEN DID I KILL MYSELF? TELL ME PLEASE ARE YOU THERE? WHEN DID I KILL MYSELF? I would have never done such a thing. I love me. I love my family. Someone did this to me; I would have never done this to myself ever. How did I get here? Oh please. Just once answer me. Please I was hoping and praying with my lips for Derrick the paramedic and Sharon who was driving the ambulance truck to swiftly get me to the hospital before I die again

Then Suddenly I froze in time as the dark shadowy image hovered on my left side. Its deep voice spoke into my ear "Do you believe in heaven or hell? Do you believe that your soul belongs to me? You haven't learned anything still blaming and pleading out to for someone to save you. As his voice got stronger and more powerful and scream unto me YOU SHALL BURN IN THE FLAMES OF FIRE. FOR YOUR LIFE MEAN'T NOTHING. SO, YOU BELONG TO ME!!!!!! LET'S SEE HOW YOU EXACTLY GOT DELIVERED TO ME!!! It smacked me back into the darkness alone in my thoughts....

10

MEET THE CLIENTS

I woke up that morning in my hotel room to Rocky stroking my hair asking me "how did you enjoy your night according to what I heard you a bad bitch Moe" I looked back and him and told him your money is on the night stand as he picked up the envelope took a couple bills out of it and tossed the rest to me on the bed. He walked towards the door and said "hey rest up you has worked to do tomorrow. I got up and asked him" Hey do you think you can push my appointments back for two days I have to go out of town to see my girl tomorrow is her birthday and I believe I'm driving down with her mom to meet her. I already told her I was coming I can't cancel at the last moment. He looked at me Glaze if you keep bringing in money like this you can make your own schedule, that's cool I will push them back just remember it's going to be double Sunday so remember that rest up and get your mind right. I have a car waiting for you downstairs to drop you off at home remember not a word of this to no one. Scared money doesn't make money you feel me.

I got up and got dress took the elevator downstairs and seen an all-black Yukon Denali truck waiting for me, the tall light-skinned man opened my door and said here you go Mr. glaze. I threw my bag of clothes in first and scooted myself on the seat. He got in the driver seat and said "where would you like to go? I laughed and said Hollywood, sike Naw take me to Presidential halls off Paxton Street. I turned my regular phone back on and waited for it to load and realize I had 7 missed calls from Lauren and twelve messages. Some of them stated the usually baby, where are you? I miss you and love you, call me baby when you can. I miss you so much I can't wait to see you. I didn't want to respond right away I wanted to wait to after 2 o'clock that way I knew she was in class and couldn't really respond back to me. I arrive back home place my key in the door and all I could hear was Chocolate screaming bitch where the fuck you been at? I told you that rent was due you can't be doing disappearing acts your ass is not grown you only fucking seventeen years old. Where were you? I snapped back on her ass bitch you aren't momma, you damn sure don't look white to me. I reached into my back pocket pulled out the bundled of money I had and pulled a couple hundred dollar bills out of my pocket tossed it at her, now bitch back up off me I answer to no one.

Hershey came around the corner from the kitchen I know where he was at he was with Rocky. Chocolates eyes got so big I thought they were going to pop out of her head. You mean to tell me you were with Clarence jones. Who the fuck is Clarence Jones? I don't know anyone by that name. "Well that's his real name and Maurice you don't want to get caught up with someone like that. He's no good and will get you caught up into some shit. He used to be a pimp and beat the shit out of females back in the day. Well, bitch don't worry about me, he likes me and says I'm beautiful and treats me well, he bought me a brand-new wardrobe and I didn't have to pay a thing. She looked at me and laughed that's how it all starts. Look I don't have time for your shit I am already late I'm going out of town to Virginia to meet my girlfriend I will be back tomorrow mom.

I grabbed my car keys and jolted out of the door. I got in my car and drove over to the East Mall and the first store I went inside was Victoria secret. I bought my woman a two-suit set with a red blouse and red heels since that wasn't something she was use to since her playing basketball she was rarely dress like a lady and always a tom boy. I walked passed kay jewelers distracted by all the shiny diamonds. I looked at a princess cut purple diamond with two smaller cut diamonds on the side. Then looked at the price and seen that it was $4000.00. Man, I was like got damn I can't afford that. The sales woman came over to ask me if I needed anything, I looked at her and said with a price like that I don't think I could afford that. She told me "well if you open a line of credit it's only $1200.00 down and you can make monthly payments on it, So I said bet let me get that in a size 7 and a half please, At least that's what I thought her size was. She wrapped the gift up in a box and I drove over to meet Mary J, out her house in Susquehanna Township. She was already in the drive way in her white Volvo car. She looked at me get out of my car and said "I almost left you go ahead and put your bag in the trunk. I hoped in the front seat and she looked at me and said are you going to put on your seat belt? I responded yes.

I am going to be completely honest the whole ride down there felt uncomfortable. We stopped in a gas station half way down there I opened the trunk and grabbed the bags out that was Lauren's to show her mother What I bought her. I opened the bag showed her the heels and outfit, her lips pressed together in disgust. The look she gave me brought my spirits down and made me second think my gift to her. Will she really like it? I looked at her and said wait I got one last gift for her. I smiled from ear to ear as I got it out of the bag, I took the tiny like pearl looking box and opened it up she looked at me and said "That's gorgeous I hope you aren't planning to propose because she needs to finish college and not focus on little fairytales. To be quite honest I don't see what stink sees in you. Stink was a nickname she called her daughter at times. As I sat beside this woman in her car and got so discourage all I wanted to do was to simply smack the shit out of this bitch. See let me give you the run down, this woman was a fake Christian that only spoke the bible upon other people's life yet very rarely did she follow her words. She hated me since day one and never really liked me. She couldn't stand the ideal that her daughter was with a boy that couldn't do anything for her daughter. It bothers deeply that her daughter loves me and I returned the same passion despite my flaws and hidden agendas. To tell you the truth Lauren knew I couldn't stand her mom, this woman didn't even like my family, up-bringing or my background. I only tried to get along with this woman just on the strength that I simply was madly in love with her daughter. All I ever wanted was for Mary J to accept me and like me. I would never forget the moment her and I got into a debate, I wouldn't call it an argument because with her it isn't. I remember it like it was yesterday.

Lauren and I got into argument a serious one, it got so bad that we were on the verged of losing everything we struggled through and build through the years. However, she was the type of girl that told her mother everything and talked to her about anything. Sometimes this troubled me. I didn't want her mom knowing about my past. I didn't want her judging me for the things that I done. That woman was bias and only seen one side of things. Which in my opinion was neither fair nor correct, you can't simply judge people based on what you hear about them. You should allow yourself to get to know a person. So moreover, Lauren told her mother about me being raped as a child and my curiosity with men. Her mother approached me on the porch of their house and stated to me "I think you are gay and my daughter doesn't quite see it yet, if you sleep with a man that's exactly what you are there is no coming back from that lifestyle, I know and have a lot of friends that are and you, young are gay. It's best to accept that now and leave my daughter alone to find a real man. You guys don't know anything about love... real love that is that pours out of your soul, that makes you work hard to be with someone. You don't understand the struggle that comes from hardship, tears, and pain. (in my mind, I was wondering like bitch how do you know; your husband is only there for you to fuck because your too Christianly honorable to buy a dildo). I believe Lauren will graduate college and find someone a real man that will treat her like the women she is and wants to be. You're still learning about life in High school and don't know anything yet. Just leave my baby alone and continue being a faggot. Man, when I tell you all the rage in me just wanted to smack the shit out of this bitch.

From that moment on you could just say her and I played the good game pretending to like one another. I never had someone dislike and hate me so much. I didn't care so though, falling in love with Lauren was the best thing I could have ever done. She didn't judge me for mistakes even when that hurt her at times. She had a way of seeing inside me no matter how hard I tried to hold the truth back, somehow in her own way she pierced the core of my soul with her love, kisses had a way of giving me flashes of our future getting over the adolescent stage, having careers settling down getting married and having kids. She was my best friend that I could talk to about almost anything. The one thing I admire about us was that we shared a deep connection. Although at times we were distant we yet we could talk for hours about everything. Sometimes when she would spend the nights with me or I with her I would wait for her to fall asleep and stare at her amazed by her beauty inside. I love everything about her from her dark skinned and the things that simply make us unique as a couple she loves me and I simple love her I'm just waiting on the day she graduates college and we can consummate our love for eternity. I didn't consider sex with men as me losing my virginity because it was against my own will, it was something that I had to do to survive and have money. I mean think about it I wasn't living at home anymore with my parents, I was living with my best friend's aunt who did nothing but use me for rides, get drunk and smoke weed all day and start fights with people I wanted to save enough money to move out and get my own place at least so when Lauren got home from college I can return to school get my GED and get into college for Nursing. I wanted to become a Registered Nurse. I enjoyed working with the elderly people and had a general love and concern with those kinds of people. My heart is kind for that kind of job. Lauren held the kill to my future and deep down I knew if she toughed it out with me, we both would have the life we longed and desired for. I just needed her to understand me more and have enough faith in me to stick by me...

We arrive at Lauren's college at Virginia state University where she played basketball at we got there just in time to catch the rest of her game. Her mother got out of the car and stated "well are you coming?" After the game, I saw Lauren and she saw me our eyes locked and I caught butterflies in my stomach and smiled so hard my dimples appeared. She ran into my arms and hugged me so tight she smelled of sweat and jasmine. I placed a gentle kiss on her lips and sucked her bottom thick lip and she whispered to me "stop nasty my mother is right there, I chuckled and said "I don't give a fuck" Man I couldn't wait for us to have some along time. I kept thinking in my head today will be the day we finally make love.

We went to dinner that night, as she was talking to her mother and I was stuffing my face at Damon's restaurant I couldn't help to notice that her mother was talking about me and the only thing she was doing was listening. I was mad that she never spoke up against her mother about me. I always defended her no matter who it was or what it was about. I didn't tolerate that disrespect bullshit. Yet because I knew the strong bonded relationship that her and her mother shared there was nothing that I could simply do but keep my mouth shut and keep stuffing my face with cheese fries and my burger. Although I had the image playing in my head of her mother choking on her food and me laughing hysterically while I distracted them both from their mother and daughter conversation, they both gave me a crazy look and I kept my eyes golden on my plate. I try not to disturb the conversations they both indulged in plus it was never really my place.

My phone started to vibrate hard in my left pocket, thinking it was chocolate asking me when I was coming home I just ignored it. Yet three more followed behind the previous one. I excused myself from the tabled to step to the men's restroom, as I pulled out my phone from my life pocket I seen that it was Rocky so I called him back to see what the emergency was. "Hello, what's up Rocky? He responded to Mr. Glaze my little diamond so how's the girly doing you guys making sweet little nothings. I laughed and told him Naw nigga we good what's up you called? He laughed at me also and said "I don't mean to bother you however, business call I had to get rid of two other employees of mines and need you to take their clients tomorrow night on top of yours I mean we talking about close to $15 G's my nigga." Call me stupid however I really didn't understand what $15 G's meant all I knew it was a lot of money within 72 hours. I told you that I would be home first thing in the morning let me finish tonight with my girl and her mother and I would touch bases with him soon as I left Virginia and got back to Harrisburg. He replied back to me saying "see that's why daddy can always count on you, keep making me proud I'm going have to spoil you some more. I giggled oh is that right, I will text you when I am on the road. He said good bye to me in a low sexual tone voice and had a way on pulling me in and trust every word he said to me. You see I wasn't like those other little trashy boys Rocky recruited, I was unique I was special my beauty and body made me one of a kind. I had a way of making men putty in my hands without having an emotional conscious. Majority of the other men that did things or worked for Rocky were dirty fucking strippers and prostitutes and barely brought close to a thousand to the table, however me on the other hand if they choose to do sexual acts with me the price was very high and well worth it. He knew that he could count on me because I for one will become a legend in the game an icon, a trophy the true Mona Lisa bared in front of all men to lavish over my forbidden fruits... I couldn't help it, yet money was on my mind hard. I was fantasizing about cars; more clothes trips out of town. I craved money, power, and respect... Most of all I wanted to prove myself to Rocky that even his senior boys are what you can call them twenty-five and up couldn't touch what I can bring to the table. Once I take up the remaining of those clients and my own I would have officially earned my spot at the winners table. Just wait and see Maurice you will demand that men respect you and people know exactly who you are nothing to be fucked with because you had Rocky to back you up.

I left the bathroom got back to the table Lauren looked at me and asked if everything was okay I said yes, just had to take care of somethings about work. She looked at me with a stern look, which deep down she could tell I was lying or hiding something yet to bring that up right in front of her mother wasn't the best thing we could possibly do for neither one of us. She gave me one of those looks like, nigga don't think I'm going to forget about this we going to talk later. She had a way of raising her eyebrows and moving them like the rock did. Sometimes it made me smile inside sometimes it place me with caution like damn do I want to pass go and collect my $200 dollars. Her mother rolled her eyes at me and kept on going with the conversation. I knew that Lauren wouldn't let me forget anything she was sure enough to bring it up to me when we got back to her dorm room. I remember walking ahead of her through the hallways and her looking at me and asking me. "Do you want to tell me what's going on or do I have to speculate that you are up to something." Deep down I was bursting inside with the truth yet, from the twinkle in her eyes she gave me there was nothing I could possibly do but to lie. So, I did exactly that, I told her I was just stressed out from not being back home with my parents, living with chocolate, losing my job at the nursing home and not properly getting sleep some days. She looked back at me and said you do seem a little tensed and tired maybe when we get back to the room we can cuddle and relax. "Well I don't know where I am going to sleep since Mary J will be in the room with us also. She laughed back at me saying "Don't worry about her just as long theirs no freaky stuff though as she winked at me that made me become overwhelmed with joy.

We laid in the bed of her dorm room while her mother took the other bed to the left of the room. I remember slowly going to sleep drifting off as I heard her mother snoring due to her allergies. I could feel Lauren gently rubbing up and down on my chest. She placed her waist and left leg over my body and whispered softly in my ear. I love you baby and I pray to god your life gets better. She woke me up before there could even be a deep sleep by kissing and biting down tenderly on my bottom lip. I returned the invitation by pulling at her top lip attempting to kiss it with love. She let out a small sigh. Somehow when I kiss her and was around her it seems as though all of my cares and worries in the world slipped away from my mind. She was like my angel, at times I felt as though she knew that I was up to no good however, she had so much faith in me to change and be different. Even when I didn't deserve it her love was just one of a kind to me. She believed that I could do better if I tried hard enough. She told me that I was special and that somehow God had unique designed plan for me that one day everything will be revealed to me when the time is right. I just had to keep praying, read my bible and keep enough faith as a mustard seed and allow god to come in and take care of the rest. She knew what I was going through and often never asked me about the whole chocolate situations and living with Hershey the whole gay thing situation. She knew it was difficult for me to talk about at times.

Moreover, I even didn't like it because I knew I never belonged there. Someone told me much older that love sometimes has a boundary, it never gets old, and it never dies nor withers' away. I was told that if you truly love someone despite what is going on in the world, around you, influences and yet love is so powerful and strong it can with stand anything even when its being attack even when troubles and trials come. Love is phenomenal, rare, a gift of creation, moreover with every scary obstacle comes a true lesson and purpose of inner beauty. I sure hoped to feel this one day even for myself inside because cavernously within

I don't feel such poise. Who really knows? One day I won't wake up feeling so useless and down as if there is no such real thing like this for me in the real world. I need to place my head out of the clouds and focus on reality that some great things always happen to people who don't really know the meaning behind pain or to suffer in life and worst things happen to those who are already hurting.

We got up early the next morning on Sunday to head back to Harrisburg, Pa and I was already missing her, I thought to myself when is the next time I am going to possibly see Lauren again. Her mother barely spoke to me the whole ride back and Rocky was just blowing up my phone like crazy. I really didn't want to go back to the things he had me doing, yet I had no choice. However, I knew that this wasn't something that I wanted to do long term and I had to try and find a way out if possible. At times the kindness and innocent heart I had inside me didn't like the things that I was doing nor did I like the way Rocky treated the other people meaning the other guys that worked for him. Majority of the people didn't like rocky nor could they tolerate his personality. Moreover, Rocky never gave me a reason to consider him a liar nor a thug. He was always so kind towards me and practically gave me all that I asked for although it wasn't much.

I arrived back at home chocolate's house charged my phone while I took a shower. I let the hot water drops smack my body like pellets as I got ready for tonight's events. I heard Hershey come in the bathroom and sat on the toilet lid and asked me if I wanted to hit his blunt, I pulled the shower curtain open as he gazed my body up and down. "Did you want to hit this or not? I said "Yes, pass it too me and my towel also please. He stared even harder at me saying, "Your changing man and I'm afraid you won't like who you become. Being a vogue queen is one thing however being a man's bitch is another. I smirked at him and laughed. "What's wrong Hershey as I was pulling my hair from my back to my shoulder; do I sense a little bitch cunt jealousy coming from you? He rolled his eyes at me and stated no not at all just remember things that you do with that man or anyone in general comes with a price! You are so right just like the price I had to pay lying to my girlfriend about you placing a hickie on my neck when I was completely drunk and pass out almost cost me everything. I told you just like I tell every other nigga you don't matter to me they don't matter to me, yet what does matter to me is simply surviving and pushing forward, so think whatever you want or like about me trust me your weak pathetic ass doesn't even phase me.

Eventually Glaze she will find out I promise you that this is a small city and everyone in Harrisburg knows everyone's business as he yelled behind me as I was walking away from the bathroom into my room. I pushed past his thoughts as I rolled me a blunt I texted rocky and let him know that I was ready to be picked up. I smoked inhaled hard as fuck and began to get my chill on. I heard the black escalade truck pull up in front of the apartment. I grab my Togo bag and cell phone, as chocolate was coming through the door I was pushing my way out. She even screamed back at me Uh no bitch please don't think you are coming back to this house, I told your yellow ass you can't just come and go as you please. I looked back at that bitch in disgust as I was hoping into the truck. I told the driver take me to where I am going just anywhere but here.

I hated staying at that place sometimes, yet where else could I possibly go. My mind was bottled up and stressed to the max; I could hardly concentrate what I had to do tonight. I arrive at the Sheraton Hotel got out of the truck and walked inside to the entrance lobby where this skinny pale, blue eyed blonde hair guy was standing. He asked me my name, I almost blurted out Maurice but I forgot I was somebody else at that moment. Jamel as I cut my eyes at him, He smiled back at me saying you are on the tenth-floor executive suite room 1014. I took the card between my two fingers and got on the elevator. The elevator design was so elegant very upscale and classy the music made me laugh because it was playing Mariah Carey's song hero. I got to the 7th floor when it stopped and a tall man 6'4 light skinned guy got on with tattoos cover all over his body. He was drenched in sweat and smelled like usher's obsession cologne. He pulled the head phones out of his ears and re-pushed the lit button for the 10th floor. He turned and looked at me to start a conversation. "So, you come here often he asked me? I took my eyes from the day dream gaze I was in to look up at him green eyes thick brown beard, full rounded lips. I responded to him "yea sometimes I'm here on business." He smiled deeply at me with dimples that looked like half crescent moons and replied nice dude me too. He kept staring at me and then asked so what do you do? I giggled back at him because in my mind I was screaming dude I'm a whore a filthy dirty little whore. Yet, I didn't react to what my mind was saying instead I blinked my eyes slowly and looked at him customer service. He smiled again and said nice dude really nice. The elevator door dinged as it open and I quickly got off and he followed behind me I forgot we were on the same floor. I looked at the signs on the wall to direct me to my room. He turned right to walk down the hallway and stop and stated to me "Are you lost by any chance the numbers here seem to be a little tricky? I shot him a quick response, didn't your parents ever tell you not to speak to strangers? He chuckled so loud at me. Well I was just wondering if you needed any help sorry to bother you. I hesitated and said "wait I didn't mean to be rude, as he stood still gazing at me and took three steps forward, I usually don't do this but my name is Romeo and I will be here for the next three days would you like to possibly go out for a drink sometime in the lobby downstairs or go for a morning workout with me. I paused for a second, got sad and told him sorry I can't my work keeps me very busy and my schedule is always hectic. His facial expression went to a grim look as he slowly steps back saying "ok well it was at least nice meeting you... and your name was again? I laughed at him; I never gave you my name sir. He chuckled again this time letting out a tiny giggle. Can I at least get your name? I winked turned around and said maybe one day but not right now. We parted ways I continued down the left hallway and he the right. He shouted from down the hallway by the way I think you are crazy beautiful. I glanced at him grinned a little bit and place my card inside the door. I thought to myself well at least he was very nice. I flipped on the light seen my king size bed with red long stemmed roses on the counter with a card. The greeting inside of it said "Enjoy yourself the next three days relax, have fun and text/call me if there are any problems much respect my nigga, -Rocky" Sometimes he can be so sweet when he wants to be and I had the hardest crush on him and he had swag. I loved how he showered me with gifts. I took the vanilla envelope next to the flowers. I opened it and pulled out the instructions:

"Tonight, you are taking on extra clients so try to rest up and be mindful these are higher up white folks at least majority of them and they enjoy what they like with hush-hush under the rug type shit. There are two costumes in the closet for you for two of your higher end clients. You have a total of sixteen clients for the next three days. Soak your body, dress to impress and remember its money time. I couldn't find too many photos of these men since some of them are married and like to be discreet about the products they keep from their personal lives. It is okay each one has been doing business with me for years and are very excited to meet the new gem behind the glass class in which that is you tonight.

P.S you meet with Mr. Espino tonight IS THE MOST IMPORTANT BEFORE ANYONE OF THESE CLIENTS. THERE IS A PAGER IN YOUR ROOM IF HE PAGES YOU, YOU GO TO HIS ROOM IMMEDIATELY WHATEVER HE WANTS HE GETS, NO QUESTIONS ASKED."

I flipped over the next page and seen the list of room numbers and times and at the very bottom was the 11th floor penthouse no number just said penthouse. I figured that's the special client he spoke of. I looked at the time across the room on the night stand it was going on 7 o'clock and my first client was at 8:15pm. I walked to the bathroom and seen more roses and under garments, and a box of 36 count of condoms picked out for me. I grabbed that shit and threw it on the bed. I ran the shower water began to undress myself in front of the large mirror that hanged over the black charcoal marble looking vanity. I began to get depress because at that moment I really didn't know what I was doing. A part of me felt so fearful inside and embarrassed to exactly what I was about to perform and do tonight. I wasn't singing in front of a crowd. I wasn't operating on anyone. I wasn't doing a fantastic event or charade. However, I was committing a sin to go out and be a whore. I didn't feel right so I believe somehow, I should get on my hands and knees and say a prayer.

Dear Heavenly father,

I come before you as the sinner I am. Lord I ask you to see past my ways and look inside my heart to see what kind of person that I truly am. I asked you to increase my courage yet you have made be weak as a mere insect antlike and to let go of my strongholds that keep me bound yet they are still attached to me like glue. Father I ask you to allow me to find a way out of the sanity that I have manage to get myself in. Lord you stated in your word that if we confess our sins, he is faithful and just and will forgive us of our sins, and purify us from all unrighteousness. Have you left me? Have I forsaken your grace? Do you still believe that there is goodness in my heart? Oh, God please just speak to me I have no one and so very alone these days. I am constantly battling the silent whispers inside my head. What is my purpose? What do you see for me in the future? My mind is so conflicted these days on what to do and where to go. I feel like I going to start losing my mind if I haven't already. Can I still believe in you? Can I still be a Christian being a faggot a man who likes and does sexual things with men just for money? God oh please just hear me, you always were there when I was a child. I forgive you for allowing me to make mistakes and not jumping to every time I call. Yet, Lord sometime I need you to lift my spirits, speak to my heart, and change me for the better.

I remember growing up as innocent children do and constantly hearing your heavenly voice in my head. I feel as though the devil himself wants me more than you. Why is that? How come you are comfortable with that? May I ask you was I ever yours to begin with? How could you allow this to happen? Am I being put to a test? Please hear me because right now this isn't where I would imagine my life. You said you may not come when I want you and that you will always be there on time. Yet, you haven't come at all. Faith is something I believe that doesn't exist anymore. Strength is what I lack, although I want to just repent and be made new again you are not allowing me or healing me to do so. Is there something you are waiting on me to do, show you? Why must this be so difficult? Why is it constant temptation and struggles of the acceptance of my inner me? Do you think battling these demons alone is stress-free?

So, I didn't want to upset you I just need to vent to someone and although I am praying aloud with words to you like everything else you won't hear me and by time you finally do get this message it will be too late for me, and the contents of my spirit... Thanks again for not hearing my sorrow cries.

Sincerely,
The Whore
Amen...

After cleansing my body from the shower water, I threw on my ebony jeans, white V-neck T-shirt, and my all white air force ones. I place a peppermint from the night stand in my mouth and opened up the box of magnum condoms and stuck a few in my back pocket. I rolled up my blunt of weed that rocky had gotten me for 3 days got damn. I'm going for the hall of fame of all whores. I walked over to the mini kitchen that was inside of my hotel room and opened the mini fridge to see a bottle of Patron. I cracked opened the bottle and made me a full glass with the plastic red cup you know the one's you use at your cookouts when you don't want to do dishes. I would say about twenty minutes or so went by and I started to feel my influences and the cocktail mixer of them both. I grabbed my hotel key, pager and my fitted all black hat and paper for hotel room numbers and walked out of the door. As I thought to myself in that moment, tonight you're no longer a child of god, your no longer someone's boyfriend, you're no longer a son, your no longer you. Everything that you ever thought you are no longer exists. At this moment, you are not even a whore but a prized escort. Open your mind let the beauty be in your reflection and let elegance show in your stance. Always walk with authority and demand respect. Remember tonight counts for its all about the money.

I walked down the hallway and stop at the entrance for the elevator and couldn't help but to think about the guy Romeo I previously met that day. Then suddenly I heard a noise of someone opening their door and coming out of there room. I didn't stay long enough to see who it was, the elevator door dinged! And the doors slid open, I got on it pressed the number four to that floor and started to sing along with the Mariah Carey "Oh when you walk by every night talk and sweet and looking fine, I get kind of hectic inside. Oh, baby I'm so into you tell me if you only knew all the things that come through my mind." I began to laugh at myself because I was alone and pretty sure people could hear me singing the wrong words to the song on another floor I was beginning to get loud. The door opened to the 4th floor and stood a white older gentleman and his wrinkly old wife. She looked like a Liberian with her deep googles on her face. Lord have mercy someone save her sight.

I excused myself from their presence and continued to pull out the paper from my back pocket and see that I had to go to room 402. I looked at the sign pointing the directions too odd and even numbers of rooms and made a right. As I was walking down the hall I could hear people inside their rooms listening to music, screaming at the football game and even arguing. I reached the second door to the last on the right at the end of the hallway. I knocked on the door three times and heard a wheezing coughing voice come to the door. As the door knob turned and slowly opened there was an older gentleman around his late forties, athletic built silver gray hair with emerald hazel eyes, white teeth as he smiled at me. His shoulders were even broad with medium horse shoe imprints in his arms and solid hairy stomach with ralph polo pants on; a pointy nose with no lips what so ever. His faced looked smooth with high cheek bones. "Are you just going to stand there or are you going to come in"

I walked inside and looked around his room, I could see he was messy because there were clothes everywhere and suitcases opened. He stared me up and down and was like got damn dude you are so beautiful. "Sorry about the mess it's been a crazy work week and I have a lot of stressed built up would you like a dirty martini? Sure, why not as I responded back to him" My name is PJ by the way. I looked at him and ask what does PJ stand for, as I projected my tender voice back at him? It means phat junk as he laughed from being slightly intoxicated making a joke that wasn't even funny in my opinion but I giggled anyway to lighten the mood. As his back was turned to me while he was making my drink and I walked over to him took my right hand and slowly ran it down from the top of his neck to the middle of his back. He let out a small sigh as if he was about give a small coo for me like a baby that is nestled between his mother's breasts. He turned around looked into my eyes that were glossy from the blunt I smoked. I reached out and grabbed the dirty martini and took it all back. I through the glass behind me and stretched my hands across his chest clinching my fingers against his pale skin leaving marks of my presence of me being here. I leaned in forward towards him even more and uttered on his lips "What do you desire? "Just make me feel good and please don't tell my wife as he responded back to me." I pulled my head back from him and cocked my head to the side looking at him with a devilish look, grinning on my face I managed to say "Don't worry baby it's only a fantasy. I unbuckled his pants and rapidly sliding the belt off watching his pants drop while the bright whitey tidies shown. I picked him up my hands wrapped around his back, placed him on the desk, his assed arched and back faced the rest of the room. His hands rubbed down my back as he was breathing in my craving sexual scent. I stretched my mouth open and bitten tenderly on his neck as he let out a growl. I swirled my tongue into circles moving and pressing down harder and going back and forth. I then knew that I wasn't any longer in control anymore, that my sexual beast, alter ego has come forth to finish the job. I c-clamped down on this neck feeling his pulse throbbed in my hand, as I whispered again to him "What is your inner desire?" "Make me your bitch he stated" He pushed off from me with a twinkle in his eye. I need to go change really quick it will only take just a second. I told him to hurry up because his time was running out. I grabbed his glass of martini left and finished it up. He came out of the bathroom with pantie hose on and gold pumps with a collar around his neck. I sighed and grinned even harder this time swaying my hips from left to right as I walked towards him. I grabbed the collar with my hand and tugged on it in a fast motion saying "Nice I always wanted a bitch now get down on your hands and knees, suck my toes. He did exactly that walking and panting like a dog. I commanded him as such because I had power to do so. I pulled out my bone and told him "now be a good boy and play dead on this bone" he licked the bone up and down, and even gagged on it a couple of times until he came up for air and asked please to place it all the way down his throat. I shoved his mouth down on it so hard even my balls were deep in. I released my sweet cream that shot off like cannons, as tear drops started to fall from the corners of his eyes as if he was eating habanero sauce. I pulled all the way out, grabbed his collar into my left hand and smack his face with my bone. I told him to go lay down and don't move. He was a good boy so I placed my bone back in my drawers in which it came from and grabbed my money from coffee table and left out of the door. I felt as though I wanted to gag and throw up yet there was no time for that I had to go to the next appointment in 20 minutes which was right down the hall.

I took the elevator back up to my room quickly went to the bathroom to clean my dick up with soap. I rolled a fat blunt and began to toke on it as I pulled the paper from my jeans. I read that I had to pull the costume out of the closet for this one and head down to room 426. As I was smoking my blunt I unzipped the black bag that as in the closet. I pulled out the black G-string thong and black and red ribbons, the baby oil. There was a note from Rocky saying "Hey you have a birthday party to do, this is all you will need he likes feminine guys so it would be nice if you were to drop your hair down a little. Remember no matter who you meet or see tonight discretion is important you feel me. I pulled this tiny piece of triangle thread out and pulled the blunt again as I thought to myself how in the hell and I got to pull this shit off, fuck that I pulled the patron out again and drunk the entire bottle. If I knew what I knew this wasn't going to be an easy client or clients. Somehow, I would have to do the unexpected. I went inside the bathroom pulled my hair out of a bun, took my flat iron out of my bag and began to curl the ends to my long Brazilian like hair. (yes, bitch all natural) I pulled the G-string up on me and immediately the thread got lost between my ass. I place to large pins to hold my hair back into position while I Chris-crossed the red and black ribbons from my ankles going all the way up to my thighs and hips. I placed my light blue eyes in, rubbed baby oil all over my body until I became a light bright glowing in the light. I left out of the bathroom and took the robe from the back of the door and swing it over my body and closed my beauty inside for tonight's presentation. I re-sparked my blunt and left out of the door. I reached the elevator got on it and got back off on the fourth floor. I made a left and reached my destination and could hear the music outside of the hotel room. I knocked on the door and a tall dark skinned man answer the door. I walked inside covered with my black robe and seen 3 familiar faces out of the six men that were there. I recognized Shyla-mar he worked at the boys and girls club on the hill where I use to play basketball at in the summer. I really couldn't tell the only one I knew use to show out this phrase "YEA BOY!!!" He looked me up and down rubbing his hands together like a junkie ready for its next fix and blurted out "YEA BOY!" Looks like that confirmed that one. He was six foot dark skinned, with a slow down syndrome look, stupid but perfectly sane, he was already sitting on the edge of the bed in the room with a stack of money rolled up into a knotted rubber band holding it together. The man to my right was sitting down on the couch he was my height and I recognized him as Riche yet he was known as LD in Steelton aka little dick. At least from what I heard from the girls from the block. That thing is Harrisburg is so small that everyone knows practically everybody. LD was slender with big lips and a bright smile. He had a peanut shaped head with barely enough facial hair to look like a grown man. His voice was so low key you could hardly hear him at times when he spoke. There was another man standing up rolling a blunt in the mini kitchen area, you could tell he was already fucked up. He looked up at me trying to figure out who I was but I was too good because he just kept smiling at me. His name was Chino... Big Chino that is, he stood at 6'4-foot-tall, brown skinned with tattoos that covered his whole entire body, with three different baby mamas and you could always find him uptown at emeralds ordering chopped chicken wings with rib tip sauce and shrimp fried rice. I never knew he was into this kind of underground scene. The men in the room turned on some music as the song by "Juvenile" back that ass up "played in the background I began to throw back my robe letting it slide off my shoulders and back hitting the beginning of my ass. There

121

was another knock on the door and four additional men came in and I knew all four of them.

The one in front was Logan aka Reese is what you could call him, I am not sure he recognizes me but he is Lauren's cousin and put chills down my spine because I didn't want him to recognize me. Last time I check he was in college yet somehow, he was here in this exact moment. The one behind him was Ka-seem who also had a twin brother that hung around a lot on the hill towards 19th street or piccolo's which was a local old head hood bar. The third man before the last was Joshua Plows also known as Josh; He was tall also light skinned, big lips that were always chapped with dirty fucking finger nails. He also had three baby mamas but was mainly know for fucking a lot of women around the burg. Last but not least, Quan Williams who live out the south in hall manor who old to every fucking body. Some people knew him as Phats the weed man. Quan was dark very dark that's why some areas people also knew him as black as well. He was good looking and played basketball for years for the Harrisburg aka the High also known as cougars. He was a smooth talker yet he had that heat for you. I never heard people really cross him because you rarely live to tell the story about it. I began to glance around the room connecting my geisha like eyes with every man in there so I could remember the faces majority of them was either rolling up blunts or drinking E&J straight out of the bottles. The one guy Chino was breaking up powder on top of the counter. I went through the double doors of the suite room that they rented out to see a silver pole attached to the ceiling. In my mind, I was nervous for this shit to go down and with this many of men however, dancing wasn't going to be much of a problem for me. I took the two pins out of my hair and watched as my curls dropped down and hit the beginning of my ass. I turned towards the men and said "So whose birthday is it today?" They all looked towards big Chino as they started to get rowdy saying "That's my nigga over there, come on and grab you some ass nigga, It's your motha fuckin birthday my G. He looked at me cutting and breaking down the white girl and said to me "What's your name? I ignored him and said "pour me a shot and I'll tell you. The right side of his face cracked a smile as he created 6 lines right in front of me. It's my birthday so can you make me feel special? I took the rolled up hundred-dollar bill he uses to snort up his nose and did all six lines while he looked at me in shock. I glared at him with desire and leaned into him saying" I won't just make you feel special but I guarantee you will cum special. I never did coke before however I wanted to throw up and cough but I couldn't this was part of the game you see.

I flipped my hair to the right and gazed into his eyes to hypnotize him with lust as I took him by his twice as big hands to the living room area. I grabbed a chair and told him to sit, the rest of the men followed gathering around in the giant room that was built for a small cocktail party. I told the nearest dude who was standing next to the music player to hit play so the music could change into the vibe I was feeling, the song by Jeremiah came on which was "Birthday sex". I took my hands to the pole and twirled around it like I was a spinning dial going up and down. I pulled myself to the very top wrapping my left leg under my right upside down while I was slowly going down the pole. I made sure to keep eye contact with Chino the whole time. I climb back up to the very top and sled down the pole fast and dropped into a full spilt, I got up crawled to him on my knees did a hand stand placing my legs on his shoulders. I could feel his big hands rubbing on my thighs. I pulled myself off him flipped my hair forward placing my hands on the ground as my ass clapped in his face. I gently sat in his lap placing his hands deep inside my inner thighs, the rest of the men I can hear them cheering him on telling him to tear my ass up, as he placed his face on my shoulder I can hear him whisper in my right ear. Got damn boy you're so beautiful with all that damn ass. I turned around wrapped my legs around him as I blew on his neck. I switched to the other side and licked his neck and softly spoke in his ear "What's your fantasy daddy?" During this time the music was going on and the niggas in the room was getting jealous yelling out at him. Damn nigga share the shawty. He responded back to me in my ear, I know who you are, I tried to pull away from him but I couldn't his hands were wrapped around my back as he began to talk more into my ear asking me to calm down not to draw attention. MAURICE! LISTEN TO ME, I grinded on him to play it off like he was liking the rough shit, he began to say to be its okay I'm not going to hurt you daddy relax. I always found you irresistible no one knows who you are here just me, collect these niggas money like you came here to do. I was slightly panicking a little bit I really didn't know what to do. He kissed my neck and told me to calm down and enjoy myself. I will never hurt you Maurice; I love your Aunt Chocolate too much to fuck with her FAM like that.

I could feel the rest of the men stare at us. He whispered in my ear you're at the wrong place at the wrong time. You don't deserve this shit man, Why would rocky set you up like this? He knows what these parties are like. He knows what goes down. Listen you need to break away from Rocky before it's too late before you lose your life. I kept grinding on his dick making the others around him crazy. He said to me don't worry I'm going to look after you tonight at least while you are here, just keep entertaining my boys real quick then me and you are going to have a private dance again "is that okay with you? I smiled while my face was buried in his neck and nodded my head up and down agreeing to yes. He stood up and places me on my fee, as he went over to the music player and played another song I was used to hearing by mystical "Shake it fast" He turned back around pulled his gun out my heart dropped to my stomach at that moment, he swings it in all their faces and said "FUCK WITH MY BIRTHDAY PRESENT IF OU WANT TO, SEE IF YOU DON'T GET YOUR SHIT BLOWN OFF, TEST A NIGGA IF YOU WANT TO. They all smacked their lips telling him to calm down and chill as if he was drunk yet he wasn't he seem very relaxed to me. He looked at me and winked his left eye and bit his bottom lip as in confirmation to keep his word he would protect me tonight. He placed his gun back and grabbed his dick and blew me a kiss and went back towards the kitchen area to drink as he watched me from a distance. I went on to shaking my ass in front of niggas and letting them slap my ass like crazy. They were pulling out bundles of hundreds as I was splitting on the floor. All I could see was moneys falling on me, yes it was raining in that bitch and I was loving it. Niggas was pulling their dicks out and slapping their shit on my ass. The guy Shyla-mar pulled his dick out and it felt like I had bat on my back. He pulled out two rubber band bundles like a stack of cards and said" I let you have both of these right the fuck now if you let me lick that thick pussy." He was dead ass serious. He was sitting on the couch in the room, I snatched the stacks out of his hand and pulled my ass up in the air and let his tongue enter my ass whole. He pulled my G-string to the side and began to clean me out. My dick even got hard, I couldn't tell you if it was the coke or the liquor but all this attention began to turn me on and get me hard, my own dick began to be stiff as a board. I began to literally be addicted to the money being thrown at me. I mean don't get me wrong I knew exactly all of this was wrong but what was a boy like me to do when I had to eat, survive, impress a girlfriend that was in college, pay rent at a place I really didn't feel like being at because I no longer live with my parents. I just kept thinking to myself that I had to do what I had to do simple as that. Although all the dick swing around me made me quite uncomfortable I just kept my eyes on the paper and plus this dude sticking his tongue in and out of my ass was really started to get on my nerves with my legs spread wide open as he was tasting my passion fruit of my hidden treasure inside of me. There was a big BANG! At the hotel door. Everyone stop and pulled out their bangers and even turned down the music. Big Chino answered the door and asked "Who is it? The deep voice responded "Kellz" Chino answered the door pissed and the tall light skinned man stepped through the door framed and starting ranting about a dude named "T-Rell being beat over some drugs and the niggas out Hall manor had beef and shit and was talking about dropping niggas on sight. Big Chino responded "Oh yea niggas don't want his A-Kay my nigga, ah yo! We out this shit nigga get yawl shit lets ride, smoke these niggas and hit Savannah's, drink and smoke. First these niggas need dealt with and they shall. Big Chino walked over to me and told every nigga to step out of the fucking room he had to talk to his birthday present in person and alone. Those niggas weren't even worried they began to check themselves for their guns and throw back shots and clock back their pistols and shit. Big Chino looked at me with his big hazel eyes and gently said "It was nice meeting you again Maurice. Will I ever get to meet you again on different terms? I smiled at him and responded nigga don't you have baby mamas and kids as I laughed. He leans into me gripped me up softy placed his hand around my neck and took his big lips and gently kissed me leaving my bottom lip quivering. He stepped back and said here as he placed two additional stack of twenties rolled up into a rubber band in both my hands and took out his back pocket another stack with hundreds rolled on it peeled back a hundred-dollar bill walked over to the music player and grabbed a pen that was on the floor and wrote his number on it and gave it to me. He looked me straight into my eyes directly and said" If you need anything at all or have any problems I mean any problems at all please call me don't hesitate. I promise you I will be there. I giggled at him and said "sure you will". He smiled, I'll let you be shawty and clear these niggas out so you can grab your money and go without being hassled. I cracked up laughing and said "I know right." He left out of the room and cleared the other room telling every nigga there let's ride. I waited for all the men to leave out before I went into the other room.

Soon as the door closed I locked the door placed my robe around me and began to pick up the money around on the floor and even took the money that was hooked onto the straps around my thighs and placed it all in my bag and realized that I had to count this shit when I get back to my hotel room to see if there was an extra cut I could keep to myself without giving it too Rocky. I looked inside my black duffle bag I came with and realize that the pager went off twice and that I was going to be late for the special client which I still didn't know anything about. I grabbed everything I came with and made sure not to miss a bill laying around. Bitch I needed all my coins okay. I even grabbed the rest of the EJ bottle and swiftly ran out the door. Fuck taking the elevator I couldn't I was already late. I forgot that Rocky stated that if he pages I go running. I took the stairs and sprinted away to the 10th floor again placed my key in the door and dropped the whole entire duffle bag in the closet. I looked at the note on the counter to see if I had any special directions for this man. Only thing Rocky stated was to dress sexy and conservative. In my mind, I didn't know what the fuck he meant by that what the hell is sexy and conservative. I turned the note on the back and there it was in bold stating "There is an outfit in the closet grab it and remember have fun. I was all oily and sweaty from drinking, doing coke and striping,

I jumped in the shower and used the Moonlight path bath and body works product to smell seductive. Washed my hair with it as well. I quickly got out of the shower dried off. Placed some coconut and jasmine oil in my hair and even rubbed a little bit of it in my pubic hair and on my chest hair. I walked out of the bathroom back towards my room and went inside the closet and pulled out the outfit hanging on a hanger. I unzipped the protector around it and there was a red see through underwear and a red see through robe with a red and black rosary. Yea that was kind of awkward to me as I thought I hope I am not about to fuck no pastor with sick fantasies of having a little church boy to turn out. I heard a vibrating sound again and there it was the pager going off again. I sprayed a little Versace in the air and walked through it grabbed the pager and hotel room key looked in the mirror to make sure my blue eyes were still in because they began to feel a little blurry to me. I took some eye drops and placed a couple in my eyes. Looked at the time and realize it was already going on midnight, I ran out the door as my pecks were bouncing, curly hair catching a breeze, my red robe gliding in the air due to my movement. I reached the elevator and pressed the "P- button" since that was the last and highest floor that you could go to other than the 11th floor. After I passed the 11th floor the elevator music playing Whitney Houston's song "I have nothing the same song in the body guard actually stopped. I arrive at the top and the elevator actually said "Penthouse" The door opened and there were gold lights six of them in a row on each wall leading to the only door down the hall. The floor was white marble and looked crystal clear. I started to choke up in my throat praying and hoping in my head this is not an old white man that will kill me because this will creep me the fuck out. I knocked on the door and the voice yelled at me from a distance and said it's open, just come in. I walked in, I was amazed to a crystal chandler hanging from the ceiling a full bar on the left side near an open opened window that you can see all of Harrisburg's city lights. There was an all-black grand piano on the right-hand side. I could hear the voice tell me in the back ground there is champagne on the bar counter just pop it open and have yourself a glass your kind of late I am just getting out of the shower. Your name is Glaze right Rocky told me so much about you give me a second I will be out. I couldn't see his face I could only see his shadow from the glass French double doors that seem like to hide his bedroom and bathroom or guest area. I walked over to the neon light bar that was black marble top and took the champagne out of the bucket it was sitting on ice. I popped the bottle and poured two glasses. So, I asked him do I at least get to eventually see you or at least know your name. There was a brief pause and he responded sure you can when I get done getting dress if you don't mind Mr. late Treasure can you at least make yourself useful and hand me a glass of champagne I mean it's the least you can do. Right as I thought to myself here we ago another smart ass. I walked over to the doubled doors and knocked on the door and a light skinned hand reach out a skinny hand and grabbed the glass and closed the door behind it. I giggled. He said what's so funny. I responded nothing sir. Sir? I am not that old. I walked back over to the bar grabbed my own glass and chugged it back and pour another I had a feeling that tonight was going to be very strange and mysterious. It seems like to me this client was different than the rest of the men I have encountered. I hope he doesn't plan on hiding behind them doors all night. Fancy guy or not I was beginning to get sleepy, just wanted to fuck and get all of this over with. Just tell me what I need to do and let me get it done so I can get the fuck up out of here. He started to make small talk with me asking me about my life and bullshit. I was honestly getting annoyed so I just sat at the bar and continued to drink. So, I made small talk back and asked so what is it that you do because I have never been in a lovely Shafto place as this. "I see we have a funny guy on are hands well, mister if you must know I am in sales and stocks that's all. I began to whisper to myself, is that right all sarcastically. I placed my right hand on my cheek and began to get relaxed because I been here already for it seemed like twenty minutes and this nigga still didn't come out. He yelled again at me and said "Hey can you reach behind the bar and press play for music. I did exactly as he told me and pressed play on the remote and soft jazz music came on. All of this old people shit was starting to put me to sleep. I even began to slowly dose off. I could hear the doors swing open and toes cracking as they walked on the floor. He said "I'm so sorry to keep you waiting however, I waited two hours for you to get here and you were mighty late. My head was down in my arms on the bar like you use to sleep in high school with your head on the desk passing out to the teacher lecturing.

Oh, my god you have such long and pretty hair what are you wearing if I might ask. I didn't respond to him because at that moment I was tapped out of energy, yet his voice sounded so familiar to me as if I heard it before. "Hey sleepy head, I'm sorry are you going to wake up and at least say hello to me. I still didn't respond. He spun my chair around. And my head slouched over. I picked my head up and looked at him as he looked at me. I WAS COMPLETELY SHOCKED TO SEE WHO IT WAS STANDING RIGHT IN FRONT OF ME, LIKEWISE AS HE WAS SHOCKED AS WELL. We both stood there for seconds glaring at one another in astonishment. I was speechless and lost for thoughts as to how this was even possible. How are you standing in front of me? Most importantly how the fuck did you know Rocky? At this moment, I had questions and needed answers....

11

A WARRIOR OF GOD?

The people that walked in darkness have seen a great light: they that dwell in the land of the shadow of death, upon them hath the light shined. Thou hast multiplied the nation, and not increased the joy: they joy before thee according to the joy in harvest, and as men rejoice when they divide the spoil. For thou hast broken the yoke of his burden, and the staff of his shoulder, the rod of his oppressor, as in the day of Midian. **FOR EVERY BATTLE OF THE WARRIOR IS WITH CONFUSED NOISE, AND GARMENTS ROLLED IN BLOOD; BUT THIS SHALL BE WITH BURNING AND FUEL OF FIRE...**
     -ISAIAH 9:2-5

FINALLY, MY BRETHREN, BE STRONG IN THE LORD, AND IN THE POWER OF HIS MIGHT. PUT ON THE WHOLE ARMOR OF GOD THAT YE MAY BE ABLE TO STAND AGAINST THE WILES OF THE DEVIL. FOR WE WRESTLE NOT AGAINST FLESH AND BLOOD, BUT AGAINST PRINCIPALITIES, AGAINST POWERS, AGAINST THE

132

RULERS OF THE DARKNESS OF THIS WORLD, AGAINST SPIRITUAL WICKEDNESS IN HIGH PLACES. WHEREFORE TAKE UNTO YOU THE WHOLE AMOUR OF GOD THAT YE MAY BE ABLE TO WITHSTAND IN THE EVIL DAY, AND HAVING DONE ALL, TO STAND. STAND THEREFORE, HAVING YOUR LOINS GIRT ABOUT WITH TRUTH, AND HAVING ON THE BREASTPLATE OF RIGHTEOUSNESS; AND YOUR FEET SHOD WITH THE PREPARATION OF THE GOSPEL OF PEACE; ABOVE ALL, TAKING THE SHIELD OF FAITH, WHEREWITH YE SHALL BE ABLE TO QUENCH ALL THE FIERY DARTS OF THE WICKED. AND TAKE THE HELMET OF SALVATION, AND THE SWORD OF THE SPIRIT, WHICH IS THE WORD OF GOD. PRAYING ALWAYS WITH ALL PRAYER AND SUPPLICATION IN THE SPIRIT, AND WATCHING

THEREUNTO WITH ALL PERSEVERANCE AND SUPPLICATION FOR ALL SAINTS;
-EPHESIANS 6:10-18

Sometimes we walk among the world as if we have everything figured out. We say to ourselves as people we know what we are doing and where we are going. It is believed that we have the ability to change the course of our actions in what we do, how we proceed things and how we operate as human beings. Although it is without purpose we don't fully understand what nor who we are or have been called to do. Many have been called to counsel with wisdom among the world, rulers of judgement, warriors for battle and healers for those who are broken in the depths of their energy or spiritual core. Power is uncontrollable, knowledge seems not enough and greed destroys humanity and the warrior is left without battle. Have you ever thought what the meaning to it all is truly unknowable? Have you ever wonder from your childhood what is your divine purpose? What are you breathing for? What designed plan have you been placed in? Is there life after death? Why are you only able to remember 7-10 years of your memories at a single moment you try to recall an event in your life? What is the meaning of your life and what part do you play in this world of a billion people? I dare you for one second think right now if you have never known about heaven or hell nor life or death, what or where would you be? How could you recall a time in your life you made an impacted on someone else's and didn't expect anything in return? Yet can you recall a time in your life you considered the world and seen how everything was connected even your energy from your spirit? Can you tell me right now readying this book that you have already developed and assume your opinion of a mere person you have never saw a day in your life that you can already predict the outcome? If so tell me exactly the meaning and value of a single soul? I thought so…

I lied there in the hospital watching dreamlike as the paramedics handed me over to the nurses and doctors. I could hear them screaming in panic adrenaline to page the surgical doctor and get and MRI stat. You see I didn't quite think of this at the time nor was I aware of my full surroundings. Yet what I could tell you is that I was slipping away from life itself. My breathing and heart that I could hear inside my ears was slowing down. I was trying to fight and hanging there but a piece of me just wanted to let go. Could I really think that I staying here would make a difference on the poor life decisions that I have made? Who would I be leaving behind? Parents, sibling's so-called friends, a girlfriend, a promised future of son from a fairytale dream. I think not these people couldn't begin to understand the battle that is buried within me. For a couple of I always love you's and miss you's and don't do this to yourself. I beg differ. I am ready to go and leave this place and start new again. Ashes to ashes and dust to dust I've always said. What good is a pure heart if it is not cherished? Why must a pure soul be trialed and displayed to be tainted? Honestly, I really couldn't tell you I laid on the hospital bed looking up at the flashing lights on the ceiling as tears of emptiness hit the corners of my eyes waiting for my maker as I silently laughed at these doctors around me speaking false hope into my body saying "It's going to be okay kid, hang in there you're going to pull through". Silly folks you may be able to fix my body but can you fix my soul. Can you mend my spirit? Can you make me whole again was the question that was bouncing around in my head?

Sometimes you just want to give up the battle and call it all quits. We get tired of living at times, paying bills, tired of love ones dying, tired hanging in there, tired of believing things will change, tired of war, tired of politics, tired of fighting to survive, tired of waiting for god to show up. Speaking of God, we get worn out in our faith. We know that he is there all the time yet we get impatience because we need when we want and need at that very moment. Yet, right now I didn't want him to be there with me. I wanted to be left alone. I am ready to go to hell or whatever you go when you die. I am fine dying without hope, without love, without peace without being a parent, without grace and mercy. Allowing these doctors to rush around me like little ants it didn't seem like they really knew what they were doing. I looked at a woman that was in front of my face with a mask covering her mouth saying "I going to give you something for the pain, try to count back from ten if you can." I was struggling to do so I could hear her but I didn't want to speak. So, I began counting backwards in my head ten, nine I could feel the room getting even colder around me as the room itself started to get dim and dark like. Eight, seven There it was again the inner fragment of me that was hanging on speaking inside of me. Six, five "Maurice! Can you hear me? Don't be afraid my child. I will always be here for you. Four, Three

Maurice! Keep fighting my son I am here for you. Two...
I'm sorry but I can't anymore. One... Then I will fight for
you. I will carry you the rest of the way... It's not over, it's
not finish, it's not ending... This is only the beginning.

This might be the hardest thing you have ever done, I
know it hurts but it won't be too long, you're closer than
you think you are and closer then you've been before. Look
unto me my son, let me heal you, let thy seal your vessel
picks thee up and make new... You have suffered
enough... Let your spirit speak for you. There is no limit
when I begin working on you. I command the Holy Ghost
to enter inside of you. I command the fire to explode inside
you like never before. I command your spiritual gifts to
awaken and aid you in your time of need. I BREATH LIFE
INSIDE YOU. For you are a warrior of me in this world.
The fight is not yet over my son. There is much to do and
there is much that is waiting for you. Do not let this world
corrupt the essence I given you upon thought of creating
you. Don't let your wisdom be fooled. Let not the world
taint what I have sent you to do. There are people counting
on you that your paths might cross. A warrior even to the
very last drop knows when to find more strength to carry
on. The time has come for you to rise up and continue on
your journey. I am not done with you yet. You do not get to
decide when you are done here or not. You do not get to
waste my creation. For I am the lord 'Al mighty hear my
words Maurice! This is not the time and you are not done.
There is much to do my child... Let me carry you the rest
of the way. Let me show you what is in the making for
you...

12

THE GAME IS OVER

"They say beauty is pure in its rarest form, it walks among the world catching the eye of every beholder. Beauty is indestructible, unstoppable... Question lies ahead who has the purest beauty... Where does it hide?
    -Unknown

Growing up I never consider myself a masterpiece I dwelled in the shadows as a middle child, unsure of affection and attention. I long to be rare, much more then intelligent, I wanted power, fame and most importantly I dared to be different. However, as I grew into manhood I realize I bitten off more than I could possible chew. Deep down I had an old soul that was searching for something that I wasn't sure that was yet created for me. I wanted love and the origins it came from. To feel unconditional breath taking love was what you can say I've been searching for since birth. Yet to be filled with so much love it breaks the barriers of doubt in phenomenal ways. I slowly learned that everything and everyone comes as a price. I also learn what the price was...

We both stood there looking at one another shocked and amazed that we couldn't quite believe that a little meet and greet in an elevator would soon bring the foreplay for us to meet later on. Romeo stood there looking at me asking questions that I didn't have the full answers to so I answered them the best I could. As he looked at me again and asked "What was I doing here and how did I get caught up with Rocky? Far as me being here currently in this present time I would call myself an escort however you would call me a prostitute and how I got into bed with Rocky was that I made him lots of money based on my beauty, my body and most importantly the way I walked with confidence drawn a man's inner desires out into light. I had to asked him how in the hell did you know rocky that you would be paying $4,000.00 just to fuck a random stranger and have them for 24 hours? As he responded to me I knew Rocky a long time ago from selling drugs on the block of 6th street uptown way back in the day and I even took the heat for his brother a long time ago and did 5 years in jail. I pulled away from him shocked in amazement how small Harrisburg truly was. I was filled with rage and I shouted on him do you know who I am? Do you know my name? What is it that you exactly want so I can do what I came here to do and collect payment in full? He shook his head and said "do I at least get to know your name?" I rather you don't and just call me Glaze and keep it professional, you hire, you pay, I deliver simple shit. "Please just give me your name". I sighed as I let out a deep breath. My name is Maurice Mayo there are you happy. Wait a minute the only Maurice Mayo I know is Miguel's little brother that ran and track and field years ago, Congratulations would you like a blow job for $300.00 Alex. No I don't damn it I would like for you to tell me what the fuck happened to you dude, you were so talented and beautiful kindest person I have ever met. A wholesome church going young boy that would had a smile that light up the world. Now it looks like you are washed up and living a lifestyle you don't belong in. You use to be a church boy singing in the choir and love the word of God. As my back was turned to him, his look of pain seemed like a destroyed face as he was speaking to me? I grew up and realize that life and people aren't shit. I am what I am now so could we please just do what we came here to do so that Rocky doesn't get pissed off at me. If you know him well enough, then you know that he doesn't like his money being played with and I need to collect in full before he comes in the morning to break bread. Wait! Maurice I have so many questions. I don't understand why I didn't recognize you from the elevator or why you label yourself Glaze. Bitch! I didn't come to play 21 questions with you ok. I came to do a job and that is simple. So, either we are going to fuck and get it over with, because I have other clients to see and get to. There was an awkward silence for a moment. Since your paid by the hour and the money is already pulled out and sitting on my night stand. I will make you a deal. "I don't think you are hearing me loud and clear nigga I am not interest in no damn bargaining." Please just here me out! I don't want you leaving and going back to this whoring shit. I'll text Rocky and tell him I was very pleased and throw an extra $5,000.00 on the deal and tell him I want you all to myself. That should cover your other clients, all you have to do is stay the night with me and talk no sex, no oral nada nothing. Just spend the night with me and talk is that a deal. Yea the fuck right as I responded to him ignorantly with no regard to his feelings, everything comes with a fucking price what is your game man because you're playing right now and I'm not in the mood for games.

"Maurice, we can do whatever you want talk, watch a movie, laugh, and joke around. Yet, I rather you stay with me for one night and I will take care of the rest." In my mind, it sounded tempting but I had to weigh out my options. Either way if I stayed, it wouldn't really matter Rocky was going to be paid and was fine with making his money. However, I couldn't read him like I could with majority of the men. Somehow, he was different as I turned around and looked at his eyes across the room from me. It seems as though he was tearing up and wanted me to stay. How could I really know that he was being genuine? What is so special about me that you are willing to toss money on a worthless conversation? Are you just doing this out of pity because you know my older brother? What are you playing at? Where is your weakness? Everyman has one and I must find yours to break you. I couldn't stay in my head because seconds went by and he was waiting on my response. I could hear a clock ticking inside trying to decide what to do. There then it hit me. I know how to get him and see if he is serious. I responded to him" I'm sorry Romeo but I have to go don't worry about the extra money I just rather continue on with my clients and keep myself busy for the night, but if you don't mind I really need to leave. As I started to turn back around and head towards the door to leave. He quickly walked up behind me and softly grabbed my arm and I flinched out of fear. "No, no please don't do that Maurice I am not that kind of man papa. I would never place my hands on you." I apologize I wasn't trying to but it's a reaction lately. He spun me around and pulled me in closer and wrapped his long arms around my neck and head. He kissed my forehead and said "If you change your mind tonight I will be up all night just encased, I'm so sorry that you are going through this and I pray that god places protection around your life".

He squeezed me even tighter and it felt good sort of. His approached was different and his chest felt like security, every ounce of me wanted to leave but somehow, I couldn't. I pushed my head through his arms and said" If you send Rocky the text and he confirms I will stay the night until it is time for me to leave but I have to be gone by 5am... He looked down at me smiled and stroked my hair through his fingers. Deal he said "I will text him right now so he did so and shockingly Rocky responded back quickly and said "No problem told you he was my rarest diamond." He looked at me and said" So now that is done would you like more to drink or watch a movie with me. I declined the drink because I was still fucked up a little from the stripping party I just came from and I just wanted to relax and rest my body which is something I barely get the chance to go. "You look tired he said "Why don't we get some rest"

We walked over to the double doors of his back room; he opened it and asked would I like to lie in bed with him with our clothes on. I grinned a little and said yes. He placed on the movie "First wives club" and said this is one of my favorite movies from the 90's. I didn't let him know that it was my favorite too because I always use to watch this movie with my mother. He lay down on the bed first asking me can I please just hold you for the night. I shot him a look of confusing and said "sure agreeing to his terms. I didn't know what to expect from him, wondering in my mind if he was going to keep up with his truth and not wanting to have sex of any sort. I crawled into the bed and laid between his legs as my left cheek of my face lied upon his fragile chest. As he stroked my head while playing with the length of my hair and allowed the movie to watch us as we engaged into conversation. "Thank you for spending the night with me Maurice I really appreciate it I know you didn't have to but I am very glad you did. Can I ask you a question? I lifted up my head as I looked into his eyes again because they drew me in like looking at emerald green trees. I said "sure ask away".

What happen to you? How did you get this way? Do you want the truth or would like the sugar-coated lie? "The truth please" I really don't know where to begin Romeo honestly. My memory is quite faded but I guess I can start by telling you I grew up regularly like normal kids. I went to school, I worked hard, I played sports, I had minor friends and suddenly one day I got molested by a family member and raped once I moved up here from Washington D.C. My mind evolved differently and I developed an attitude towards everyone that crossed my path. It was like I wasn't myself anymore and I just belong to someone as property. I suffered to find out what my identity or sexual preference is and I still struggle with it now. I have a girlfriend that is currently in college and doesn't even understand nor know half of what I deal with or begin to struggle with as far as my inner demons. She wouldn't even understand that her cousin black mailed me into sleeping with him all to hold the secret of me being raped and being curious out in the world. I had to constantly have sex with him on demand to keep her from knowing my secret. Another burden you can say. I fight each and every day for survival. My parents kicked me out you can say over a high school rumor. I live with my best friend Monique's Aunt called Chocolate. Moreover, I really can't stand living there because I have to date her best friend Hershey in order to live there or yet he's a cheater himself, and I am just another trophy face to him. That's all I am to any man. Although every time he and I engaged into sexual activities I gag and throw up. I just felt sick inside and my insides would curl to the thought of even kissing him. I been getting tested for HIV/STD's since I got rapped and literally going to free clinics by myself so my parents don't find out since I am under the age of eighteen still. Well what else can I say? Oh, every person I have come in contact with wants something out of me and it seems as though they take more of me each time. I use to be in church at Redeem United Church of Apostolic. I use to sing gospel music and hear god's voice inside my head and in my spirit. I no longer sing nor have my faith. I kind of believe I stop believing in god. "Wait a minute, I don't think you lost your faith nor stop believing in God. However, I just believe you lost your way that's all and God is currently working on you." As he stated to me. What do you know about Christ aren't you sitting here in a room with a prostitute you just paid for, as I snapped back at him? Hold on mister calm down I never said I was perfect as he laughed at me. My momma raised me in the church and my daddy use to say this scripture to me all the time, a doubled minded man is unstable in all he does" I don't remember what part of the bible that came from but my daddy was a strong Christian man and always believed in the lord. It's from the book of James I believe chapter one verse seven through eight. Don't quote me on that though it's been about 8 years since I picked up the bible. I'm afraid I might burn alive. Moving on because I don't like talking about Christ and my sins all in the same topic.

Where was I? Oh, yeah, I got into voguing through Hershey and dancing and that's when I met Rocky. I dropped out of High school my senior year or you could say my parents signed me out and I basically been hitting cities allowing old dirty men underground to company them to dinner, plays, musicals, work trips, stripping parties etc. It didn't matter if the men were married, hiding their sexuality, pastors, doctors, lawyers. Hey even color didn't matter to me, it was all a part of the job. Get in, get out was the philosophy. Rocky has always been kind to me and treats me differently than the other boys that work for him. He has never placed a hand on me nor made me do something I didn't ever want to do. I get 40 percent of the cut from the money I make him and it's a very nice price once it is all said and done. "Listen to me Maurice Rocky can't be trusted you are nothing but a number, a product to him, pawn on the board. You must learn how to play chess instead of checkers. Always be five steps ahead of anyone. He is a very dangerous man; trust me I know Rocky and I have past encounters. He is only nice to me because of my jail time. Rocky has killed people before; I don't know how you have to do it but you need to find your way out of this game. Why do you think people don't cross him? Why do you think he has the temper he does? The nigga is straight thrown the fuck off no lie. Do me a favor Maurice the moment you cross Rocky or he even suspects that you have crossed him is the moment you are no longer alive or walking" Well he's not that way with me he promised and I'm his shiny new diamond. I make him too much money for him to do any damage to me. "BOY! Are you that dumb wake up and realize this is life and it's not a game. The game doesn't work that way it's either kill or be killed. Either get hunted or be the hunter, you have to be much quicker than that. You are very smart Maurice and always cautious and play dumb very well but I am telling you wake up before it's too late. Enough about Rocky! I am more interested in you honestly. Have you ever had any dreams papa? I mean use everything you been through to motivate you in life to be different and improved. Start opening your eyes to get an understanding of what your worth is. The moment you realize what natural beauty is the more divined you will become. Never be boastful always stay humble, doing this will allow you to appreciate even your weaknesses when you are at your strongest. Just remember that.

Yes, I had dreams of being a Nurse working and taking care of sick kids. I wanted to fall in love and get married to my wife and have three kids. I wanted to raise my children in the house of the lord. I want to travel the world and see exotic places. I wanted to write a book about my childhood experiences so that some kid one day like me will pick it up read it and dare to be diverse. Maybe write a story line about my adventure and obstacles to adulthood. "And you can do all those things Maurice you just have to trust in yourself. What would you call your book? I never thought of it before honestly it was more just a hobby thing to me back in high school. Yet, if I could write a book and explain to the world my trials, tribulations, fears, and struggles, I would call my book "A Silent Cry" ... Or a Series of Tears... Who knows? Maybe I might write a sexy erotic sex book for gay men called "The Glaze Chronicles" yet like I said "Always remember these men are always dysfunctional with a weakness. Its best if you become immune so that you have the upper hand is what I have learned. Yet silent cry sounds better. Why do you choose that title I mean couldn't you just say stripper Glaze gone wild? No bitch! Nice try! See that's why I didn't want to talk in the first place. "I was just playing around with you please tell me go in detail, I really want to know" I don't know I feel like my whole life since I been a kid something inside me has been soaring and is only getting louder and louder as I am getting older. I feel as though no one hears me that one day when I am dead and gone finally God or someone will understand my silence in a cold world. "Your silent cry of what?" Tears of pain... No loneliness, that's just a mere thought that isn't any hope for someone like me. "I believe you can do it if you wanted to Maurice half the battle is trying the rest will always fall into place." You really think so? I know so!

145

I laid back on his chest as we both watched the movie until we both went fast asleep. I woke up before him on the left side of the bed. I looked over to the clock on his night stand and the time read 6:00am. I slowly creeped out of the bed trying not to wake him. I closed the doubled doors behind me in the mid dark hotel room because there was only a little light that shinned in from the windows. I grabbed the envelope on the bar which was Rocky's payment. There was a letter next to it with my name on it. I opened up the letter as it read:

Maurice,

I know that you have been through a lot and I know this is not the life you always neither dreamed of nor imagine. I hope that one-day god looks down on you and change your life for the better. I hope and pray that one day you find that special woman and settle down and get married. I want to give you a gift to help you along your journey on bettering yourself and doing what you love in the future. Inside is a check for you to start making your dreams comes true. Please use it wisely and always remember. God never puts more on us than we can bare. With love and understanding.
-Romeo

I looked back and the doubled doors and smiled and silently thanked him for keeping his word of respecting me that night. He was different and lifted me up on a pedestal. I will never forget you Romeo and I pray god watches over you my friend. I walked out the penthouse room and went towards the elevators. I came down to the 10th floor and got off the elevator and walked down the hallway to my room. I reached inside my robe and pulled out the key to open my door. It was too early in the morning and all I wanted to do was sleep. I looked at my cell phone and realize I had 12 missed calls from Lauren and 5 missed calls from Rocky. I placed Chino's number that was sitting on the counter inside my wallet and wrapped my wallet in my Togo bag, which was what I carried all my personal things in. I turned on the radio in the bathroom that, Sunday morning and listened to gospel music play in the background as I was counting all of Rocky's money to make sure I wasn't short because I knew he would be calling to collect. After I got done counting $20,000 plus the $8,000 Romeo gave I realized Rocky made out really good. I didn't touch any of it I wanted to wait until he got his cut first. I opened the letter again and read Romeo's letter to myself again to replay the moments in my head and a piece of paper fell out. I picked the paper off the floor and turned it over and there it was a check for Maurice Mayo written out in my name for $50,000 and the memo stated for school. Tears formed in my eyes and I began to sob and rejoice. I was excited because I was ready to get out of this game and start a new life. Tell my girl everything and pray that things change for the better. Beg her forgiveness... Suddenly there was a knock at the door. Man, who the hell could this be this early in the morning? I asked from where I stood who is it? The person responded who do you think it is nigga? I recognized that voice it was Rocky.

I walked over to the door answered it as he walked inside followed by his two goons the big men they always came with him no matter where he went. If you saw them then you saw Rocky. "Hey my diamond Gem how did everything go? Did you make me proud? I sure did as I responded to him everything is in the black duffle bag. He walked over to the bed and grabbed the bag and put on the biggest smile in the world. "Nice that's what I'm talking about, I heard nothing but great things about you." Is that, right? I was walking around the room packing up all my belongings and throwing them in my bag. Rocky? What's up beautiful? I wanted to ask you something if you don't mind. Sure, you making me money like this shit you can ask away as he was looking at the taller gentleman to his right.

Rocky, I don't want to do this anymore; I want to go back to school get my GED and go to College and make a name for myself. I want to change people's lives. He looked at me and started laughing so loud at me along with his two bodyguards. They all began to laugh. I rolled my eyes and said "Rocky I am serious I want to do something with my life other than sleeping with men and being a profit. He stopped laughing and his voice got deep. "Are you not happy with what I been providing for you? I gave you a family when you didn't have one. I gave you money when you couldn't even pay for a pack of gum. I placed you into finer things in life when you were just a bottom feeder. Have I not treated you and took care of you and did so much for you? HAVE I NOT!? As he started to yell. Yes, but Rocky I am tired... "That's all you had to say Babyboy if you need a break then take a break and come back to work that's all. No Rocky, I am tired of this lifestyle of tired of doing this. This isn't what I wanted out of life. You can keep my percentage if you like just let me better myself and be different that's all I want.

He walked up to me and starred me in my face and said "Where are you going to go? Who is going to look after you like I have? I will I responded. I will take care of myself. I will build myself. I can be much more than a whore. "You think your better than me is that what this is? Oh, Glaze here thinks he's better than Rocky. Do you hear this? Rocky please. Don't please me boy as he looked meaner at me and snatched the piece of paper from my hand which was the check Romeo wrote for me. "Oh, I see how it is now, you were fine with letting me have my money but was holding out on a check for 50 G's for college tuition. You aren't going to any college. I wasn't holding out Rocky it's a check and there's a possibility it won't even go through. He ripped up the check in my face into tiny pieces. As he turned around and back handed the fuck out of me. Naturally at that moment I would have been scared yet I wasn't I tilted my head back to him and gave him a look as I step towards him and said "I bow down to no man, you're not god, as I balled up my fist and struck him right in his jaw. I shouldn't have done that once I did his two body guard men stormed towards me grabbing my arms and held them back as Rocky uppercut me in my stomach causing spit to fly out my mouth. He was more furious then what I have ever seen him before and I couldn't believe right now that this was happening. He directed his goons to stand me up and he struck me multiple times in my face blow after blow. I could feel my face swelling up and getting tingly as if my cartilage was crushing. Rocky screaming at the men to strip me of my clothes that he provided for me, so that's exactly what they did ripped my shirt off of me, placed me in a head lock until the point I couldn't breathe while they took off my pants and underwear. They even through my shoes across the room. Rocky took off his belt and struck me on my body with his belt buckle which looked like it weighed about 2lbs. The goons walked around the room trashing shit just because even took the liquor bottles on the counter and began drinking and spitting liquor on me. While Rocky just sat in the chair and watched in amusement. The whole time I just couldn't understand what did I possible do wrong for him to betray me like this. All the sexual things I have done for him making him lots of money it seems like all of that was for nothing. He was exactly what everyone said "He was savage and only cared about making his money and that was it.

The taller caramel skinned one think his name was Brock kept getting drunker as he was gripping and smacking my ass. I stood there shaking as my body was cold from the liquor that was spat at me and even the blood dripping from my mouth and side from when the buckle hit me too many times. I looked over to Rocky please stop this what do you want from me I just want to go home. Please just let me go. He got up from the chair in the room walked over to me and gripped me with his big hands around my neck saying "Oh poor Glaze, I had such high hopes for you to become something different, you were my star and my prize procession. Your damage goods now. What can I possible do with you? Now who wants to see your body now, who wants to fuck something that is dried up? Ok I'll make you a deal if you continue to work in my night club I'll let you, heal your body and keep majority of your tips on weekdays. What do you say? As he was pulling my head up by my hair. Sounds like a deal to me. He gripped me by the back of my head even tighter and lifted my head up to hear my answer. I was trying to find the energy to speak and at first I couldn't but something inside me had to make a stand. I spit from my mouth blood and saliva and said "Fuck you!" He spat back in my face screaming you will always be nothing but a filthy little faggot. FUCK ME! NO NIGGA FUCK YOU LITTLE BITCH. Brock, Jay hold this little nigga down throw his little ass on the bed and hold his hands down. I could hear him unzipping his pants and spit on his dick and rimmed his shit inside me I began to scream. Rocky directed Brock to shut me up. He took the pillow case off the pillow and shoved it in my mouth and placed his knee on the back of my neck to keep my head buried in the bed. Rocky kept fucking me harder and harder as I was in so much torture screaming in the inside. He pulled out as Brock got in line for his next turn as if I was a wild bull wiggling to break free from them. Rocky took the belt and tied my hands together and placing them in playing hands style behind my head. The more I tried to move the harder they took turns gang banging me vigorously. My body hit the shock mode when everything feels numb, everything in the room was spinning so fast even my vision started to get blurry. That moment Rocky told Jay to pull out his dick and piss on me. Jay laughed and said "Fuck this little nigga, he does have some good ass though. All three of these men started to urinate on my back and ass as if I was a urinal to void upon. I barely had energy to move. In my mind, I know I had to get up and make a run towards the door as best as I could. Soon as they stopped I took my hands from behind my head as I could hear my shoulders pop out of place as I made an attempt to the door. While they were trying to reach for me and zip-pen up their pants at the same time. I made it to the door but had a hard time trying to unlock the door. Rocky pulled me back by my hair and threw me to the ground. My mouth was still covered as I was crying and just wanted to go home and leave this whole life behind me. I tried to stand up then suddenly Brock took the lamp out of the wall and bashed my head in twice. I dropped immediately as I felt blood pouring from the back of my head. I think I was panicking from that blow that I was blacking out or in shock of some sort. Rocky leaned down and turned me over on my back as he looked over into my face and said "I hope you die motha fucker from crossing a real nigga like me. Like I didn't make you." I could see the color of the ceiling as it looked beige, the foul rotten smell of his breath as he spoke to me, moved my face from side to side and I had and empty stare. I had no reflex to him doing this. Jay said from the background "Rocky is he dead? I heard Rocky shouting at both of them one of you cleans up this mess. Brock wrap his body in those sheets and through him out back of the ally take his bag also, someone would just think he's a crack head that got fucked up over a bad fix. Brock went to go speak yet, Rocky yelled "DO IT NOW BITCH OR YOU'RE NEXT! Jay leave no prints behind and clean up everything. Brock don't take the elevator it's too early in the morning someone might see you take the back stairs and when your done both of you meet me in the car.

As I lied on the floor of my room, there I seen Rocky's shadow pass my body. As a white sheet came down over me as Brock picked up my body. I could still hear the gospel music playing in the background on the bathroom sink it was Fred Hammond's famous song "No Weapon". It seems as the words drifted along with my body as he exited the room and took the first exit on the left I could feel my body bouncing in his big arms as he was running down the stairs quickly. He kicked open a door and dropped my body near a green dumpster behind the hotel. The sheet brushed passed my face as I could see the grey sky out my right eye. At that moment, I thought okay I can hear my voice inside my head am I dead? I couldn't move my body at all. I heard people walking near the street. I tried to speak however I was only speaking in my head. Get up Maurice! Something inside me screamed. Get up Now! I can't though it hurts. Don't die Maurice. Get up now! I looked up to the sky as I was waiting for God to come down and help… I let a few seconds go by and still heard nothing from him. I couldn't muscle up the energy. Get up my Blue Jay. Grandma help me! You have to get up baby. I began to blink a couple times as if I was waking up out of a dark slumber. I rolled on my stomach. Looking out to the street as it seems as though everyone or thing was moving in slow motion. I pushed myself up with my elbows, pulling my knees up to the concrete floor. My balance was unstable as I tried to stand on my feet and walk. I slowly began to walk dragging the sheet covering my body with my blood and tears on it. Trying to push to get someone to help, yet I was talking help me someone! Please! I couldn't scream. As my feet was dragging from the weight of the pain my body was in. I got closer to the street leaving the back alley from where I was. I saw five black men get out of a truck parked on the same street I as was on. I reached out to them with my hands as I fell to the ground crying in agony please just help me! As my head laid on the cold ground as I saw the men running towards me in a rush. One of them turned me on my back and picked me up cuffed me under my legs and back. He had to be tall because it felt as though my body was ascending into the air. He was walking me over to his truck and said "Hey man it's going to be okay we're going to take you to a hospital. Just hang in there. He said "I'm Chino but everyone calls me Chris. I took my left hand and squeezed his chest hard as I could. He looked down at me and said "Don't be scared I promise you little homie it's going to be okay." As we got closer to the truck I squeeze his chest hard again he looked down at me and said "What is it you want to tell me something? I leaned up to his right ear, as he brought it down to my lips and with all the energy I had inside me I stuttered MMMY Nan- NAME- is MA MAUR- RICE. He screamed to his boys running next to him somebody get the truck now. This is little homie from the Ho-telly. NOW!!! I looked up at him although he couldn't recognize my face; somehow, I was calm that he knew it was me. I could feel myself getting inside the car and my head laying in Chino's lap and the men in the car asking questions who did this to him. I was fading in and out I couldn't speak anymore. I looked at chino as he looked down at me asking who did this to me. I took his hand and spelled out "ROC" with the blood I had on my hand as I started spitting and coughing up blood. I could hear Chino screaming and saying" T man get us there to downtown". Take us to Harrisburg Hospital Bruh come on push this shit nigga... Everyone's voice around me seems to fade away because it felt like I want to just go to sleep without waking up. All I could hear inside my head was Fred Hammond's song again as the lyrics and melody started to ring inside of me loudly. "No weapon formed against me shall prosper… It won't work, Saying God will do what he said he's going to do, and He's not a man that he will come through. It started to repeat in my head over and over… Yet the questioned lies still in my head, where were you father?

Oh! Father,

I am speaking at the most desperate time of need. Can you hear me? When is, it going to end? Why must you taunt me like this? You said if I have faith as a mustard seed you would take care of the rest. You left me again time and time again. I don't think I no longer need you. This time was too close for me and I needed you to show up in my time of need during the midst of chaos. You chose again to look down at me and did nothing. I don't know why I am praying to a pretend God who has no power who can't even help one of his children. Do you laugh at your children up above those clouds and if we are all screw ups? What is the whole point of being a fucking Christian if you can't even have an ole powerful being assistance you when you need it the most? TALK TO ME DAMN IT I AM HEAR!! Speak to me you false God. Is it because I slept with man that you can't even hear me now. I'm I that much of an abomination you no longer need me on earth that you sent this situation to take me out. I laugh at you and your funny little conscious riddles you give me. There is no inspiration. No Muse guiding me but a false prophet such as yourself. I tell you one thing right now if you don't answer me I will kill myself. Don't test me father for I will ruin your very creation that you neglected. FATHER!!! Dad please… You told me I was special you told me I was different you told me I had gifts that the world needed me… WHY CAN'T YOU ANSWER ME!!! Must I go to your other fallen angel that cares more about me and actually listens to me when I speak? Should I give him my soul so that he can grant me my every desire? Should I call out his name and know that he will listen to me. Is that what you want? Should I speak the language he has spoken to me in my dreams? Every time I need someone he always shows up no matter what. Should I have called him when I was being raped? Should I have uttered out his name?

You still choose to be stubborn. COME OUT COWARD WHERE ARE YOU? There is no point you see God does not exist, God isn't real. I believe I have been playing a mind game this whole time and me praying right now wouldn't even mean nothing because I am on my own like I have always been, I'm tired of believing I am meant for something greater and different truth is I shouldn't have never been born. Tears of a broken soul cries through my spirit and aches for one day I will be made whole again...

Amen,
Says the victim...

13

FALLING SHORT

It was once said "That everything happens for a reason that the natural balance of life holds a light and a dark." It is believed that karma is what goes around comes around. Yet, if it doesn't go around and stays attached to one person, does that mean it never comes back around... What a cliché I say. Its simple trouble doesn't last always nor does it. Can one truly take a break from a series of unfortunate events?

I couldn't begin to tell you everything in detail as my mind likes to play tricks and remember only the things my consciousness allows. However, I woke up in Harrisburg Hospital as my eyes opened to adjust to the morning light bouncing off the white walls of my room. I saw my Aunt Chocolate sitting down in the chair in the room by herself. "Your finally up I see glad you are okay, so your crazy ass will maybe listen to me when I speak about shit that I know. Don't scare me like that I almost called your parents and had to tell them, their son has died." As she scolded me mildly. What day is it I asked? Its Thursday she responded laughing. "That's the first time I ever saw you sleep for a whole week straight. The doctor says you are going to be fine, I told them you got into a street fight so they didn't ask weird questions. Although the scares on your sides and cigarette burn on your back won't go away. Don't worry we can put some cocoa butter and fix that right up. They had to pop both your shoulders back in place since they were dislocated. I waited to the doctors left the room to clean down there on you." I was trying to make sense of it all everything felt like a mere dream. I turned my head to the left looking out the window watching the sun orange like rays place me in a daze which seemed like I was day dreaming.

Maurice! As she called my name, I turned my head back to look at her. "I realize when I was cleaning you up down there on your private area you have bruising and swelling it will go down but you have to take it easy and ... What is it chocolate? You're going to have to use baby wipes to clean yourself down there for a little bit. I had to stitch you up so you got about twelve stiches down there. It may take a couple months for you to heal and you might not shit normally for a little but a little vinegar and warm water should do the trick. I mustard up the smart remark, bitch just because you were a nurse aid and watch scrubs don't' make you a fucking doctor okay I am not one of your fucking experiments I see how you like to make projects around the house. Bitch I'm not an Mr. Potato head okay you can't just pull and pick pieces and stick them anywhere. That lip of hers curled up and said" Oh no honey you won't talk to me like that! After you have got my pressure up sugar foot having me almost come to this hospital in my panties when they called me saying your nephew's in critical condition. So, I grab my pretend doctor's bag because you needed a real nurse okay you know Harrisburg hospital kills people and I couldn't let you die without collecting my rent and bring you beef curry and white rice bitch. I chuckled trying not to laugh too hard because I was still in a little pain. Chocolate! "What Hun? As her hip was pop out to the right side like all ratchet bitches do, head cocked to the side as she smacked on her fucking bubble gum that drove me crazy. Tears shaped in my eyes as I seen her change her whole mood and came to my bed side "don't you dare shed a tear bitch man up, don't worry Rocky got his, it's time for you to get back to what makes you happy in life. This was never supposed to be your life. I told you there is something strong inside of you that this world has never seen. You have to create and build yourself and change for the best. I'm always here for you. Bitch if you knew you was doing something like that why didn't you talk to me and Hershey about it first or let us know where you were at. At least we could have been your back up. At least we could have known where you were at. Damn Maurice you had me worried and I just thought you was stripping and drinking. I had no idea you were being force to fuck men on the low- low. That shits not cool and it's not right. At seventeen you should be living life, going to high school picking out colleges, watching movies over friend's house, having girlfriends, going to church praising the man upstairs. I had no idea you were doing that. Speaking of girlfriends, yours keeps calling my house phone asking for you and catching attitudes with Hershey because you know he cares about you so you know his mouth has no filter honey.

My eyes got super big "Fuck Lauren" what did you say? Was she upset? Does she know what I been doing? Who told her? Bitch relax okay I told her you lost your cell phone and was working doubles a lot at a warehouse job and the only phone you have is the house phone until you get a new phone. Calm down we all know how much you love that girl and how much you care about her. One day you will have to tell her Maurice coming and speaking as women, it's better to know than to not know and who knows she might forgive you, but that is between you both. Maurice if you want a better life you have to change and start off fresh no one has control over your life but you. No one can tell you how to love and be different. Don't get me wrong nephew you have a lot of pain and unsettled demons you deal with but no one can fix those things for you but you bitch. If you want to build a life with that girl you have to start by being honest with yourself. Figure out what it is you are looking for and what you want. Whether you are straight or gay and don't tell me it's the attention you get. It's much more than that. Love is a powerful thing; it can be used for multiple things either to create life or destroy. "Last time Lauren called was yesterday, I told her that you were working a double. So, the doctor says you can go home you just have to take it easy walking and moving around. I'm going to say this then I am done... "I don't know how you made it but thank your lucky stars you are here someone is watching over you. I love you I'm going home to get you some clothes, I will be back in a couple hours okay try to get some rest okay. I smiled back at her and inhaled a deep breath and laid my head back on my pillow, staring out of the window. I couldn't help but to let my mind drift off thinking about my future.

Sometimes they say our dreams are ways for us to unlock things that are to come in the near future. Some experience it as Déjà vu, for others it's a nightmare, a chance to be a superhero or a simple dream that you can't remember. My dreams always started with me battling inside myself. I remember before I woke up and started talking to Chocolate my dream was so real, I think that's what woke me up truly.

I dreamt that I spoke with Satan himself until an angel intervened. I was surrounded by darkness and really couldn't see anything. Until I was Astor-projected it seem like that I was on a cliff as the clouds were grey as lighting and thunder hit the sky. The wind was as strong as it felt while being on the edge of that cliff. I called out to air "Is anyone here? Can anyone here me? Hello? "I heard a deep voice speak out to me "I am here Maurice like I have always been. Where are, you I can't see you as I call out to the voice again as it echoed in the distances? "I AM HERE...HERE...HERE... Show yourself please. Suddenly the ground rumbled where I stood and there was suddenly a black image merging down from the grey clouds. It appeared to me speaking to me and with its voice I heard it ringing in my head and my thoughts. "Maurice, aren't you tired of this world. Haven't you suffered enough? Do you really think that you were born to suffer in this world that doesn't care about your spirit? Why is it that God never answer when you called him? For a person of peace and mercy never seems to grant you nor forgive you of your sins. Why must you be told to have faith? Do you believe it to be false words of encouragement? The son of man, the son of God, don't do this or don't do that. This is a sin that is abomination too many rules and restrictions if you ask me so why worry about it. Trust in the lord. Honestly, where has that gotten you but raped, beaten, and thrown out to the shadows. I have always protected you. Remember you cried out to me and asked for help. You cried to me with your spirit so I lend you my tongue. You were afraid, ashamed, hurt so I took all those feelings away and gave your mind a fresher way of looking at things. Don't worry revenge is the key. Those who are violent with us we must be violent with them. In the world, it is killed or be killed. Shouldn't you not want to be violent, nor seek death against those who have doubled crossed you?"

160

Yes, but I don't think that is what god wants me to do. I don't quite understand everything but something inside me says that it is not right to do those things. Somehow inside there is something roaring deep within me and I don't know what it is. "You must ignore that feeling Maurice that is nothing but bad energy. It will feel you up with hope that your life can be different, it will cause you to love when there is no love to receive. It will cause you to grow and speak life into things that doesn't require your spiritual connection. Listen to me you must never give into that inner voice of yours. Never open that door, nor listen to the words that stir up inside you. It is called a calling many are always called; you see the true battle is when you answer to be chosen. I say to you that you are not chosen to be anything. There is no divine destiny for you. I have done my best in healing you, pushing you to have the finer things in life. Tell me you weren't happy stripping receiving attention and power, tell me you weren't excited being in the center of all that. Tell me that you crave more and I shall deliver more unto you. The way of the wicked is always righteous my child always remember that and keep that in mind. Maurice, I have always stood by your side and guided you the best I could. I allowed your mind to be free from that internal voice you speak of. I have lifted up your thoughts into understanding what it truly means to live without sin. That man upstairs in those happy little clouds you see doesn't truly love you. You trust in something that doesn't speak clearly to you. You place your trust in a being that walks on water yet doesn't grant you the same power. How many times have you cried out and no one showed up to your time of need. How many? ANSWER ME!!!

A lot as I responded to the shadowy being in front of me. "Then you now know what must be done. You must move on forward with your life and forget that god exists. Forget that he will here you. Forget that faith is believing in things you can't see. Did I not just show myself to you? Did I not just appear before you my child? For I truly love you Maurice and care about the eternity of your soul. Allow me to take control of things. Allow me to fully direct you in the direction of where your life is going so that one day you can truly be with me and I will pick you up my child and carry you to my world. You won't have to suffer on this world anymore. You won't have to question if people are sincere in their actions with you. There is no trust in the lord. There is no believing in Christ that all things are simply possible. I am the true lord and savior. As I always promised I can take more than just the pain away my son, allow me to be in your head conceal your thoughts. Let me wrap your heart in coldness. Let me make you numb so the way of the world is opened fully to your eyes so that you may see what it is you need to do. Trust in me and I shall guide you as promise. Have I not kept my word? All you have to do my child is fall from this cliff that you are stuck on. Fall so that I may catch you, we shall soar through the night skies. Fall from that inner peace you think you have. Drop those feelings of love, warmth and peace. Ignore the battle you feel within yourself. Listen only to the calling voice of my will. Enter into my world so that your eyes are no longer blind to the false prophet. I shall make you powerful, knowledgeable, and stronger to my purpose and will. All you have to do is fall. Fall from this hope and there will be a change. Come my child I can teach you so much. There is much to be done.

"What will happen to me if I fall off this cliff? I asked the being. It was silent at first. The thundered and lighting stopped and the clouds began to be clear. I could see the sky pure white and blue. The ground even stopped rumbling from underneath me. I could see mountains in the distances, valleys below and rivers that flown pass the cliff I was on. The sun looked so pretty red, warm and the air seem as crisp as I could breathe and smell the cleansed serenity around me.

I looked over back to the being and saw myself hovering in the air. "I looked at myself as I called out to it. Who are you? You look like me but I am me. It smiled back at me and was silent for seconds and then responded with the same voice before. "I have many names and I have been called many things, yet that is not important my child. Are you ready to follow me? The version of me started to step down in the air as if he was going down stairs. He stepped onto the cliff with me and grabbed me by my hands. Look at me he said." "You are so special and unique you don't even understand the power that is inside you. The gift you have inside you is so rare, why waste that here. Look out to the promise I am giving you and we can change so much. The both of us can do some much. If you truly want what I promise Maurice all you have to do is fall. Leave this cliff and I shall carry you on my wings. He held my hand and we both walked closer to the cliff as my toes were hanging off and I felt the wind trying to push me.

He turned to me and asked me "Am I ready" I couldn't help but to be scared and crying at the same time. I don't know what I am doing, this is doesn't make sense to me. "Maurice do you trust me? I hesitatingly said yes. "Then trust me close your eyes and let me be your guide. Don't open your eyes until you feel me lift you up into the sky. We both edge even closer I was only hanging on the cliff by soles of my feet. Are you ready as he asked me again meaning me? I couldn't speak as I was hesitating again while tears were falling from my face. On three we both shall fall okay. One... I looked to the side as I was looking at the mirror image of myself smiling at me. Two... It's me

I should be able to trust myself right? I mean we both are leaning forward at the same time. Three... As I leaned a little more, he let go of my hand and as I tried to shift my weight backwards to not fall, looking at myself grin. He gave me a little nudge and said don't forget to close your eyes it's a long fall, remember to clear your mind and let me in. Just like that I felt myself falling what felt like through clouds in the sky. I didn't open my eyes. I was falling and I couldn't feel air in my lungs.

I could feel the weight lifting off of my shoulders and heart. I could see the imagines of everyone that did me wrong. I could see them hurting me and me conflicting pain on them. I feel the fiery rage burning inside my mind it felt good. I was smiling as I was falling was breathing in the desire to make them all punish for hurting me. SOON THEY WILL ALL KNOW MY WRATH. SOON HE WILL LIFT ME UP AGAIN AND I SHALL NOT SPARE ANYONE.THE POWER IS MINE TO CONTROL... I say to you enter me now. I was falling faster and faster. I could feel the speed on my cheeks. Tears were falling heavy from eyes while I still kept them closed. All the flashes from my childhood, pain, and hate all began to STORM my mind at one. BLUE JAY!!!! "You have to open your eyes at once." I CAN'T!! He told me not to. The voice called out to me again "Listen to me Blue Jay you have to open your eyes before it's too late. But I am afraid I don't know what to do anymore. This is the only way. BLUE JAY!!! This isn't right trust me focus on my voice, Think of me, and picture me. Think of the laughter. Focus on the love inside you, Remember the first time God spoke to you, Remember the first time he filled you with the Holy Spirit. Focus you are running out of time. YOU NEED TO OPEN YOUR EYES!!!! Trust in the lord, you can do all things in Christ that strengthens you... Look inside yourself... Please just open your eyes. I CAN'T!!! I'm too afraid help me please! As I was falling faster than the speed of light in the abyss, I suddenly felt. A lot of hands wrapped around pulling me backwards. The hands covered my entire body as a whisper said "Maurice! Just open your eyes if you don't you will be stuck here." I opened my eyes and there I was lying in the hospital bed… Another attempt of an estrange dream. Someone or something wanted me in its army. I could feel the darkness ripping inside of me. I wasn't sure how long I have, yet what kind of time frame was going on. What I can tell you is that, Death wanted to kiss me? Was I to open or return the favor with my own lips?

A CHANGE IS COMING

Sometimes in life we go through so many differences. We deal with so much as people. We never truly let go of the past and pain because we are afraid of healing. We want to cleanse ourselves of the negative impacts as well as start new. However, temptation, greed, lust, hatred and evil tends to lurk around the corners as we try to progress and ascend from the place we once were. Trying to get to that next level of self-awareness and appreciation of our inner being is quite tedious and problematic sometimes. Can people truly change? Better yet can we ultimately change are wicked ways? Can we be reborn again and start fresh? Yet, is it the ways we change, the speech that we carry, the thought process we have adapted to? Ask yourself have you truly changed and made yourself new. Have you truly broken the chains that have held you bound in your own captivity? Have you? Or did you just adapt and change the course of your direction instead and learned to change for the sake of others not truly seeing you for what or who you are? I never believe in change only adapting into my next stage of life…

I left that hospital with Chocolate never the same. I stayed two weeks there and moved with a relative of mines to Pembroke. I was still in my relationship with Lauren, although I told her only a few things that I felt as though she could handle. I told her that I was raped as a kid which is the reason why I didn't want to have sex with her right away which was the truth wrapped up in a lie. I also told her that I left my parents and in order to stay with Chocolate I had to be in a relationship or pretend to date her best friend Hershey. She pretended to listen to me while we talked, her lips pressed together as her one right eyebrow always raised up in a sign of her frustration. She came forward to me crying in tears lashing out on my chest asking me why I didn't tell her. Why didn't I come to her with my problems? She told me we could fix are problems and work hard on them together. I knew deep down inside I took a piece of her security and comfort level that I could possibly never give back to her. I knew deep down there was rare kinetic love energy we shared, yet all I could think in my mind is that you weren't never truly here. Don't get me wrong you being in college was a good thing however, when I needed advice you rejected my calls, when I needed a simple I love you my texts were ignored.

As more time went on with Lauren's and I relationship I learned that it wasn't really worth the fight to strive to change things. I moved in with a relative of mines such as my Aunt Chris to make sense of this double lifestyle that I have been living. If there was anyone who understood me or what I was going through it was her. I manage to get a job at best-buy working in the warehouse. I was working on getting back into church and ready to be a different person. I was hoping by moving to my aunts that my past wouldn't be able to follow me there since my aunt liked to live low key. I was still drinking a lot with my older cousin spam which was an insider nickname we would call each other. It didn't matter what brand of liquor it was we was drinking and enjoyed every drop. Every day it seemed as though we got buzzed. Soon as I would get off work I would drink and pour a glass or five. I wasn't talking about shot glasses. I was talking about 4-8 fl. oz. of liquor down the hatch. Drinking felt so comfortable to me and it kind of took my mind off of things. Sometimes even at work I couldn't function straight without having a least finishing a bottle. I became useless in my relationship, a dumb ass whore of a boyfriend. I hated things that I put her through however I felt that there was nothing I could do. Darkness consumed more of my soul than I actually thought. Even praying to god seemed so hopeless at times although I wasn't tricking anymore a part of me still felt drained and tiresome.

I couldn't tell you how many friends I thought I so called had to reach out for help and even guidance; at times, I just really needed someone to talk to. Deep down I thought I could change for her and change for the better yet somehow, I knew deep down there is nothing truly going to change... If anything, something much darker was hiding in the midst for me... The question during this time was what?

Dear Father,

I have truly missed hearing your voice. Have I truly let my pride get in the way of my own salvation? What is it fathered that you seek from me? You once said to me in your own words father that you value me as your child. Are not five sparrows sold for two cents? And yet not one of them is forgotten before God. "Indeed, the very hairs of your head are all numbered. Do not fear; you are of more value than many sparrows. (Luke 12:6-7) yet lord a

168

*sparrow is what I feel like. Uglier the more I am
overlooked. It appears to my heart that you're no longer
there for me and the shadows have consumed me entirely.
How could you allow this to happen?*

Amen,

As time went on I became more aggressive to drinking
and smoking weed. I cared less about my own goals and
place a perfect image around many people. My own
girlfriend no longer knew me. She only knew what I would
allow her to know. At this moment, I didn't give a fuck. I
was alone and help wasn't going to come in my aid not at
all. I later on got arrested for robbing cars and stealing
property from people and caught 17 charges with my
favorite cousin spam and even had my own Aunt beg me to
take the charges because it was my first offense and the
only thing I would get was probation and maybe a slap on
the wrist. However, when you are in jail the only place you
can call is home. So, I called Bernice and she paid my bail
and told me not to take the full blame that my cousin and I
both played are parts and both needed to own up to our own
mistakes. So, I did exactly that, I owned up to my own
mistakes and truth be told I could hardly remember the
whole night. I was too drunk and high to remember
anything. So, months later I got placed on probation,
community service of 1600 hours and also, I had to go see
a therapist to speak and talk about my problems and
careless attitude.

Lauren stuck through me the whole time with
judgement as usual from herself and her mother. It sickened
me at times to think that she only thought of be as a fuck up
and not how she use to look at me. Although it didn't
matter to me, I was still glad to have her by myside. As
more time, pass of me living back with my parents being a
good boy and not speaking to anyone but Lauren I manage

to get another job working at a group home with elderly people. I enjoyed this job and tended to calm me and settle my negative thoughts. I also learned That Lauren was pregnant and we both were excited. This changed everything for me. I was so excited nervous and scared all at the same time to be a dad. I put in extra hours working at my current job. I wanted to be different and better than my own father and love my child unconditionally no matter what.

I began to go see my therapist Dr. Walker uptown on Division Street. He was a tall, athletic built, brown hair with hazel eyes, with an Adam's apple that stuck out far from his neck, more of a Caucasian light skin white man mixed with little Latino... He wore glasses that always glared in any light. I remember walking into his office the first time and feeling out a stupid ass questionnaire sheet. There was a basic question what is your name? How old are you? What brought you here? I just went down the list, my name is Maurice Mayo, I am 18 years old. I was brought here because of court. He took the questionnaire from me and laughed and said "nice you scribbled on the rest of the questions I guess we can talk about them in our sessions. I looked at him and stated "Look I really don't want to be here, I am only here because I am court order so can you just so kindly right me off and send me on my way. He smiled at me and said "I do see that your impatient, attitude problem and have a bit of a temper. Dude whatever let's just get this session over so I can get back to my life. I'm not really interested in doing all of this. He told me "The easiest way for you to get over all of this is for you to speak, talk about the choices you made in life and how you felt about them that lead you to this moment of getting in trouble with the law. It is important that you and I develop a relationship with each so that we can work through some of your issues or dilemmas together. This will all get a little better as you begin to converse more with me in our sessions will determine if I will sign off with the court if you are stable enough to be back in among your peers or if the court needs to place you under more probation until you can learn to clean up your act. So Dr. Walker what would you like me to say sir? Maurice! Please Dr. Walker is not needed please call me Kyle. Alright Kyle what would you like to know I am pretty much an open book within means. Good Maurice start from the beginning or wherever you would like to start from that makes you comfortable.

In my head I honestly didn't understand what this shrink was possibly looking for me to really tell. What is it that you really want to know? I could hear us talking back and forth with one another yet somehow I still was having a side conversation all within my own little world wrapped in my head. Somehow, I believe this man was trying to crack and break barriers inside of me. I've seen a lot of movies and knew deep down that no good will come from these so called sessions that he wanted. To dabble inside of my head is something that you really don't want... Yet if a battle of the minds is what you really want, then I shall give you what you are looking for. Never play in my mind for you just might get lost inside.

15

DANGEROUS MINDS

Every mind is so vast and different in its own way; the mind can be beautiful and roam with imagery. The mind can empower and even place us under misery. If the mind is so powerful, that it can even force others to do it's bidding against their will. Then why is the mind so free to roam? Does the mind not have barriers? Are there no laws protecting the mind? The mind will always battle between what's real and what is fundamental...
-Poet Mark Anthony

I never quite understood Kyle with his nonstop scrupulous questions trying to confuse the hell out of me against my own personal feelings of things. We began that session January 16th, 2009. So, he started off by asking me "Tell me who you are? And how do you feel about your life and family?
Family is nice and their very smart and supportive, my life is exactly the way it's supposed to be living and learning

and far as whom I am… I … I could say I am still figuring that out. He looked at me with a puzzled look and said "I find that strange that everything is okay with you and your family. All families have their dysfunctional ways and issues to address. Fine, if you must know my father and I rarely got along. My mother would try to shelter and love me enough based on me and Senior's relationship. Who is Senior? As he interrupted me right in the middle of speech. Senior is my father his real name is Miguel Anthony Mayo and senior is easier then calling him dad. Plus, his eldest son is named right after him making him a junior. I have another brother and two sisters. They aren't my real sisters just adopted however I consider them my real sisters. So, you could say I am the middle child. Hmmm… What else as? I pondered my thoughts. The only thing that Kyle was doing was simply writing on his clip board. As he asked me follow up questions. So, Maurice what is your religious background? I was raised inside the church; we grew up in Washington D.C. There was basically church three to four times a week and sometimes twice on Sundays. I am baptized so I do believe in Jesus Christ however; he and I don't really get along these days anymore. And I quite like it that way to be honest with you. Wait Maurice? What do you mean you like it that way? You mean to tell me that your relationship with Christ is different? As Kyle looked at me with this curious look, as if I said something that would confuse him.

I will get to that in a moment on why I feel the way I feel about Christ. Growing up the middle child I always sort of felt singled out not sure on my position of where I was placed at in times of my life with the relationship with either one of my parents. My mother would often try her best to show me more love in my interest of hobbies such as books or writing which was something I often enjoyed doing as a kid. However, I grew to hate her and hold a grudge against her as I even got older. My brothers became my road maps to comparing myself to them. My older I use to look up too yet as I got older I wanted to kill him to be honest. I was always jealous of him and the simple fact of him touching me in private area disgusted me. Yet I said nothing too Senior to know that his precious favorite child was doing ungodly sinful things would be the death of him. My youngest brother Sam was always daddy's baby boy and often at times could do no wrong. Yet among my family I seemed more of a black sheep. So, I grew even more hatred towards both of them each and every day. Don't get me wrong I love my brothers now and the older I got I realized it was just best to simply let things go and forgive. Dr. Kyle: Have you truly forgiven them Maurice? How about your older brother? Honestly doc if you must know their own guilt of their lives would be the death of both of them. One will become an alcoholic, the other a drug addict and me either I will die from depression or be killed in a lifestyle that I couldn't quite began to understand. What do you mean by that Maurice?

Sigh, well after the molestation of the incident from my brother I grew up kind of different. My mind changed and I didn't quite understand what I was attracted to. I found myself being attracted to boys my age or a little older. I moved up from Washington D.C to Steelton, Pennsylvania where I had a best friend and to make a long story short. I spent the night over his house his dad ended up raping the fuck out of me and gagging me like a little toy. How did you feel about this? Go back to that moment and tell me how you felt what you can see around you. I rather not go back I built barriers around in my head blocking that out but if I can paint a picture in your head doc here you go. I was in Harry Potter P. J's I believe. My butt poked out more than usually boys it's sort of a family trait comes with being a Mayo. I walked in the bathroom that smelled like vanilla sugar cookies and cigar smoke. I turned around got struck across the face then tied with a shoe string with my hands and feet gagged with a sponge or some type of washing cloth, He spit on my ass and on his dick and what can I say the man penetrated. Can we please not do this I don't want to discuss Shawn anymore? Who is Shawn Maurice? He's my rapist, my shadow the image that keeps me up at night. He's my downfall and watches me even when I am not paying attention. He started the venom that poisoned my mind, that raptured my soul into a sinful bliss. Where is Shawn now? Have you told your parents? Shawn died when I was 15 years old from lung cancer. I didn't tell my parents until I was about 18, by that time it was too late I was too far gone. My mind had already begun to change for the worst I stopped believing in god, I gave more into the craving of men and began to do more sexual acts because I consider that being the norm of things. I mean I have a girlfriend so I guess there is some type of hope for me. What do you mean by hope? Explain? I mean hope as in I won't burn in hell for being a faggot or loving a lifestyle without even fully understanding it completely. At times, I knew doing these acts being a stripper, doing drugs, lying to my girlfriend, fucking men just simply because it was a way of survival. Honestly If I could take it all back I would. Sadly, doc I can't somehow, I knew my life would be like this I experienced it so many times in my dreams as DÉJÀ VU.

Tell me something Maurice! If you could be any kind of animal what would you be? And Why? If you could go anywhere in the world where would you go? If you could have anything in this world what would you want and tell me why? That is your homework assignment and I will see you tomorrow at the same time and be prepared to discuss and talk about those questions.

16

I DREAMED A DREAM...

I went home and later on that night I couldn't get the images out of my head of how I felt about my past. I had work the next morning and was becoming to get even more tired working about three jobs why Lauren was pregnant and working her summer job at her church. I decided the next day after work that I would go out with my friend Terrell to catch a couple of laughs and get my mind off of things since I was going through so much stress. I was becoming a father soon and although I was so excited a part of me didn't want to become one. Trying to understand and prepare myself mentally for the journey that waits for me is something that still clouded my head at times. We went out that night. To go chill at some folk's house that he knew out Chest Nut Pointe.

Although I knew I shouldn't have been smoking and caring on with people I was enjoying myself. Terrell was celebrating his son's year birthday and I was celebrating my expecting surprise with my girl as well. A dude there by the name of Tony, I believed his real name was Anthony he was a friend of a friend of Terrell's and he also was celebrating his unexpected surprise of being a father. Yet he was talking about getting his ex-girlfriend pregnant and shit, because apparently, her boyfriend she had was playing around with her too much. So, during the midst of us sharing stories, I told him I believed I was having a son and he stated he believe he was having a girl. I was happy for him and then I told him yea "They said my seed might be here on September 11th. He looked at me and said word "Lauren just told me our son will be here on the 11th also. Whoa! My nigga what you talking about? Even Terrell got quite and looked at me and said calm down Maurice! It may not even be the same girl. Naw Rell, the thing is that you're not understanding is that this is a small city come on man not too many girls around here got that name or from the same growing up area. I text her that night I didn't get know reply.

So, we left that night and only thing I wanted to do was smash that nigga's face in but I couldn't without checking with her first. I was at work that morning when she got back to me. So, I asked her Lauren what is your ex's name? Anthony, she responded. Okay let me be clear what is his name that he goes by? Tony why what's up she replied. When was the last time you guys talked, or hung out? About a couple of months ago, why are you drilling me with these entire questions baby as she replied to me. Are you fucking him? WHAT!! AS SHE RESPONDED TO ME IN ALL CAPS? Are you fucking him yes or no answer the damn question? She replied to me NO!!! Fuck out of here don't come at me over no shit like that, when I am caring your baby. I snapped on her well the word of the mouth is bitch it isn't my baby. I got too upset I threw my damn phone at the wall at work. I knew I shouldn't have lost my cool at work especially working around those who are mentally challenge however I didn't care I was hurt. A part of me felt like she was lying. I was so sick and tired people playing fucking mind games on me. I wanted to get even and hurt her as much as she has hurt me.

I left work driving to my therapy session and smoking a cigarette all at the same time. I walked inside the office and waited in the waiting room. It seemed like Dr. Kyle already has someone inside but my appointment time was coming up. All I could do at that moment was feel myself up with anger and rage. The door opened and then Dr. Kyle was standing in the door way looking at me with those weird seductive eyes as he called my name Maurice come in! Doc I got so much to tell you and so much is on my mind it's like you're my own personal diary. This bitch got pregnant and then this nigga claiming my baby. My folks are getting on my fucking nerves I am ready to just off everybody and they fucking mom real wrap Bruh, Maurice!! Slow down, have a seat and did you work on your homework assignment like I asked you too? I sure did doc. You asked me some weird questions about some animals, etc. right?

"Maurice the importance of your growth depends on you doing half of the work and understanding yourself more as a person. Now relax and clear your mind we are going to try some exercises today. I want your honest answers and don't think how silly or weird your answers are just being yourself ok?" I will try doc. If you could be any animal what would you be and why? I paused for a second and told him that I wanted to be a blue jay bird. The reason is because doc there peacefully birds and there always flying around singing. You rarely get to see them and when you do they are so beautiful to the eye. I also wouldn't mind being a blue Jay because I would love to just fly whenever I want, be free and overlook all of god's creation as I am above soaring through the blue sky. "Okay thank you Maurice, now if you could go anywhere in the world where would you go and why? Truth be told doc I always loved the ocean growing up as a kid and often felt if I could breathe underneath water I would live there. The reason why the ocean is the place I want to be is because it's impossible to hear the voice I hear in my head. It's impossible to feel agony around you. The ocean is so deep that I would become my own shelter. "Okay interesting, now if you could have anything in the world what would it be and why? I honestly don't know that one is very hard. Take your time and tell me. Well what I've always wanted since a kid is for true love, someone to love me for me and not what I look like; I would rather fall in love with someone who is deaf and blind rather than someone who is going to mistreat me. I rather love freely in the world without judgement or hatred. Then to have false love from family, friends and relationships that could lead to my own self destruction. Can I ask you a question doc? Sure thing! Ask me, as he looked at me with his hand to his cheek pondering over what I just said to him.

Do you think we as people know what the future has in stored for us? Like for some strange reason do you believe that are dreams can subconsciously unlock pieces of what we are to experience in the near future that we call it DÉJÀ VU because we are reminded of a word or phrase, person, place or thing that simply just jolted the piece of the future we experienced. "Good Maurice I am sure that it is possible and that there have been scientific studies that have possibly proven that, is there a particularly kind of dream you would like to discuss? Well, sort of I really don't know what it meant if it's a dream or a warning but it felt so real like I have actually been there and experience it all before multiple times.

Tell me if you don't mind sharing? I looked at doc straight in his eyes. I don't really know where to begin. I dreamt that I saw myself grow up past the age of thirty. I suffered a lot of pain; I became homeless at times and had multiple relationships. I also saw myself weak and sick like. I dream that I ended my relationship with my current girlfriend because her destiny was no longer tied to mines but of someone else's. I saw that I became a drug addicted and self-destructed which was one part of the dream. I also saw myself being a wonderful father to a beautiful little boy. I say myself getting married and finally finding love and being happy. In this dream, I was battling my soul between life and death or you could say heaven or hell. I was placed on trial by God and Satan for the pain I caused others as well as the sinful things that I have committed. At times, I seemed happy and also at times I seem depressed and hurt. I saw that I killed myself in my own dream and God was upset with me. The dream I had no longer made sense to me because every time right before I would kill myself I would wake up. Often at times the dream felt so real that sometimes when people are speaking to me that I have encounter in my dream flashes from my dream appear in my head. It's like my mind already knows what they are going to say, then I say something and it sparks the whole experience that I have been here before. I didn't understand it all but I would wake up in tears some nights because I don't want that to be my future at least the bad parts. I want to be a good person and help people.

Yet, doc this dream I seen myself losing my child. I saw his mother taking him from me to satisfy her own pride and agenda. I saw her being married and living the life she was supposed to. In my dream, God explains to me that I was going to hurt her severely and that there was nothing I could do about it because the pain I caused her would alter the way she is supposed to be. He told me that one day I would have to make the decision on letting her go for her own future or holding her back in misery and pain. As long as she was with me all that I saw in her future was set backs. I knew deep down inside that this was true because I often felt it. I remember the first day we had sex, I saw a bright future with us both having kids and succeeding in our careers however, I also seen myself dead and killed by the lifestyle I chosen. Doc, I realized that everything that I was dreaming would soon come true, the reason is because I felt the emotions there, I could smell speak, walk, and talk. And somehow everyday seems closer to the mark of when it all happens. "What do you mean by that? I mean Doc; each day that I wake up and go on my daily routine is one day closer to the day I died. Somehow, I don't remember how it happen, yet I could see people grieving over my body that looks like a funeral. Have you prayed on this matter, sometimes pray has a way of relieving stress and reassuring us that God is still with us! That the lord will keep his promise. Maurice, have you talked to your church pastor about this. Doc, I left the church a long time ago when my pastor forced me to give him oral pleasure one Sunday after service. I did because it was easier doing that then him telling my parents that he basically caught me trying to kiss a boy out back on the church porch. "When you experience these things Maurice how do you feel"? I feel Cheap like a dirty filthy little whore as if I am only a product of service among people instead of a human being with feelings and emotions. A mere sex object or toy. Every person that I have come in contact with that see's my attractiveness only wants one thing from me to fill their sexual desires. Sigh... Truth is doc, I am tired, I don't want any of those things. Good Maurice what is it that you truly want besides love? I want... I want to be happy and free. I want the simple things in life to roam and create memories. I want to travel the world and see different cultures. I have an inner love for people to help them and feel their pain. I want my gifts back from God. I want to have anointing in my voice again, to see what's inside of people's hearts and minds. I don't want this life anymore. I want to control my anger and temper. I desire to possibly live on a ranch or out in the country away from the world. I desire to live without the guilt of my past sins. I don't want to be in love nor fall but I just want someone that is meant for me that's all. So far, I been loving and seeing me go through so much hell and complications in my dreams of people I was in relationships with that by time I found him it was too late.

What do you mean found him? Sigh... Well a part of me doesn't believe that it is a sin for me to be a homosexual. I saw myself as that, as I am older in my dreams with a 12-year old child. I also saw that I went through hell to find false love and agony of those only wanting to be around me just because I could offer them something or do something for them. Wait! Maurice, you mean to tell me that you've actually seen yourself in your dreams of what you look like and how your future is supposed to be and this all seem real to you. Yes, before you mark weird and wacky notes on your clip board and I don't expect you to understand me nor believe me yes, I have and I know it all to be true. In the near future if I am not dead. I will no longer have long hair. I will no longer have a fit body yet, I was older and little more with wisdom, and I will have cut off my family completely. I am not sure if I have a son or a daughter all I know is that I am pushing a kid on a swing. I have tattoos which is something that I would have never agreed to period I don't believe in those. I also seen that I was a different person from when I was in my teenaged years. Somehow a part of me was healed externally yet and often still felt pain from my past. Unfortunately, my dreams never allowed me to see what I wanted only what I was allowed to see. This is exactly why the future for myself seems so vague and unsure of its meaning. "Hey doc, do you think you can make sense of it all to me? Good Maurice it sounds like to me that you have a lot going on and that you need to try and focus on staying goal oriented. You need to also get back into church and allow God to use you and guide you through your troubling times. We as people always go through a series of tests and trials, yet with faith and guidance we always seem to make it out of the mist of any storm. The bible tells us we must have faith of a mustard seed and constantly call on the name of Jesus. Maurice if your faith is strong enough you can overcome anything. I believe you can have enough faith as small as a simple rain drop. I do believe you have so much to offer the world and so much love to give that it overwhelms you at times. I also believe that you are destined for great things in your future. If your dreams of your future scare, you then I want you to pray more and seek understanding and direction of where you are heading in life and going to become. When was the last time you prayed to god? "I really can't say it's' been a very long time I believe. Doc!

I never knew you believe in Jesus Christ? Maurice I don't. Doesn't mean that I can't connect with my patient's religious beliefs. If you feel comfortable praying to something you cannot see or understand to submit to a higher power, I say go for it. Try this I am going to leave the room and I want you to begin to feel the power that is inside you to begin to pray and you just come out of the room whenever you are ready, I will give you the last ten minutes of our session to pray and speak with your savior on whatever it is that is on your heart and remember just always remain to be true to yourself. "Sure, I will give it a try doc. He left the room and the entire room was silence. I folded my hands and closed my eyes and began to call upon his name....

Dear Father,

Hey big guy you up there in the sky I haven't done this in a while could you be so kind to listen to me and hear me out. I am not sure what is going on with my life or how you like playing with it yet, I need you to stop, your confusing the hell out of me. What is it that you want me to do because I no longer have guidance. I no longer am sure on what's ahead for me anymore. All I feel deep down inside me is pain and guilt. I thought that a father is supposed to protect his children. I thought a father is supposed to hear his children. I am lost in a storm and no longer hear anything I am left without a hand to hold. Can you please hear me and you talk to me before? Answer me!!!

DID YOU REALLY THINK HE WOULD COME? I was shocked that God was answering me I haven't heard him in a while or at least I thought it was God. Oh, I am not the lord but I have been listening to you the whole entire time. I have never forsaken you however, I am sad to tell you but you are going to die soon and there is nothing you can possibly do about this. Tears began to fill my eyes what do you mean? I don't want to die. Are you serious did you not forget that thy has done an abomination unto the lord. Thy shall not lie with a man as thy lie with woman. Did you really think that your sins could be forgiven? Did you really think that you were destined to be something so blissful? Can you tell me who you are? I think you already know why I am Maurice I been here inside you since you been a little boy. I have always guided you on making decisions. I have lifted you up when your pride has been broken. I am the shadow that lurks in your soul. The moment you utter my language as a child was the moment you allow me to enter inside you, be one with you. I am you and you are me. You're speaking in riddles and that doesn't make sense. If you must know Maurice there is no

185

hiding or escaping me I will take over and help you always you just must call out to me that is all. No get out of my head; I do not want you to be here. You are the reason I have gone through so much pain. Maurice! Open your eyes I have been the only one here for you the sooner you understand that is the sooner you can begin to change and be even more better then you were before. I SCREAMED! At the voice inside my head to get out... get out. I ran out of the office crying because he wouldn't leave me alone. Dr. Walker stopped and grabbed me by my arms and said "Maurice! Look at me! Are you ok? I can't get him out of my head he wants me to hurt myself, he wants me to end it all and I can't. I'm sorry I can't. Dr. Walker hugged me and said" SShhh not a word. Shawn popped in my head and I pushed Dr. Walker off and yelled at him get away from me please your just like them. I ran out of the building and got to my car and drove off in a dash. I was panicking in my car smoking a cigarette crying my eyes out and suddenly the voice stopped out of nowhere. I knew deep down inside that my life truly really meant nothing I was just wasting time...

17

REMEMBER SEPTEMBER

Sometimes in life we are unsure of the things that keeps us back from the destinations we are meant to be at. I know by reading this you seem confused possibly on were this story is going but I promise you it will all make sense soon. Often growing up I question a lot of things and even myself you could say it's the part of getting older. By now my life has completely went into chaos and I wasn't aware what was up the road. My girlfriend was pregnant, my family I felt isolated from and everyone I basically came into contact with did nothing but use me or took something from me. My faith lies on the balance of either life or death. I was so destroyed mentally I had no way out. I grew tired of mind games and life's struggles that I wanted to start all over again. Although I never believe that you could be reborn again or reincarnated yet, I just wanted a reset, a do over a second chance to make a difference and have something different for my life. For all that is reading this soon you are about to see exactly what I was talking about. You will be able to feel what I felt…

I went to work like usually going back and forth the past couple of weeks taking my clients out on outings to see the inner city. My communication with Lauren was slim to none and honestly, I stopped caring about our relationship, I gave up hope that we could be a family. I lost sight of our own dreams we have together to hear talk around the city that she was caring another man's baby, it hurt me deeply. I felt as though she was better off without me anyway since her family never really liked me. Her mother hated the shit out of me. It felt as though my whole entire life I knew has just been one big mistake and lie. I didn't know what to think nor do I just know that I now longer wanted to feel the way that I felt.

It was that Saturday on July 9th 2009. I was going to see a friend of mines that lived on 17th and Regina Street. I saw a boy walk by and normally, I never pay attention to men; however, he looked me straight in my eyes and asked me my name. I told him my name was Maurice. He smiled at me with an innocent look and said nice to meet you my name is Renee but some people call me Mena. "Are you from around here? I responded to him and told him no. He took his phone out and took my number down and said do you smoke weed? Although in my head I was saying no but I didn't mind smoking a blunt with him. Something about him caught my interest and I couldn't figure out why. Inside of me my mind was screaming who exactly are you and where did you come from? Days and weeks went by with us texting back and forth especially when I was at work I would drive my clients out with me to go see him and keep this all a secret from Lauren. I felt as though since you cheated paybacks are a bitch. I remember telling Lauren that I had to work overnight one Saturday just so I could go and chill and hang out with Mena. I took him over one of my friend's house where we got drunk and basically had sex on the first night. To tell you the truth I could hardly remember it. I was there for one thing only which was revenge. Yet, when we were done fucking he manages to tell me that he grew to love me. Now imagine I never knew what this boy's age was and finding out he was only 17 still in high school. I felt so shocked as if I was a child molester. I mean majority of the men I came in contact with was way older that I was equipped to handle them not a young one. He was fresh meat on the block and I know if I was to send him out there in the world like that he would be crushed like I was. So, I grew to love him too. (If you are reading this, this is not to hurt you but to explain my downfall.)

If this book serves as my diary, then let's just keep it all the way hundred. As time grew on us I fell in love with him. I broke up with my child's mother and left her doing her second trimester all over a rumor of her having another man's baby. I was sick in the head for what I did to her yet a part of me didn't care. I was too way far gone being back on drugs again that I couldn't even get help this time. Mena and I's relationship became so toxic with lies, cheating and betrayal that it was more of a situation-ship. Every day we were smoking, drinking popping mollies. I was doing coke in crack houses on the hill and every time my phone would go off from Lauren about our baby or updates I would ignore her, not because I wanted to but because I really couldn't speak correctly being high. I knew deep down Mena was cheating on me so much and there was nothing that I could do about it. I left my woman for a piece of ass and a cute face. I believe she was willing to accept me back if I agree to go back to counseling and fix some things. No matter what I didn't, every time I wanted to break up with Mena there was a fist fight or an argument and a psychotic magnetic pull he had on me. He even dropped out of high school for no reason when all I wanted him to do was to better himself. I had a tender spot for him because I knew what it felt like for men to only chase you for your beauty and no matter what you are in the inside. I tried to break it off as friend's multiple times however; I was tired of the way I looked like a bum. Dirty finger nails, kinky braids, same clothes on for 3 days. Smoking in the morning and night I dropped so much weight you knew I looked sick and this wasn't what I was used to. Going to other gay parties were people actually knew my baby mom embarrassing her with my flamboyant ways and telling people fuck you and you can tell her what you want.

True of it all was that I no longer wanted to be here in the madness. I wanted to come back home. Moved to another state start fresh. I realized that I truly fucked up at this moment and there was nothing that I could do to resolve it. I often tried to hide the truth from Lauren but her eyes had a way of knowing the truth about me anyway. I soon found out who Mena truly was. Just because he was slim, short, Hispanic with paw prints coming up his stomach, a smile of gold with a soft gentle voice with brown eyes and slick Rican hair. He was my baby and my strong hold at times I simply just couldn't let him go but I knew I had too. I told him that I will always love him and that one day when the time comes if I have to let you go to be a parent I will because that is my job. Your mind isn't mature enough to handle what is about to happen with my life. You're not ready for kids because you're a child yourself. I believe deep down he understood that in his own way.

I was lying down with him on my chest at a friend's house when I got a call from Lauren telling me her water broke. I was nervous and excited all at the same time. I ran so fast down to the Harrisburg Hospital. The wait for the baby to get here was time consuming. My whole mediate family was there my mom, dad, sisters, and brothers and even her mother and relatives were there. No later than me being there after 4 hours Mena showed up, somehow Lauren find out and the epidermal they gave her to induce her labor wasn't working she manage to be so stress out from the information of Mena being there it was affecting the baby and they had to prep her for an emergency C-section. So much was going on doctors weren't fully explaining to me what was going on. I began to get so angry with rage I snapped on doctors and her mother. I DON'T GIVE A FUCK WHO IS WHO I AM GOING IN THAT ROOM WITH HER NO QUESTIONS ASKED. They rushed her down the hall through the double doors on the 11th floor to do the C-section. I remember them telling her they are going to numb her so she doesn't feel anything. As see looked at me, I went over and kissed her on her forehead and told her that "I love you and I wasn't going anywhere. She utters to me please make sure our baby is okay. They pulled out our baby and all I could hear was silence for a second. Come on baby breathe. My heart dropped down to my stomach and soon as I heard this loud cry we both were eased. She had tears coming out of the corners of her eyes and closed them in relief. I followed the nurses over to the changing station where they let me cut the umbilical cord. September 09, 2009 at 7:03pm we had a beautiful baby girl, I was shocked I thought it would be a son. I never felt so much joy in the world; I stayed with Lauren that night because that's all that matter to me was her and my baby girl. She came out 7lbs and 3oz and 19 inches with a head full of hair. She looked so light skinned orange looking that she was like my little pumpkin.

Lauren was so pumped up with drugs far as morphine for pain that she could barely move. The nurse came in with the paperwork while she was sleeping and I filled out as much as I could. They asked me what would be her name and I said Maliyah Latrice (Which is her mother's middle name) and I waited for her to get up from napping to decide if she wanted to give her my last name or hers. I mean I was a coward I left her when she needed me the most she didn't even have to put me on the birth-certificate. Surprisingly, she agreed to give Maliyah my last name. I was shocked and thrilled all at the same time. I let her hold her for a little until she took a nap again and I took the night shift so she can rest. I looked at my baby girl in her eyes and mines were filled with happiness and tears as well. It is family tradition that I give you my blessing. So, in that room I held you in my arms against my warm chest and prayed over your life...

Maliyah-

Happy Birthday! Today is the day you were a miracle and a blessing for us both. You were made and created out of love. There is nothing in this world your mother and I wouldn't do or give you. You have made both of us the happiest people in the world. I pray that protection will always follow you. I pray that you never have a heart break. I ask God to always watch over you and shield you from the ignorance of the world. Pray that you always understand that you are loved. Father in heaven, watch over my blessing and give her. Her hearts desires. Embrace her with spiritual gifts and favor. Ignite the light that is in her and began to break the curses of previous generations. Claim her in your name and always guide her to do what is right. I ask that I sacrifice my heart to purify her. I pray that we have a rare bond that will never be broken. Lord I suffered a relationship with my own father, so I ask that you grant me the discernment to understand her at difficult times. Father who is in heaven, please always keep us together, for she is mines and I am hers. I pray no harm comes against her. On this day of birth, I vow to give her my whole entire life.

As I looked at Maliyah in my arms humming to her, the day is done it's time for bed. Let happy thoughts fill your head. So, cuddle up and snuggle in and let the happy dreams now begin. My beautiful sweet little girl, daddy loves you this is my blessing unto you. I would rather die than to have you go through discomfort or let anyone hurt you in any kind of way that goes for family or foes. This is my promise to you I will always love you and be here no matter what it takes. I am excited to be a new father and knew at that moment there was a lot of things I need to change in my life and make for the better. Seeing her looking into my eyes made a lot of things clear for me. I need to seek help and guidance so that I can be there for my daughter. I need to stop my foolishness and get my act together. I knew I needed to break up with Mena although it wasn't something that I wanted to do yet it was something that I had to do deep down inside.

Something troubled me though? Would he just really up and let me go? Or would I have to wait for our next argument for him to simply break up with me and for me to walk away. This wasn't something that I thought that far ahead yet I knew that our time being in a relationship has to end quickly so that I can fix my mistakes and get back to my normal life as soon as possible for Lauren and our baby.

16

PLAY WITH FIRE YOU GET BURNED!!

We often believe that when we love someone truly that we can never be broken hearted or scorn by that person. Yet right there in that very moment we proven ourselves to be so wrong. Love can heal as well as it can destroy and sometimes we hold on to things we love and our inner truth is simply telling us to let it go. You often find yourself holding on to the damages of a broken love that you begin to become broken and damage yourself. When will learning it's better to not love at all then to love all over again...?
-Anonymous

It was time to get my life back together so I cut off Mena for a couple of days and told him that I need to be with my daughter so that I can get a proper routine schedule. I made a call to Dr. Walker's office to make an appointment apparently, they always left my slot open so I had a session within the next hour that Friday evening around 7pm. I prepared myself and got in my car and went over there. It was so hard driving in the rain that felt like a strong storm. I did manage to arrive back at his office

soaked and wet. "Maurice! How have you been? Long time should we pick back up where we left off or would you like to start something new. To be honest Doc I just want to vent to someone and explain how I feel is that ok?
"Sure, Maurice shoot for it".

I really don't understand how my life got to this very moment, I love my child's mother and I have a beautiful baby girl and I not sure on what life I should choose. I mean, I met a guy I really do love and care about despite him lying and cheating those are things that we can work on but I just have never felt this way about someone before, I am just not sure he is ready for the kind of love that I can truly bring. Lauren is great and such a sweet woman. She is bold, confident I just feel bad leaving her broken hearted that I left her for a man instead of telling her the truth and I feel like karma will bite me in the ass later on in life. However, I was told that if I didn't let her go I would only be holding her back from her purpose of finding true love and happiness. Unfortunately, I don't live in a world where I can have both and I have to choose. Although I don't want to choose because that is the hardest decision I have to make. I wasn't raised to create and make a child out of wedlock and leave. What would my family think? How would my parents react? Why does this burn so badly?
"Why does what burn so badly Maurice"? Love Doc... Love. I feel like I was born with a curse to never truly be happy in love because I am never really supposed to have it. Help me figure this one out doc. If I don't choose her my life will be hell and I know it. I will struggle, work multiple jobs, be placed on child support, argue with her future boyfriends about maintaining a relationship with my daughter, Men will treat me like shit because that's what I see in the near future for myself. There has to be a way to correct and fix this. There has to be a way that we can still remain good friends and raise our child in a loving and healthy environment. There just has too. "Maurice! You're

not making sense your speaking in terms of the future that isn't here yet. Don't insult my intelligence, I know what I know I am not stupid nor do I think it won't happen. Damnit, I know things before it gets here, don't ask me how or why I know because I can't begin to make understanding of it either. Why doesn't anyone believe me? It's a gift from god I always had it as a kid from God, Sometimes the dreams aren't too vivid and clear but doesn't mean they aren't real. I thought I was going to have a son and I dreamt that I had a daughter and look I have a daughter. I thought I was never going to be touch by and man and looked I got touched multiple times. I also thought I was never going to find a girlfriend and look she came to me and I responded just like the dream showed me. Maybe I am only meant to be here with her in general for a certain period of time. Could it possibly mean that I am her hardship to pave the way for something extraordinary for her? It's possible you know. God never said for sure she was supposed to be my wife. He did explain to me that one day would come that I would have to let her go and open the door for another opportunity for her to love again. I was never supposed to be here permanently and I understand that now. BUT WHY ME! WHY MUST I GO THROUGH THE TRIALS?

Maurice! Please try and calm down, you are getting yourself overly excited. He stood up and came around from his desk and told me to come close to him so I did. He reached out his hands to me and said "Come here you have gone through so much in your life from a boy to man and I believe no one has ever told you that they care about you. Let me give you a hug. Tears were streaming down my face and all I wanted to do was simply let it all go. I came close into him and laid my head on his chest why he hugged me. I knew this whole chemistry was wrong because I was his patient, I just wanted someone to understand me and be here for me no matter what without judgements. I went to push back from him and he tilted my chin up to look him in his eyes and he brought his face down to kiss me on my lips. I pushed him off. "What the hell do you think you are doing? You're supposed to be my therapist, and you know that this isn't right. A hug is one thing but you're taking it too far. "Come on Maurice! Why must you play these games with me? You know deep down you actually like me and have an attraction to me.

What the fuck are you talking about? You're supposed to help me through my issues. You told me if I opened up and discussed my pain you will write it off to the judge that I am fine. That I am stable enough to be back in my normal life. "What makes you think I would do that when you haven't given me what I wanted yet? I began to slowly step back from him because the vibe in the room drastically changed. His look even change. He took off his glasses and placed them behind him on his desk. He began to walk closer to me. I was beginning to get scared. "Are you afraid of me? You're walking away from me Maurice and I have done nothing but try to help you and listen to all your complaints." That is your job Dr. Walker. Please I insist call me Kyle. I think Dr. Walker is fine to me. Come here don't walk away from me. I began to step back again and he lunged in and grabbed me by my arms and held them down by my waist. Look damnit boy, I am not looking to hurt you. You're too gorgeous for that. Let me go Dr. Walker this isn't right and we both know this. You can lose your job over this. You're older than eighteen we are both adults. Its fine it's okay I promised. As the look, he gave me in my eyes troubled me with fear now. He pulled me into him and ripped my shirt open and began to try to kiss me on my neck as I was fighting to push him off of me. He smacked the shit out of me and yelled at me and told me to give him what he wanted if I didn't the judge was going to get a bad report. I yelled at him and told him that I didn't care. This is wrong and we both know this. He pushed me against the therapeutic chair that clients lie on to release their thoughts while in session. I fell down on it and he climb on top of me as my hands were trying to push and fight him off yet he had an advantage with is height and weight I found it hard to struggle to get him off of me. He began to reach for my pants to unbuckle them. I tried to yell and he took the small oval pillow and placed it over my head to the point it was hard for me to breathe. I reached behind me to see if I can grab anything and my hands caught onto the lamp that was on the stand next to the chair. I grabbed it firmly and struck him over the head with it and he rolled off of me and fell to the floor. I got off the chair and began to kick him why he was on the ground. There was blood coming from his head. I panicked and called out to him Dr. Walker are you ok? Doc answer me. Kyle please oh god please let him be okay. I heard him let out a small sigh of breath and I ran out of his office. The waiting room was dark with no one being there in the office as if the office was now closed for the weekend. I was shaking so badly in my car I couldn't manage to get my keys in my hands to turn on my car. When I did I spat off out of the parking lot and reached for my cell phone. I was contemplating on what it is I should do to call the cops. Was he dead? I heard him still breathing. Omg am I going to go to jail what is going on with me. What did I just do? Oh, God please help me I need you right now God please. I unlocked my phone and called Mena so that way I would have an alibi if anyone asked me where I was I could say I was with my boyfriend the whole entire time and I knew he would have my back. I called him and he didn't pick up the first time then he called me back. I guess he could hear it in my voice that something was wrong. I told him can I just please come spend the night with you. He told me yes. I asked him where he was and he was at his grandmother's house uptown at Cumberland Court Apartments. I speeded down 6th street trying to get off the streets so badly and every cop car that passed me drop my heart to my stomach and I couldn't deal with the pressure of one of them mistakenly pulling me over.

I reached the parking lot of the apartment complex and reached to my back seat and grabbed my hoodie and place the hood of it over my head so the cameras couldn't see me going through his window. He looked at me and hugged me and said" Baby, what's wrong your shaking. Is everything okay? I couldn't quite tell him what just happened. I told him that everything was fine I just needed to take a shower and get myself clean. He went inside of his closet and pulled out a towel and pulled some of my spare clothes from his dresser and told me to go ahead and get cleaned up. I went inside of the bathroom and couldn't even look myself in the mirror. I turned on the shower water and began to let the hot water burn my back and turn me red. The whole entire scenario kept playing inside of my head over and over and I couldn't believe what I just did. Dear God please forgive me. Please let him be alive and okay. Please Dear God I beg of you. I can't go to jail I have a daughter. I don't want this anymore. I pressed my face against the cracks of the shower wall crying deeply covering my mouth not to make any sounds. I felt hands on my back and I jumped petrified in shock. It was Mena. He wrapped his body around mines holding me telling me "Baby whatever it is it's going to be okay I am here for you till the end. I turned around and wrapped my arms around him crying baby it's all my fought all of it. Why me? What did I do? I should have never been born. God is punishing me? He looked me in my eyes as water was dripping from his head and said "I know you, you're the softest gentlest innocent person I have ever known. You don't deserve to be treated badly by anyone and you know that you're special. I'm sorry baby if I ever took you through anything. I'm sorry for coming down to the hospital when your daughter was born and if you need to leave me to be with your family then so be it just know that I am always here for you no matter what. I love you Maurice and never forget that. He pressed his lips against mines so gently and placed his tongue in my mouth. We were French kissing and both are hands were roaming on each other's bodies. He dropped down to his knees and placed me inside of his mouth and began to send me on a plane of pleasure. It was taking my mind off of the situation and felt different for me.

He then got back up and turned around and place me up inside of him. My hands wrapped around his waist and chest as we began to move and slow stroke to the rhythmed of the shower water hitting our bodies. His head tilted back to me in pleasure and I whisper in his ear with tears coming out of my eyes" Baby, I love you and I want to spend my life with you. He started to cry also and for once it felt good to connect for once with a man on that type of intimate level. He arched his back and I ran my hands down his spine pushing every inch of me inside him and gently taking my time. I pulled myself out of him and told him go head it's your turn. He rimmed himself inside of my, yet as it hurt I took that pain into numbness and silence my pain inside of me. Everything I went through in life was playing in my head like a movie. Every time he thrust inside of me painfully and rough. I clenched down on my teeth and gasped in agony and terror. At that moment, I wanted to feel agony because it was all that I was use too in the world. It was all I had to give myself. Ache of being unwanted, Pain of being hurt, Hurt of insecurities and pain of being with people that only consider me as a pleasurable object. I also knew that this would be my last time seeing him and holding him and caring for him because I have to go and be a father and fix my life.

I woke up that Saturday morning early as he was sleeping I kissed him on his forehead and when I left that house, I left him in mind of never coming back and never seeing him again. The thought of this along made me choke. I had that knot in my throat but I couldn't no longer cry anymore. I had to man up and become a man that I was meant to be. Although I would never forget him, I would never forget our bad times nor our good times. Our laughter with one another and the way that we are connected because we know what the struggle was with one another. He was my friend and the love I gave to him was unique and I hope and pray to God that no harm ever comes his way. I will always remember Mena as the man who pushed me to be different. The boy who took me as a confused man in a relationship and gave me a little hope that this lifestyle isn't so bad. There is hope out here that I can find real love with a man, that it's basically all what you make it. So, for that I will truly always love you and miss that about you.

A week went by and Lauren and I had to sit down and talk about somethings about our relationship. Were we together or not. Can we fix the broke damage with us? Could we possibly mend all the pain we caused one another? I meet her at my parents' house that night and we began to sit down and talk. She explained to me how she felt about me hurting and leaving her. All I could do was hold the tears in my eyes because I didn't want her to see me weak. I knew I had to come clean to her about my therapist but I felt as though I deserve to hear her side of things. I been shutting her down emotionally for months and even throughout her whole entire pregnancy and I was pretty sure there was a lot that she felt. She kept a lot of emotions inside and I knew it was time for her to fully release it all on me. She placed our daughter in the crib and looked at me and said "Maurice I love you but I can't wait for you to get your life together. Every void can properly be filled just know that me and my daughter will be fine with or without you. I sat back for months and couldn't stress myself or the baby out and saw you self-destructing right before my eyes. I took your lies and you're cheating. I'm sorry I couldn't be there for you while I was in college. I was trying to better myself and you knew that before you got in a relationship with me. I am sorry my mother thinks differently of you but you are not in a relationship with her, you are in one with me. Who cares what she thinks eventually she will come around. Baby I love you and I meant it when I said that I want to spend the rest of my life with you. Don't give up on us. Don't give in to the devil. You know that you are stronger than that. If you need me stop letting your pride get in the way of our happiness. I'm right here with you. I'm no longer in Virginia in college. We can both work together to fix us. We can be a team again. Tell me you don't love me and I will just walk away. I told you and always told you this if we aren't together cool... Fine with me. I won't place you on child support neither will I ever keep your daughter away from you. Yet this back and forth shit is killing me. I'm dying inside because you don't see how much I love you and care about you is just ridiculous to me. I'm standing right here in front of you confessing my love that I am here Maurice. You left me for a boy in the middle of my second trimester and I still had faith in us.

The tears began to burst out of her eyes and I could feel her pain for once. After being together for nearly four years I could finally sense and feel her pain. I could see all that I took her through. I could for once feel her love that I couldn't feel being in a long-distance relationship. I finally understood the type of women she was and was proud of her courage. I knew I fucked up as a man and she didn't deserve a man like me she deserves so much better. I finally understood my dream of what God was telling me. Even if I wanted it to work with us our child and our future. There was no way that it could work. You see here love is so strong and uniquely pure because of the heart she has that it made it impossible for her to fix me. It wasn't her job to do that. She couldn't fix something she didn't create. She couldn't love me entirely because I didn't love myself enough. At that moment, I knew that it all made sense for once. She was no longer the girl I saw at 15 but a molded potential woman in the making. Lauren Latrice my sweet love was destined to be what God created for her. Her future was brighter than I ever thought or could imagine and the more I held on to her, the more she would be trapped in my web of deceit and sin.

I took my hands around her face and kissed her like I never did before. We both stood there in tears kissing one another. I kept apologizing to her telling her that I was sorry that I didn't want to hurt her. I am sorry for all that I have caused you. Please forgive me and I will try my best for it to never happen again. She looked at me with her big bold brown eyes and lifted my shirt above my head. I took off hers as well and unsnapped her bra. I placed my hands on her back and rubbed her soft skinned that felt like shea butter and silk. She smelled like coconut mist fragrance. As I gently nibble on her neck I could feel her breathing on my ear. We walked backwards to the bed as I laid her down on it, while on top of her I kissed gently from her neck down to her stomach licking her. Placed my hands on her breast and began to massage her nipples and as she looked at me with teary eyes, I could feel tears streaming from mines as I was making love to her lower pussy lips. I swirled my tongue inside her completely feeling the ripples of her walls. I sucked on her black pearl and until I felt it vibrant on my tongue. I could hear her moan in sighs of a melody of pleasure. I began to think about everything I took her through and got deep into the aggression of creating a new love with her. I wrapped her legs on my shoulders and lifted her up inside my mouth more. Her pussy became my oxygen as there was no time for me to go up for air. She took her hands and rubbed them on the back of my head pushing me into her more craving the speed of my tongue. I finally came up with my beard soaked from her tasteful salted caramel juices as I wiped my mouth. I placed my finger down inside for another taste, pulling it back out licking my fingers as if this dessert was my last. She pulled me on top of her and reach down to grab my dick in her hands. I was throbbing so hard that I could have burst at any moment. I reach over on the night stand and open the drawer to grab a condom out. I ripped it with my teeth and place the rubbed on me. I took my hands and wrapped them around her head as her hands wrapped around my back scratching downward. I slowly teased her peach thick pussy playing around it before I placed myself inside. The moment I did, we both simultaneously let out a gesture of pleasure. She was letting off a heatwave and I was receiving every bit of it. I slowly stroked inside of her like a snake did on the ground. She bit into my neck sending electrical senses down my spine. I looked her into her eyes and said "Baby, I'm sorry I will never hurt you again." She kissed me and took her hands around my ass and pushed me inside of her even more. I began to speed up the beat as if I was beating on a drum. I took her legs and place them on my shoulders and placed my hands on her shoulders pushing her down to me as I pulled away and stroked inside her even more aggressive than before. I could hear her saying out loud I love you daddy. I returned with I love you ma. I began to beat up the box like I never have before as if we were making another baby. I could feel the inside of her pulsating letting me know she was about to reach the ecstasy of her climax all-time high. As soon as her walls clamped down unto me as she began to gasp, I than released also feeling a piece of myself leave my body and hit the tip of my rubber. I pulled out and took at towel and wiped off the remains of our rondeau vu and didn't even realized that the condom was ripped on the one side of it. I didn't mention it to her because I knew we was safe just didn't want her to get pregnant again. I immediately cleaned myself up and her and pulled back the covers on the bed and held her in my arms until she fell asleep. I couldn't sleep that night. So, I looked at her while she was sleeping I realize how beautiful of a woman she was and great of a mother she was. I prayed to god that night not just for myself but for the both of us.

Dear father,

Who is in heaven I ask only one thing from you if you have never been with me in a time of need. Please forgive me and watch over her and my child. I know that I am going against your will but I love her father and don't wish for her to go through any more. Leaving her will destroy the very essence of who she is. I am not ready to let her go. I am not ready to be without her. I know that I have caused a lot of chaos and pain yet, I am here as your son begging you to allow me this one blessing to be with her and my child. To be a better man and father to grow old with her and cherish are growth and development with one another. Please give me a sign that we can make this work. Please I beg of you.

Amen,

I woke up that morning and kissed her on her lips she woke up and returned it back to me. We both smiled at each other and just like that are spark was back. Something was different for the both of us. She didn't want me to leave but I had to get up and go to work. We are parents now and I can no longer just sit around on my ass and not do anything. She looked at me and said "go head I have to make the baby a bottle and I will see you after work." I smiled and said "absolutely and when I get home we can watch a movie whatever you like as long I am with you and holding you I am perfectly fine. I stole another kiss left to work.

Now my memory may be a little cloudy but I recall this event. I remember Mena was texting me at awkward times telling me he misses me and how was me and the baby. I was trying my best to only send him short replies because I gave her my word that we would fix and work on us. However, two weeks went by and every sense I had sex with Lauren I was feeling different downstairs on my dick. I didn't want to think anything about it so I let it go after the first week thinking I just probably bruised my dick having sex. I went to pee one day and green shit was coming out of my pee hole and it was burning. I told my boss I had to leave work because I wasn't feeling too good. I remember that day because it was a Friday and I took a double shift. I drove down to Harrisburg Hospital to the ER and told them that I was having puss coming out especially when I peed. I met with a doctor and he asked me weird questions did I have kidney issues or any soreness in my back or spine. I told him no. He then came back and ran some test on me and took some blood and I waited there what seemed like forever however it was about 2 and a half hours, He came back and ask me have I had sex recently. I told him yes. He then looked at me and said "Well okay that explains a lot so you don't have a UTI (urinary tract infection) but you have gonorrhea. He gave me a shot in my ass cheek and wrote me a prescription for anti-biotics.

Do you have any questions? "Fuck yea I do, I was confused like how the fuck did this shit happen? I just had sex last week what the fuck do you mean? How can you catch this and how long have I had this? I was in rage and began to snap on him in anger. He told me to calm down its curable, Nigga that's not the point. The point is that it shouldn't have never happen, whether it's a mistake or not I don't play that shit. He told me that I was caring it for three weeks and sometimes the symptoms show late with some people. If you have unprotect sex with anyone recently I advised you to simply let them know before it is too late. Wait so you mean to tell me that I've had this for 3 weeks so that means I been caring this around inside of me for 3 damn weeks. "Yes" Do you know who gave it to you? In my mind, I knew it wasn't Lauren I just had sex with her last week but I knew exactly who it was. I left the hospital with my prescription in hand with a temper that was on hundred. I swear to God I am going to make you pay for this. I texted Mena and asked him where he was at. He replied "Hey sexy I miss you" "Oh I miss you too muffin" Oh come see me I'm at home. In my head, I was like oh really say no more I already on my way to your grandma's house.

I pulled up to his house and he text me and told me that the door was open. I walked inside the door framed and had to control my temper. He jumped on me and started kissing me and saying I thought I was never going to see you again. Me either. As he was holding on to me I was kissing him and walking him over to his bedroom. I tossed him on the bed. "Oh, baby I love when you get aggressive. I told him I got a surprise for you. Literally in my mind he just didn't understand what was about to happen. He scooched up to the top of the bed and I said close your eyes! "Oh, baby I love surprises you know that. Oh, don't worry muffin this one is going to be spectacular. I took a tie from his closet and blindfolded him and took another two ties and tied his hands to the railing. "Oh, kinky I see what we're doing, you better fuck me right nigga." "Oh, baby don't worry I'm going to do more than just fuck you. With the blind fold over his eyes he couldn't see what I was doing. I went in his top dresser drawer and took out a pair of socks and held it in my hand, I whipped my belt off from my waist. "Now all I want is the truth Mena, did you know that you had a STD? What the fuck are you talking about? I cracked that belt on his bare chest leaving a whelp mark. He screamed so loud I stuck the pair of socks right in his mouth. Then I struck him four more times. Yo! I am tired of men lying to me and treating me as if I am common filth. You fucking lied to me and told me you weren't cheating. Your friends and everyone else was covering up all of your lies. Why I do not know? As I was pacing around the room in anger, now I'm going to remove the sock and all I want is the truth. They say the truth sets you free so let's hope in your case that is right. I'm asking you again did you know that you had a STD. He was crying No please stop! No! Your lying, I place the sock back in his mouth again and gave him 6 more lashes on his chest. He seen in my face that I had the last straw of a man breaking me and taking from me and using me despite of my knowledge of this lifestyle. Yet do you realize what you just did, you could have taken my life sleeping around on me. Fucking these niggas around on me and only using me as a mere trophy. Let's try this one more time I am going to ask you again. Did you know you had a STD? I took the sock out of his mouth to allow him to speak. YES!!! I'm sorry please stop, I am sorry as his words were breaking coming out of his mouth. My back was towards him as I was looking at the door. I began to shatter inside and my mind exploded no more ringing no more voices. My mind cracked into fragments. Let me asked you this Mena? Was it worth it?

Was I that horrible of a boyfriend trying to figure my feelings out and with your jealously of me being a father and having a baby mom. Was it all worth it? As bad as my mind is telling me to snap your neck. I am not a killer that's not in me to do, however you will suffer as much as I feel this pain inside me, but please tell me? If you knew you had a STD why did you sleep with me? I wanted to show you that I love you... Tears streamed from my eyes and rage shook my whole entire body my hands were shaking so fast. There was a beast inside me ready to bust out of the cage, I turned around my face red as ever and gagged him with the sock again. I took my pain out on his body with that belt as lashed him over and over until he pissed himself. As he was sobbing in moaning cries. I have never been with a man that I gave so much of my mind and body to that has hurt me the way you have. The saddest thing about all of this was that I was willing to let her go just to be happy with you. Truth of it all Mena I was in love with you and the whole entire time while you're listening to your friends and people thinking that I was doing you wrong, I was just trying to figure out how to add you in my life with being a parent. I hope and pray karma hits you fully like it has done me. Don't ever contact me ever again and don't come around me, my child nor her mother. I promise you this if you ever tell anyone about this I will kill you, don't think for one second that I'm not capable.

I remember leaving that day different mentally and so low and hurt that, that day couldn't get any possible worst but it did. Lauren texted my phone and said we needed to talk. I already knew what it was hitting for. I met up with her and could already see that she had been crying also. She got out of the car and without even warning punched me dead in my jaw and sat me on my ass. I couldn't do anything but look up at her with my hands up. I already knew why she was pissed. "I go to the doctors for my normal checkup and find out that you gave me a STD Maurice! Seriously like really. You told me you never slept with him, after everything Maurice you told me you wouldn't hurt me again. You told me that I had nothing to worry about and this goes and happens. Why did you? I looked up at her and said "Baby" Naw Nigga don't baby me I don't even want to hear that shit. If your ass wanted to be gay, then be gay. Don't drag me back and forth over your damn curiosity, I am better than that. Especially when I heard rumors and everyone was telling me but I choose to have your side and have your back. If you wanted to take dick in the butt like some faggot then let me go, like I said me and my daughter will be fine without you. Lauren please don't do this, I was serious, baby I stopped everything completely, I went to counseling I done things that I am not proud of PLEASE, I'M SORRY AS I GOT ON MY HANDS AND KNEES I'M BEGGING YOU WHAEVER IT IS YOU NEED ME TO DO TO FIX THIS I WILL PLEASE! Maurice! Get the fuck out of my face I don't even want to see or talk to you right now. She got back in the car and speeded so fast with her car in my direction I felt as though she was going to run me over...

I was dead inside. I guess God gave me a sign alright. That wasn't the sign that I was looking for however he taught me a valuable lesson and I knew that it was all true she was better off without me in every single way. The thought of me hurting her and my daughter wasn't a risk I was willing to take. I knew that there could be no future for us and that I simply had to let it all go now. I wanted to die deep down inside...

19

A WALK WITH DEATH

We fear not the dead for the dead cannot speak. We fear the living for the living leads us to our own death. For living is a blessing yet death is a solitude, one should never try to force the natural balance of things. -Mark Armstrong

Maurice, do you now begin to understand why you have been called here? There were choices in your life that you had time to correct your mistakes yet you have chosen to give into your own desires of lust, sexual activity, sin among all things you violated the most precious thing in life. "Sprit I do not understand please show me, I can't remember what I did wrong. "I will show you your ways so that you may truly understand the sincerity of your punishment before I take you away". From darkness, a stream of light and I saw myself on 13th and Derry Street where the crack heads purchased their drugs. I went inside of an old beat down abandon house to score an eight ball of coke, a dub bag of weed and left to drive to a liquor store. Where I purchase a big bottle of tequila and went to the red roof inn on Eisenhower Blvd. I paid in cash so the guy couldn't run my card I didn't want anyone to find me. I took my key and drugs into my cheap motel room and began rolling up a blunt and as I was smoking it I was breaking down the lines of coke on the table snorting line after line after line. I wanted to feel numb and dead inside. I called the pizza place and told them to deliver me a large pizza, I had cash to give them and just take the change. I left out of my room to go get ice but I could feel the drugs taking effect on me. I was stumbling through the hallway laughing at myself making a mockery of my own stupidity. I went back in my room and I could see myself from below watching me make a fool out of myself with the shadowy spirit looking from above right beside me. Why are you showing me this? I asked. "Look closer and you will see."

I was drinking the bottle taking it back to the head. I poured out Vicodin pills from my back pocket and didn't even look to see how many pills it was, I simply just opened the bottle and crushed a couple in my mouth and took it back with liquor. Although I was looking from above at myself I could feel every bit of the emotion and thoughts in my head. I began to cry and lash out to God. You fucking coward why me! Huh! You think your better then all of us down here. You think that you can just mess with someone's life. You told me you love me and that you will never forsake me. You told me you cared for me. Do you want me to go to hell? You probably do shit I wouldn't mind going to hell at least it's not cold there. I was laughing at myself stumbling over my own feet. I reached inside my back pocket and grabbed my blade box cutter out. I command you lord almighty to come down and stop me. If you truly care about me, you will come down and save me show yourself. I took the blade up to my wrist and slit a piece and drew blood. I didn't hit a vein but I was bleeding mildly. You like that don't you, you like seeing me suffer is, that right? I fell over on the bed and looked up at the ceiling. God don't make me sell my soul to the devil because I will. I laughed again the devil Ha-ha yea right as if he wants my ass either. You know what god I don't understand you; do you find amusement into making people's lives miserable? Do you enjoy the agony that you have put me through? What is it really that you want from me? You made me get rapped, you allow my brother to molest me, you took my woman from me and you're going to take my child. You made senior hate me for being this abomination. You made me a fucking faggot. You allowed these men to take my essence as a boy. He knew that I was going to go through all of this agony and yet he, never not once step in and said anything as I thought to myself. I got up off the bed and grabbed the bottle and kept drinking and popping more Vicodin as if it was candy to me. I walked passed the bed into the bathroom that had blue and black tiles on the floor. I was amazed on how they looked being high as hell and I bent over to touch them and banged my head on the sink. I fell to the floor. The bottle broke in my right hand as glass fragments stuck out. I rolled over on my back feeling the cold tile pressed against my skin. I stared up at the bathroom light bulb and I could hear every sound inside the room I could hear creeks in the ceiling and water dripping in the pipes. I than began to hear a loud beating sound as it was ringing in my ears. He sounded like a beating barrel... Thump... Thump... Thump. It was the sound of my own heart beat slowing down. Wait a minute are you telling me I am dying. You can't be serious spirit answer me are you telling me I just killed myself that doesn't make sense I didn't know that I die. How? I look back at myself my eyes wide open staring into the light. I know I am dying God and I am sorry and never meant for any of this to happen. I began to seize and foam at the mouth. The image stopped, everything stopped at that moment even time itself. The spirit spoke unto me. "I am death and suicide is never the answer you have killed yourself all because of your own sorrows. You are here by trial and I have been sent here to guide you through your entire past so that you may have a clear understanding of what it was you have done. Anytime you have upset and change the balance of things, you shifted the natural order. Suicides are never taken lightly by God, hence why you are here on trial. Would you like to see the rest?" Yes, please. The image of me played on lying there dying right before my eyes bleeding out. My eyes began to be dilated vision fading into the oblique. I asked the spirit could I get a closer look; it shook its' head nodding yes. I was fading away and I could hear my heart beat decreasing down by the seconds. I saw a small light inside my chest. What is that spirit? "That is your inner soul praying out to God before you go? What do you mean?

Every soul before death speaks to God It is what we call the final prayer of life. The mind no longer works, nor does the body but the spiritual core of the soul inside connects with the spiritual realm of the Lord and speaks one on one. I heard a knock at the hotel door. "Pizza delivery" ... Hello anyone in here. I was shouting from above go to the bathroom dude, He looked on the table and grabbed the money placed the pizza on the table and was about to turn around to leave back out the door. He walked closer inside the room saying "Hello, Pizza Man anyone here? I am here as I was screaming from above but he couldn't hear me. As he edges even closer towards the bathroom he saw my foot hanging out of the door way and walk even closer. OH, GOD DUDE! Are you okay? He walked up to my body and placed his fingers on my neck to fill for a pulse. He reached in his pocket and pulled out his cell phone to call the ambulance. I was screaming with tears of joy. The spirit looked over at me and said "It is too late your time is up". Wait what do you mean my time is up help is on the way. "Your body is dead and the only thing that is keeping you alive is your spiritual connection with

Christ. By the time, you get to the hospital and they operate on you it will be too late." Spirit can you take me to the hospital at this very moment currently were all of this is taking place I have to see for myself.

The spirit pushed us forward in time into me lying there in a hospital bed with tubs in my mouth. Wait I am confused you told me that I died. Am I dead or alive? Which one is it? "I can't say." I don't have the power to make that decision right now your mind is blocked with no response and your body is dead like. I am waiting on orders on where to take you. "I don't want to die, please what can I do to change this. We were standing right next to the bed side no longer hovering above the ceiling. "There isn't anything you can do Maurice it has already been decided. There was a flood of tears spilling down from my face because I made a mistake and that's not what I wanted. I knew I messed up and just wanted a chance to change and start all over. Does God hate me for doing this spirit? Does he disown me as his child? Why is there still a light over my heart? "Your soul is still crying out to God and in the midst of a spiritual battle of respiration. You're praying to God your last cry". Oh, spirit is there a way I can listen into my own prayer so that I may know what God is saying to me please? If you listen into your prayer you will no longer be out here, I can no longer guide you. If you go inside of the light you will disappear and be were your meant to be at. I don't care if I am dying and if I have the chance to speak with God himself then I would rather have that then to live at all. "As you wish, place your hands over the light and close your eyes...Remember you have one opportunity and one only to speak your inner truth and plea to him...

20

A SILENT CRY

Dear Heavenly Father,

I come to thee asking forgiveness. For your grace and mercy is the key to every mortal being. Forgive thee for being ungrateful for the life that was already chosen at the moment of my creation. Your tender kindness has always been there in my time of need. As a warrior, I got weak and stop listening to your voice. I stop speaking in tongues afraid that the devil could understand my language. I am truly sorry for allowing him to corrupt me into his wicked ways. I don't know what else to really say God. I don't want to be dead I want to live please just hear me just this once.

Maurice! As a voice of thunder called out to my name, there was a light shining so bright it nearly blinded me. Then I was in shallow water looking out at the red sun with a tree not so far from me. Its branches were a crisp shade of brown and its leaves were transparently royal blue. I saw birds above me flying about. Is this heaven I asked? Not quite my child this is more like what you have dreamed heaven is. Can I ask who you are? The voice responded to me I AM THAT I AM! Nothing less and unknowingly there's nothing more. Are you God? Lord is that you? Am I dead? No Maurice! You aren't dead... YET! I am what your mind considers to be Christ. I speak in reference to the lord God almighty on the behalf to be here in this place of trial. You have come here right in the midst of your soul preparing to depart from your body. What is it that you seek here? "I really don't know I made a stupid mistake, I don't understand why I am here. I know that I can do better God. God who is God? I stared out into the clouds and light from the sun confused on the question that was asked of me. "Well aren't you God? The voice cracked like thunder "Would you like me to be God? I don't know this is all too much for me and it doesn't make sense. If I am not dead, why am I here? If I am being punished could you get this over with so that I can pay for my sins? It doesn't matter anymore my life meant nothing in the first place.

Maurice! Is that your truth? I don't know what my truth is just please help me and tell me what I am doing here and what I did so wrong to get me here in limbo. I can't tell you what you are looking for because the answer is buried deep within your heart. I can only show you the errors of your ways in which I have, you are here because you believe that there is a small piece of faith that is holding on for you to continue with the purpose you were destined and born for. All lifeforms have a purpose and unbelievably it is all connected. Every single living being animals, plants, air, water, mankind is all a part of a greater purpose of his designed plan. When life is taken, new life can always be created, yet when life has been wasted there is no seed to grow a new creation. Maurice! Think the moment you were created you were bestowed with extraordinary pieces that made you unique, rare, delicate, valuable. The blood that was shed for you to rethink your choices and decisions in life so that you may live accordingly to God's purpose and not bend to wicked and sinful ways. You strived so hard for perfection yet you couldn't see that through trials and tribulations you learn more of who you are inside versus what you allow yourself to be. Free well always comes with a price my child to believe what is right or fall to what is wrong. You stand there as your feet lye in the clear waters of your own dreamlike of heaven and still can't see what it is that the lord has always been asking from you. You ask me if I am God. My answer is no I am only one part of the Trinity which my name is Holy Ghost. I work to correct your mistakes, I break the barriers inside your spirit so that you may be able to reconnect and speak accordingly to the father and Son. I set a fire inside you that heals and mends your broken spirit. I reach deep inside you and bind every broken vessel and replace it with the word of god. You can't blame the spirit for the choices and decisions you have made. There is always a choice and there is always an inner voice inside you that is whispering to you on what is right and what is wrong. The lord has never silence you. He has never forsaken you or neglected you. He has always been with you through good and bad. Do not think or place blame on someone else for your mistakes when it was you who decided to leave god. God never left you, you stopped answering the calls. So, let's be very clear on something you were called here for judgement and now that you have seen the errors of your ways what do you really have to say for yourself. Before you answer and speak as you stand there in the shallow water tell me what you see. "I don't see anything. All I see is water beneath me. I will give you a glance of what is or was to come hadn't you been on the verge of death. Close your eyes, clear your mind allow yourself to be open. Now look into the water again Maurice! Tell me what do hear and see!

"Daddy... Daddy, can you push me? Here I come baby I got it. I saw me walking up behind a little girl struggling to kick her legs on a swing set. I walked up to her and seen her face to face. She couldn't be no older than 8 years old. Her eyes big and brown, her smile identical to mines and even her laughter a giggle we commonly shared. I don't want to swing no more daddy; I want you to swing me around like you use to do. I was shocked and confused to what was this because it feels so real I can touch her and smell the air around me of trees and fresh cut grass. We were at a playground of some sort but, I couldn't make out the area but it felt familiar like I have been here before. I grip her up in my arms and I started to spin her around as we both looked up towards the clouds and fell to the ground both laughing and smiling. "Daddy that was so fun... Daddy? Can I ask you a question and you promise to tell the truth? Sure, pumpkin anything. That was even weirder it's like my mouth and mind already knew what to call her as if I said this name multiple times over and over. "Daddy I want you to promise you will always be there. Promise you will never leave me. Promise you will always be my daddy". "I promise pumpkin, where is all of this coming from? It started to get dark on the playground as if it was about to storm. Even the clouds got gray and the wind was starting to blow so hard that leaves were blowing in our faces. "Something is coming daddy; promise me you will be there? Don't give up daddy please I need you?" What is this? What is going on? I don't understand why is this happening? As tears started to fill the cracks in my face I looked around and seen a storm was heading our way and I turn and looked back at my daughter she was gone! Get me out of here! Please....

"You have to understand Maurice! The moment you decided to end your own life selfishly you left a piece of you behind. You neglected to protect the very thing that split from you from pain came a tremendous gift of love that you needed. We always have to keep in mind that when life is given it is not up to use to decide what happens. The only thing that is important is that we simply have faith and try to complete what we were sent here to do even if God's purpose isn't fully reviled to us. We must strengthen ourselves constantly even if we don't know how, we have to seek guidance and study to be quiet and wait upon his voice inside us. There is still time here Maurice! There is still one opportunity to correct and fix this, I can't help you the only thing I can say to you is repent and speak your truth!

"I am scared" ... With fear comes courage, the only thing that can save the soul of you is your tears of truth." That is all I must go now.

I was standing in in the shallow water still as I could see the sun going down in the dimensional place. The royal blue tree far from me, branches and leaves started to break off and it began to get colder around me. The clouds started to disappear as it looks like my own heaven around me was dying, just like I was dying. I was alone again in silence as I could hear from above doctor's still working to save my life with a constant beeping sound trying to get my heart steady. "What do I do as I stated to myself. I kept rushing my inner thoughts even then... "Remember your promise daddy never leave me... was ringing inside of me.

"GOD!!!
I Maurice Mayo call upon the father, the son, the holy spirt hear my cry. Forgive me for killing myself. Forgive me for my wicked ways of lying forgive me for not using the word when I needed it the most. Truth is lord I was afraid of standing out. Ashamed, is what I feel that the world would judge me for being different. I spent so many dark days lying to people, hurting myself and blaming

everyone around me for my problems when it was me the whole entire time. I had sex for money because I thought it was the right thing for me to do. I took my pain and anger out on everyone around me. I blamed myself for the relationship I didn't have with my father and mother. I pushed so many people away even those who were only trying to help me. I spent days cutting myself and blaming it on my aggressive clients at work. I thought smoking and drinking was a good way for me to cope, yet I realized I was digging myself deeper and did nothing to change that. I broke a woman's pride lying and cheating and sleeping around on her with men because I was the one confused on who I was. I personally got her pregnant because I always wanted a piece of me to remind her of who I use to be and I knew that was wrong. I disobeyed you lord numerous of times because I wanted to be in control and shape my own destiny. I silenced every good opportunity for me and thought it would be okay even if I prayed to the devil thinking he would treat me better, and God I am sobbing right now because I was wrong. I robbed people and slept with so many men risking my life without a care. I took a painful event as a child and allow it to crush my whole entire life and made excuses for it. I should have prayed more; I should have reached out more. I didn't mean to kill myself and I realize I was past wrong. You told me you will always be there and I thought you were lying. Now God my daughter will grow up without a father because of me. History will repeat it's self if I am not around. If she gets older and finds out that I committed suicide because I was a coward and shamed she will lose herself. God Please! If she grows up and changes without knowing the love I can bring, she will be her mother's child completely. You gave her to me for a reason. You could have given me a son yet you felt as though a daughter is what I needed. I know my role I play in this. I realize that now God. I realize why you gave her to me even though I prayed for a son and always wanted one. Having a son, I wouldn't know what being a father truly meant. I wouldn't know how to love a son or speak to him. You knew what you were doing. It was all a part of your plan. Lord, I know what kind of heart you gave me that I am the reason why I am different of this world. I know what kind of love that I am capable of which is unconditional. I simply made a mistake without thinking. I acted off impulse and truly wasn't thinking about her and putting myself first. You sacrificed your only son so that we may have another chance in this world. You loved your son and believe that people can change. I can change father. I can be different. I can fix this if you just allow me to. You told me that if I believe with my heart and confess with my tongue that I may receive the kingdom of heaven. Do this father and grant me this last wish. Allow me to live so that I can be the father I was truly meant to be. I don't care if the road is hard. I don't care if I go through hardships and struggles. I don't care if I have pain beyond what I could ever imagine. A life without her is no life at all. I choose her over everything. There has to be a way to fix this just tell me what I need to do. What can I show you that I can love her and give her what she needs?

I understand fully now God. Honestly, I do. Sacrifices are meant for the greater good. I am willing to pay the price. I SACRIFICE ALL THAT I AM TO SPARE HER FUTURE. I WILL GIVE MY LIFE SO THAT SHE HAS ONE. FOR THE LOVE OF A FATHER IS GREATER THAN ANY LOVE OF THIS WORLD. IF THIS IS YOUR WILL THEN LORD PROTECT HER FROM WHAT LURKS IN THE SHADOWS AND WHAT IS COMING... I WILL WATCH OVER HER IF NOT ON THIS WORLD... THEN I WILL BE INSIDE OF HER... DO YOU HEAR ME I GIVE MYSELF, MIND BODY AND SOUL TO YOU IF YOU JUST SPARE HER FROM

THE WICKEDNESS OF THE WORLD...HEAR ME
FATHER....

AMEN,

My eyes opened as the gift of life manifest throughout
my body.
**"I HEAR YOUR CRY MY SON, IT SHALL BE
DONE..."**

TO BE CONTINUED...

www.ingramcontent.com/pod-product-compliance
Lightning Source LLC
Chambersburg PA
CBHW032045240626
47154CB00003B/1088